CONSTANTINE CAPERS

A Song Without Words

CONSTANTINE CAPERS

A Song Without Words

NATALIE BRIANNE

Searose Press

MMXXVI

Published under Searose Press

Interior Art by Natalie Brianne

Cover Art by Natalie Brianne

Edited by Becky Tomlinson

ISBN: 978-1-965477-98-4

To music and musicians,

without whom I would write in silence.

And to Dorothy L. Sayers,

who gave me my love of ciphers.

Overture

Letter to Marc-André Souchay, October 15, 1842,

People often complain that music is too ambiguous, that what they should think when they hear it is so unclear, whereas everyone understands words.

With me, it is exactly the opposite, and not only with regard to an entire speech but also with individual words. These, too, seem to me so ambiguous, so vague, so easily misunderstood in comparison to genuine music, which fills the soul with a thousand things better than words.

The thoughts which are expressed to me by music that I love are not too indefinite to be put into words, but on the contrary, too definite.

Letter to his parents, June 6, 1831

I dislike many-sidedness, which, moreover, I rather think I do not much believe in. Anything that aspires to be distinguished, or beautiful, or really great, must be one-sided.

Felix Mendelssohn

Prelude

VIENNA, AUSTRIA-HUNGARY
JULY 8, 1878

IT WAS A RATHER SLOW DAY IN the Thaliastraße Post Office. Jannik Hass sorted through a stack of letters at his leisure, placing them in mail slots or sacks as needed. Luk and Niklas were almost late for the next delivery. He had half a mind to report the boys to Mr. Kersche. He stretched his back and turned the page of his newspaper.

The bell above the door chimed and he looked up, expecting the lollygaggers. But instead, he found a regular customer.

"Ah, Mr. Mayr. Greetings to you. How can I help you?"

Mr. Mayr shook his head, producing a large parcel wrapped in brown paper. "I'd like to send a package, Jan." His voice shook a little and he seemed out of sorts. "To my niece."

Jannik leaned over the counter. "What's troubling you, my friend?"

"Just a long day." Mr. Mayr smiled, but it was forced. "Nothing more."

Jannik noticed these things with all his customers. Perhaps it made the job more interesting. Perhaps it was because his wife liked to hear the news of all the people on their side of town.

He did not push though. It was not his business. If Mr. Mayr wished to share, he would share. Jannik tapped the article he was reading.

"What do you think about this treaty, eh? Our country may be expanding, taking control of Bosnia, if they sign it."

"They will," Mayr said, letting out a breath. He pushed the package forward. "How much?"

Jannik weighed it, clucking his tongue. He checked the address. "England? Do you have this written correctly?"

"Yes. She moved there a few months ago. How much?"

"Thirty kreuzer. Are you sure you want to send it? That's a week's wages."

"I'm sure."

Jannik shook his head, stamping the package. "You must love your niece."

"I do. Can you make sure it is sent straight away?"

"I'll send it direct with the next courier I see." Jannik said, copying the recipient's name and address into the postal records as a foreign charge.

"Thank you. Thank you." Mr. Mayr counted out the coins, each making a satisfying clinking noise on the counter.

The bell above the door rang again as Luk came in from the morning deliveries.

"Perfect timing," Jannik said, pulling the new mail sack from the wall and slipping the package inside it. "This package needs to be the first thing you deliver, understand? Take it straight to the station."

"Yes, sir." Luk took the mail sack with one hand and snagged his lunch from behind the counter with the other.

Mr. Mayr's shoulders sagged as Luk left the post office. He turned to Jannik and held out a hand. "You have helped immensely. Thank you, again."

"Of course! It is my job." He shook the man's hand. "And we will see you back soon, eh? You are always sending letters."

"We'll see." Mr. Mayr tipped his hat and the bell above the door rang out once more before leaving Jannik in silence. Perhaps Jannik was not as good at reading his customers as he thought, but it didn't seem as if Mr. Mayr had been teasing.

Niklas was still running behind. Jannik never liked to rat on the boys, but Mr. Kersche would want to know, even if Niklas was only a minute or so late. The post office demanded efficiency and the boys knew the consequences when they were not on time.

He turned towards the rickety staircase that would take him to the upper office, the boards creaking under his feet. He rapped on the door, the sound dull against his knuckles.

"Come in," Mr. Kersche said.

Jannik poked his head around the door, not wanting to fully enter. Mr. Kersche kept his office immaculate: a place for everything and everything in its place, a living cliché. The man himself was tall, but you couldn't tell when he was seated. Most of his height was in the legs. His long arms ended in spindly fingers. Jannik would never tell anyone, not even his wife, but from the moment he met Mr. Kersche, he had reminded him of a spider.

"You wanted to know if the boys were late again. Niklas hasn't been back yet."

Mr. Kersche opened a drawer, took out a folder, and flipped it open. He wetted the end of a pencil and marked a check. "Thank you. If he isn't back in half an hour, let me know."

Jannik nodded and turned to leave, but he hesitated on the threshold. Mr. Kersche was always asking about any unusual activity. Perhaps Mr. Mayr's nervousness wasn't something to comment on, but there was something else. "One more thing, sir."

"Yes?"

"Do you remember Mr. Mayr having a niece?"

Mr. Kersche looked up from his paperwork for the first time.

"Mr. Mayr was in?"

Jannik nodded. "He sent a package. To England. I don't remember him having any relatives there."

"Do you have the package still?"

Jannik shook his head. "I sent it out with Luk."

Mr. Kersche sighed. "Bring me the record, then."

Dutiful as ever, Jannik ran downstairs to fetch the record book. Niklas was there, so it took a few minutes—and a proper scolding—before Jannik could return to his errand. When he opened the record book, the relevant page had been torn out. He brought the book to Mr. Kersche.

"I'm not sure who would have taken it, sir."

Mr. Kersche snapped the book closed. "You don't happen to remember the address?"

"No, sir. I don't."

Mr. Kersche let out a nasally sigh, glanced at his watch and stood, moving to put on his coat. "Excuse me, I am late to an appointment."

"I remember the name though."

In all the years that Jannik Hass had worked for Mr. Kersche, he had never seen the man smile. Until now.

"Tell me."

February 4, 1889: Morning

LONDON, ENGLAND
NEARLY ELEVEN YEARS LATER

The sun bled through a thin gap of curtain, spread across the floor, and sent a beam of light onto Mira's face. She blinked and turned over as the last vestiges of a dream left her. The details were hazy and fading quickly, but she was left with a warmth in her chest.

The light caught on Clarisse's golden hair, the little girl still fast asleep. She'd wandered into Mira's room early in the evening, not wanting to sleep alone in a new place.

Trying not to jostle the bed, Mira slid from the covers and wrapped up in her dressing gown. Her feet were cold on the wooden floor as she moved to the window. Nero jumped from his perch on a chair, giving a soft meow and padding over to her. She picked him up and ducked between the curtains, careful not to let too much light in. She sat in the window seat, her breath fogging up the cool glass as she stroked the cat's soft fur.

It had been three days since she and her family had left Paris. A day since they had arrived in London and began the tedious process of settling into Swan Walk. While there were enough rooms for everyone, the house definitely felt full. Filled to the brim, as it were. It was good to be home, but Mira wasn't exactly certain where she fit anymore. Perhaps it was just that the house was still in a state of transition. The house and their lives. Everything was in upheaval.

After all, it had been less than a month since her Uncle Cyrus and Loretta were married. Less than a month since Emilie had died. Less than two since Professor Burke and the bridge and Durant and Circe . . .

The family was still reeling from all the changes. All the memories.

Mira's mind had been better about staying in the present, at least in the few weeks since she had told Byron the truth about her memories and the nightmares. But there was a thread of anxiety not knowing if or when something might trigger an impromptu trip to the past. Could she walk through Kensington Gardens without seeing the ghost of Alexander Durant there? Would she catch a glimpse of Professor Burke standing in the parlor?

She shivered and pushed the thoughts away. Maybe it would be best to find a distraction before her mind carried itself too far into the past. Mira deposited Nero on the windowsill, ignoring his meows of protest, and pulled a copy of *Persuasion* from the shelf, returning to her seat again.

"Sir Walter Elliot, of Kellynch Hall, in Somersetshire, was a man who, for his own amusement, never took up any book but the Baronetage; there he found occupation for an idle hour, and consolation in a distressed one; there his—"

Sir Elliot rather reminded her of the mannerisms of her

uncle. He'd always been focused on status and propriety, even when he couldn't live up to his own expectations. As recently as October he'd been blustering about social status and whether or not she and Walker would ever marry. Now, here he was, married himself and with a decidedly different demeanor and a revised view of the world.

Mira had known that things would change for her after Cyrus and Loretta were married. The family dynamic, their living arrangements, and her future all took a drastic turn. She had expected that. But her emotions were not part of that expectation and she wasn't prepared for how much the sensation resembled the feeling of being left behind.

Cyrus had a new family, and while Mira was technically a part of it, she still felt as if she were on the outside. A niece, not a daughter.

But was it unfair to think that way? Cyrus had done the best that he could in raising her and her brother. But seeing him with Loretta's children she could see a new side of him, one he had rarely shown to her or Walker. It hurt to see him acting so fatherly to the Lavigne children, when it took almost twenty years for him to act that way with her and Walker. He'd been too detached, caught up in his own grief about their mother's death, to even be a proper guardian for them.

And then there was Loretta.

The general air of the household had shifted since Loretta came. And it wasn't just because there were more voices filling the air and more footsteps running through the corridors. There was a change in energy, in purpose, in care. And Mira wished it didn't hurt so much to see what it would have been like to have a mother.

She'd never imagined that Cyrus would ever marry. When she was younger, she gravitated more towards daydreaming what her relationship might be with her future husband's family. With his parents and his mother especially.

A loud crash sounded from one of the lower landings, startling Mira from her musings and the cat from her side. She pushed the curtains aside, meeting Clarisse's wide, blue eyes.

"What was that?" Clarisse asked, pulling the covers tight to her chest.

Mira moved to her, holding out a hand. "Shall we find out?"

They found Jean-Marie and Georges apologizing profusely to Landon on the landing just below Cyrus and Loretta's room. Teacups and tray were strewn about, the china in pieces and the carpet stained. Each of the occupants of the landing were covered in the remains of eggs, sausage, toast, and crimson jam.

The bedroom door opened just as Mira and Clarisse arrived. Cyrus poked his head out, asking the obvious question.

"What happened?"

"A little accident, sir," Landon said, stacking the detritus on the tray. "I thought you might want breakfast in your room this morning."

Cyrus glanced at the mess. "A good thought, but considering the circumstances, why don't we all adjourn to the dining room?"

"Yes, sir. I was thinking the same thing."

"We didn't mean to." Jean-Marie rushed through his words.

"There is always a risk to running inside the house," Landon said, his voice warm but stern. Mira had heard this tone many times as a child, although usually it was directed at Walker. The butler stood, balancing the tray in one hand.

"I'll send one of the parlor maids up to finish cleaning straightaway. In the meantime," he said, spying Mira and Clarisse's bare feet. "I do believe shoes are in order."

Breakfast was much louder than Swan Walk had ever seen it. Even at its full length, the table was crowded with people, splayed out elbows, and dropped silverware. That isn't to say that Mira's cousins had poor manners, but in such close quarters, it was difficult to stay within one's own space; and with so many conversations happening at once, it was difficult to know what anyone was saying. Mira had a sneaking suspicion that Landon had foreseen the difficulty and had hoped to avoid it by serving breakfast to her aunt and uncle separately.

"We'll want to leave the house by six-thirty at the latest if we're walking," Cyrus said. "I want to be there a bit early. It wouldn't do to be late to dinner with the Renaldis."

"Why can't I come?" Clarisse asked.

"This is a more grown-up party, my love," Loretta said, buttering her toast. "It wouldn't be much fun for you, I promise."

This dinner party had been planned over several weeks of correspondence. Liza was anxious to spend more time with Walker and wanted her parents to have a better understanding of the family she could possibly marry into.

"But Georges is coming," Jean-Marie said.

"I would rather not," Georges said sinking in his chair.

"It will be good for you," Loretta said to her eldest. She turned to Jean-Marie. "You'll be old enough in a year or two."

"It isn't fair," Jean-Marie said, more of a statement than petulance.

"No, it isn't," Loretta said. "But I'm afraid that's how it is. Mrs. Pringle and Landon will look after the two of you tonight. So please be good for them."

"Yes, Maman." Clarisse pouted.

The conversation turned to other things, but Mira couldn't shake her nerves. The Renaldis were an older family and set a high standard as a result. Not that Mira's family wasn't respectable, but their fortune was fairly new. They had always had enough money, always been in the upper middle class. Yet, as much as Cyrus blustered about status and chided them about what was proper, he himself didn't always live up to the standard.

Cyrus had a great desire to appear correct in all social norms but was the first generation of the family expected to do so. Elias Griffon, his father and Mira's grandfather, brought the family from poverty into wealth, but couldn't provide the necessary skills to help them thrive in the new society. Cyrus compensated by traveling the world and continuing to build up the fortune. He didn't prioritize his social standing until he was given guardianship of Mira and Walker.

Suddenly, he had expectations to live up to, children to raise, and a society to fit into—and he no idea of how to go about it. He'd started by purchasing a copy of the peerage and keeping up with the news of the court. It had seemed the sensible thing to do, though it didn't give him the practical knowledge he needed.

He hadn't recognized the necessity of hiring a governess for her or a tutor for Walker. While he had sense enough to ensure a good education for her brother by sending him to boarding school, he only sent Mira to finishing school as an afterthought. Thank goodness he had, otherwise she'd be lacking in all the social graces. And then, once they were grown, Cyrus had forgotten about the need for chaperones entirely and had been easily persuaded to allow Mira live on her own.

Looking back, it was impossible to know if his leniency in raising them was due to ignorance, his own grief, or a desire for them to have some happiness after such a great sadness, but regardless of the reason it had left them with a deficiency of manners.

Loretta, on the other hand, was already working out her children's education. Georges would get an apprenticeship, and she would arrange for a tutor for Jean-Marie and a governess for Clarisse. She was making plans for dance lessons and negotiating with tailors and dressmakers for new wardrobes.

For years the Lavignes hadn't had the option to follow the social standard because of the debts left by Mssr. Lavigne. But now there was an opportunity to improve their circumstances and Loretta was primed to take it. Conforming to social expectations seemed to come naturally to her, though perhaps that was because in doing so she ensured a better future for her children.

As for Mira, she still struggled to remember everything that was expected of her. Walker did too. Would it have been different if their parents hadn't died? Their father came from a well-established family. Had their mother cared about propriety and status? Or would she have had the same attitude that Mira did about hairstyles and hats?

Would Mira be less anxious for this party with the Renaldis?

"Mira?"

She looked up at the sound. Her uncle was looking at her expectantly.

"Sorry, what was that?"

"I asked if you'd talked with Mr. Constantine about this evening."

"Oh. Yes. He should be here in time to walk with us."

"Good. Good."

MIRA SPENT THE REST OF THE MORNING unpacking and helping her aunt with the odd task. Sometime in the afternoon she hid away in the library, settling onto a rug near the hearth with a stack of letters. Most of them were addressed to Palace Court. As an independent detective, Byron had correspondence from all sorts of people. Since he'd been gone for almost three months, the letters about cases and leads piled up.

She had taken about half of the stack of envelopes to sort through, but there hadn't been time to chip away at them yet with all the unpacking and excitement. They'd only been back in London for a day. Letter opener in hand, she set to work on thinning the pile.

First, she discarded the obvious advertisements and ordered the remaining correspondence by postmark deciding it would be best to work from the earliest and move forward. Some of the leads she came across had definite timeframes that were already long past. Those, she set aside. The aim was to find any communications that merited immediate response. The rest could wait until they had time to write an apology for being out of the country.

It didn't take long before she came upon some information that made her pause. It was from the police in Reading. The two thieves Byron had helped to capture back in November, Charles Montague and Aaron Dennis, had escaped. They had worked under Selene and possibly under Circe before that. They'd broken out on December twentieth, just before their court martial trial was to be held.

Mira had visited them in early December at the prison in Reading to ask about Selene's potential whereabouts in Paris. She bit her lip as she read over the note again. Montague, or Monty as he was called, had been incredibly cooperative. Dennis was the bigger worry. Something about the man hadn't set well with Mira at the time, especially after learning that Dennis had pulled a knife on Byron. He was violent and had a vengeful streak.

She set the letter to the side, as something to be dealt with sooner rather than later. She glanced at the clock. It was almost time to get ready for the party, but she found it difficult to stop. A little lower in the stack, she came across a missive that made her stomach turn.

Detective Constantine,

If you are reading this, I am dead.

Her eyes flicked to the bottom of the page and she found the name *Selene Vermielle* in cursive script. She brought a hand to her mouth, memories of the thief's death in the catacombs flooding back. The blood, the dust, the bones. She forced the images away and kept reading.

> *Durant has just visited me, and I fear that he will not keep his promises. Even if he does, it is only a matter of time before Circe decides I am a loose thread that needs cutting. You must know that everything I have done has been in self-preservation. But my loyalty to Circe has long faded. If they kill me I do not want the knowledge I carry to follow me to the grave.*

The handwriting was shaky, as if written in a hurry. Mira couldn't imagine what Selene had felt as she wrote it. She herself felt sick just reading it.

> *That is my purpose for writing this letter. I wish to tell you everything I know of the organization. Unfortunately, the bulk of my understanding is limited to the Crescent. I also wish I knew the identity of the Serpent, but I was never privy to that information. I don't know how much you know about the Crescent, so I shall tell you everything I know.*

Selene had told them about the hierarchy of Circe in the Gallerie de Mestra back in December. The organization was split into three guilds: the Crescent was over the thieves, the Cypress over the murderers, and the Crossroads was over the smugglers. Each was headed by an individual who operated under a code name. The Serpent, the Hound, and the Charger, respectively. And of course, Mira knew now that the Charger was her own godfather.

First, you should know that there are two types of thieves: those who work independently and those who work with a gang. Both are subject to the whims of the Crescent. Most of the time gangs and independent thieves can steal as they like without some grand master plan from the Serpent. Sometimes, they may even believe that they are free of the organization. But when Circe has need of them, they are obligated to answer.

If a thief refuses to help, there are dire consequences. The Serpent has leverage on each of the gangs and has operatives that will find compromising information on any independent thieves that are too successful.

Second, you should know how the Crescent uses thefts for their gain. Circe rarely needs something stolen just for the sake of money. More often they will use burglaries as a means to cover up or distract from other crimes. You know this as distraction was their object during the Pennington mystery that brought our fates together.

Mira nodded along as she read. Selene had burglarized Pennington's flat so he would reveal the location of a secret cache to the Shadow. Then Selene had committed several other burglaries in the area to keep the police searching for her instead.

The Serpent sometimes recruits from outside the usual circle if they believe it will help the cause. For instance, the Crescent often hires unskilled thugs with the intention of them being arrested. Designated scapegoats that keep the police diverted while more dangerous operations are put in place. Circe also calls upon thieves of the Crescent when a specific item needs to be stolen or if an independent thief or gang has a particular skill that would be useful in a larger scheme.

You can assume that most gangs and thieves in England have worked with Circe at one point or another. The network is vast, but I do have a list of some key players. At least the ones I have worked with or have heard rumors about.

The Forty Elephants

The Lambeth Lads

Henry Mayhew

Joseph Carney

Norine Askew

Jonathan Wallace

Terrence Wheeler

Francis McKenzie

Minnie Porter

Felix Boltzmann

Dante Paolini

Augustin Lafaille

Mira skimmed over the list. She didn't recognize any of them, but maybe Byron would.

I will give this letter to a trusted clerk, who is not involved in Circe, to send in case of my death. If all goes well, you will never read this. But if you do, consider it my apology for what I must do later this evening. I don't wish you or Miss Blayse ill, I hope you realize that. I have no choice. If I refuse, Durant will kill me. If I do as he says, I might have my freedom. As scant of a chance as it is, I must take it.

Please forgive me.

Selene Vermielle

She tucked the letter back into the envelope. Selene was wrong. There was always a choice. And Selene had chosen to help them, even knowing that the mark of death hung over her. Now, because of her foresight, they had a lead on the Crescent! They might be able to cripple Circe even further. Her death needn't be in vain.

She stood, rushing out the door, passing Walker on the stairs.

"Where are you headed?" he asked.

"Palace Court!" she called over her shoulder.

"But what about—"

She left before he finished his sentence, grabbing her coat and dashing out into the London chill. There wasn't time to stop and chat. They had some leads! Some real leads.

She called for a cab and paid in advance, settling into the seat. Halfway there she realized her mistake. The party! Would she have enough time to make it to Palace Court and back and still have time to dress? Calculations flooded her mind.

It was ten minutes to Palace Court by hansom, twenty minutes gone with there and back. And it would take fifteen to walk to the Renaldi's, so they would need to leave by quarter to seven at the latest to still be on time. That would leave just about fifty minutes for her to get ready. Would that be enough time? Especially with how particular the Renaldis were about decorum?

Goodness, Walker was still earning their esteem. What if she didn't make it in time? Would they judge him based on her actions?

What if Byron had already left for Swan Walk? Or even worse, what if he had forgotten about the engagement and wasn't ready himself?

The cab slowed in front of Palace Court and her nerves calmed by the slightest degree. The lights were on. That meant he was home. And she'd made good time. Perhaps she would be fit to be seen for the party. She certainly wasn't ready as she was. Her walking dress was wrinkled from unpacking all day and she hadn't done anything with her hair. Her curls were bobbing about all over the place. But it didn't matter. They had a lead!

She opened the door, calling for him as she came into the sitting room. "Byron? One of your letters—"

Her words caught in her throat as she took in the scene. Byron stood by the mantle, fully dressed in evening wear, eyes wide as he glanced between her and the other occupants of the room. His brother, Castel Sherard, sat in the armchair next to the hearth with a sly smirk on his face and two women sat on the sofa that faced the window. She was in full view of them all as they stared at her.

The younger of the two women had red hair with streaks of grey in it, pulled into an updo with frizzy curls cascading down. She glared at Mira, her nose wrinkling, as if she was affronted that Mira had interrupted.

The older sat closest to Castel. She was trim and petite. Her silver hair peeked out from under her lace cap and her blue eyes betrayed no emotion beneath rimmed spectacles. She simply looked Mira up and down and turned to Byron, saying, "Castel mentioned a girl. I didn't realize she was so . . . familiar with you."

Mira's face burned, her mind going blank.

Byron cleared his throat. "Yes, Mamma. This . . . this is Samira Blayse. Miss Blayse, this is my mother, Mary Haughton Clarke Sherard, and my sister, Mary."

His mother hummed. "And what is the situation that seemed more important than dressing oneself for the day? Or knocking, for that matter?"

Another rush of warmth came over her. This was not how she intended to meet Byron's mother. Not that she had particularly thought about the prospect. Yes, she'd thought in general about what a relationship with a fictional mother-in-law might be like, but it hadn't occurred to her that it would be Byron's mother. In fact, before this moment, she had quite forgotten that he even had one. If she were to decide on the worst first impression, this was certainly it.

"I-I . . ." She drew her gaze to Byron. She had intended to tell him all about Selene, but it wouldn't do in present company. She held out the letter and Byron took it. "I brought you one of your letters."

"It couldn't wait?" Castel asked, leaning forward.

She glanced at the clock, trying to think up a good lie. "Well, there was also the matter of our engagement this evening at the Renaldi's." She looked back at Byron. "I knew you intended to arrive at quarter after and when you weren't there . . ."

"You thought I had forgotten." Byron nodded. "I was . . . well." He glanced at his family. "I intend to come as soon as possible."

"Yes. I came to make sure . . . well, I thought it would be best." Mira took a breath. "I'll see you at the Renaldi's, then."

She gave a quick curtsy and rushed to the door, escaping judgement, scrutiny, and Palace Court all at once, grateful, at least, that the letter was no longer burning a hole in her pocket.

February 4, 1889: Evening

Mira's ears were still hot as Mr. Renaldi regaled the table with a story she was certain she had heard before. She stirred her soup a little, trying not to think about how terribly she had ruined her first meeting with Byron's mother. Byron sat across from her, out of discreet earshot due to the Renaldi's ridiculous adherence to the old traditions. Mira never understood why it was necessary for the gentlemen to sit by a different lady from the one he accompanied to the table.

Georges had been assigned to sit with and attend her. He'd never been to a dinner party before and she could feel the nervousness rolling off him. Mira had already helped him to avoid humiliation in choosing which utensils to use. Walker sat on Mira's other side, and since he was assigned to sit with the notorious chaperone, Aunt Eleanor, he wasn't faring any better.

Byron and Liza seemed to be getting along alright, and her aunt and uncle were doing swimmingly with Mr. and Mrs. Renaldi, respectively. All in all, the party was turning out to be a success. Mrs. Renaldi would have to be congratulated. Not too much, of course, lest she think it an insincere compliment.

Regardless of the triumph of the seating arrangements, it meant that Mira hadn't had a moment to talk with Byron about her impropriety that afternoon, what they were going to do about it, and why his family had been there in the first place, let alone discuss Selene's letter. He kept sending her glances across the table and every time their eyes met her embarrassment resurfaced.

"I can't believe it myself," Cyrus said. The conversation had moved on without her noticing. Her uncle continued, "Why would a crown prince take his own life, I ask you?"

"And his mistress as well," Mr. Renaldi said. "I'm sure you've heard the rumors that it was a political assassination."

"Yes, but then why cover it up by saying it was suicide?" Mrs. Renaldi asked.

"We don't have all the facts, yet," Byron said. "It's been less than a week."

"Do we know who is next in line?" Liza asked.

"Archduke Karl Ludwig," Cyrus said. "The emperor's brother. And then his son, I think. Franz Ferdinand."

"The whole business is dreadful," Loretta said. "His poor mother."

The servants took the soup away and Mira adjusted the napkin in her lap. Once the main course was out, the conversation shifted towards a pleasanter topic: the move.

"It must be quite the change to be in London," Mr. Renaldi said, gesturing to Loretta. "How long did you say you lived in Paris?"

"Almost thirty years," Loretta said. "And yes, it is strange. I haven't been to London since I was a girl."

"How are the children adjusting?" Mrs. Renaldi asked.

Loretta glanced at Georges, who stiffened a little. She said, "We only arrived the day before yesterday. I'm sure it will take some time for everyone to settle."

Mr. Renaldi turned to Cyrus. "Did any of the staff come with you?"

Cyrus coughed a little. "No. There was no need."

"Not even the governess?" Aunt Eleanor asked.

"Yes, your youngest must be devastated," Mrs. Renaldi said, cutting a bit of roast duck.

It seemed the Renaldis were under a false impression about how the Lavignes lived before Cyrus and Loretta were married.

Loretta frowned. "We didn't have a governess."

Aunt Eleanor raised an eyebrow. "That is quite unusual. How did you manage their education?"

Loretta shifted in her seat a little. "After their father died, we had to put the children's education on hold for a while. I intend to remedy that as soon as possible." She picked up her glass. "Do you have any recommendations on where to find suitable tutors and a governess?"

Aunt Eleanor straightened, lifting her chin. "Whatever you do, do not put it out in a common advertisement. You shall have all sorts if you do it that way. No, for a governess you shall want to go to the Governesses' Benevolent Institution. And for a tutor, you shall want to speak with Mr. LeFranc at the Tipton Educational Agency. And make sure that the man he sends has been to university. Although, how old is your boy?"

"Just fifteen," Loretta said.

"Then you can avoid the whole unpleasantness by sending him to boarding school. Eton is good. As is Sevenoaks." Eleanor turned to Walker. "Didn't you go to Sevenoaks?"

"No, I went to Brighton."

"Oh, no." Loretta shook her head. "I don't think I could. I'd much rather have my children at home."

Mrs. Renaldi tipped her head to the side. “I can understand the sentiment. I felt the same about Liza. But, then there is the difficulty of room and board for the tutor. As well as the governess.”

Loretta looked at Cyrus. “I hadn’t considered that.”

Walker leaned over to Mira and whispered, “I don’t think the house could take another person, let alone two.”

Mira nodded. Even if she shared her room with Clarisse, that would only leave one extra room in the house. Perhaps Georges would go off to an apprenticeship or university and then Jean-Marie could share with Walker. It would be rather close quarters though. Like sardines packed on top of one another.

“What about Spenston?” Byron said, dabbing his mouth.

The entire party turned to look at him.

Cyrus took a moment to chew and swallow before speaking. “What?”

Byron said, “Sutherland’s estate. There would be more than enough room there. It is yours, isn’t it?”

“Why . . . yes. It is.” Cyrus frowned.

“You have an estate?” Loretta said.

Cyrus cleared his throat. “Spenston Park. It belonged to my late business partner. When he died, the property came to me. I intended to sell it, but with everything, well, it quite slipped my mind.”

“I didn’t realize memory loss was catching,” Byron said, a twinkle in his eye.

Walker barked out a laugh, nearly spilling his wine, and got a harsh look from the dreaded Aunt Eleanor.

After dinner, the party adjourned to the parlor for further discussion and cards. The married couples, Aunt

Eleanor, and Georges sat near the hearth, discussing the best way to go about setting up Spenston Park, how long it would take, and other particulars. That left the courting couples to play whist in the corner of the room and allowed them to finally speak freely amongst themselves.

"Good show on remembering Spenston," Walker said, turning over a card to determine the next trump suit. Spades. "If you hadn't said anything, we'd be looking at a good few months rammed to the rafters at Swan Walk. At least, until Uncle stumbled across the deed again when reorganizing his papers."

"It's a new experience for me," Byron said. "Remembering."

Mira smiled, shaking her head at her detective and he caught her gaze, expression softening.

"How does someone forget that they have an estate anyway? If I had inherited something like that, I feel I wouldn't forget it so easily," Liza said.

"He didn't have enough time to get used to the idea of having an estate. And there have been more pressing things," Walker said, glancing at Mira. "Then he was in Paris for almost three months."

Liza tipped her head, playing her turn. "I do hate to think that you'll have to leave London. Especially as you've just returned."

"Well, there's no reason that I couldn't stay at Swan Walk once the family has moved down," Walker said. "I'll still be helping Uncle with the business. It would be good to have someone here in London to keep an eye on things."

Mira splayed the cards out in her hand. Diamonds and clubs, none of them higher than a nine. "I'd rather stay in London as well. Although, just imagining the arguments to be had with Uncle makes my head hurt."

"I'm sure we could come to some arrangement," Walker said.

"Well, I'll have at least a month to persuade him, until the household is fully established at Spenston."

Walker groaned. "A month of overcrowding. Do you think we can bear it?"

Mira rolled her eyes. "A month is not that long."

Liza dropped the king of spades, taking the trick and turning over the three of hearts. "How many rounds left, do you think?" she said, surveying the deck, then placing a nine of spades to start the round.

"Two, I'd say. And I must apologize," Walker said, placing the jack of spades over Liza's nine. "But I believe I've taken this trick already."

Mira sighed, setting the two of diamonds on the pile. She had the most rotten luck. No hearts or spades.

Byron drummed his fingers on his leg and Mira wondered if he was determining his next move or his next sentence.

Walker filled the pause. "Speaking of forgetting, I meant to ask why you ran out so mysteriously earlier today, Mira."

Her stomach dropped. "Yes. Well. I had a letter that . . . well, I wasn't thinking." She turned to Byron. "If I had known that your family was visiting I never—"

Walker's mouth dropped. "Your family was there?"

"Unfortunately. And I believe you spoke too soon." With a flick of his fingers, Byron showed the ace of hearts and took the trick, turning to Mira. "There was no way you could have known. Their arrival was unexpected for me too."

"Do they visit often?" Liza asked, considering her cards.

"Not as a rule. Not since my memory has improved, at any rate. In this instance, they came round because they have a case for me."

"They do?" Mira's curiosity overtook her unease. "It's not for Her Majesty again, is it?"

"Heavens, no. Otherwise, Castel would have come alone. No, my mother and sister have been staying in Bath since Christmas. There have been a series of thefts in the area, and they became the latest victims last week. Several pieces of the family inheritance taken."

"Such as?" Walker asked, placing the six of clubs.

"My great aunt's bracelet, my grandmother's ring, and a necklace that's been handed down since the reign of Charles the II."

"Is that all?" Liza said with an incredulous laugh.

"More or less. Lucky for them, my profession does come in handy—when they decide to acknowledge it, that is."

"You know, I keep forgetting that you are a Sherard," Liza said, taking the final trick.

"That's the aim. Could prove useful to remain inconspicuous for this particular investigation," Byron said. "They asked me to come up as soon as I can."

Mira swallowed. "When are you leaving, then?"

He set his remaining cards on the table. "That depends on when you are able to get away from Swan Walk."

She blinked, looking up at him. He gave her that devilish smile he always had when he thought himself particularly clever. "After all, what is a detective without his secretary?"

"Byron, you know we can't use that excuse anymore." She glanced over at her uncle.

"Yes, of course," his expression softened. "You are much more than my secretary."

A warmth bloomed in her chest and she smiled, averting her gaze.

Walker cleared his throat. "I highly doubt Uncle will allow it."

"Oh, I don't know," Liza said, a twinkle in her eye. "I think it all rests on how we present the idea."

"It sounds like you have a thought." Walker leaned closer.

"I do, although I'm not sure you'll like it. It involves Aunt Eleanor."

Walker let out a rush of air. "Oh goody."

"My mother's family is actually from Bath. When my grandparents died they left the house to Aunt Eleanor."

Walker frowned. "If she's got a house in Bath, what is she doing living with you and your parents?"

"Well, last year much of the city center was under construction due to the Roman ruins found near the Grand Pump Room."

"Roman ruins?" Byron's eyes widened. "That sounds fascinating."

"I'm sure it will be. They are building a museum or something over top of it so people can see the ruins. But because of the construction, society is a little less, well, sociable. And Aunt Eleanor gets so lonely, I suppose she makes excuses to visit us."

"I can understand that," Mira said.

"She's been talking about going back to take the waters," Liza continued. "So I think it would take little to convince her and Mamma to go to Bath for a short holiday. And I do believe it would be appropriate to bring a small party with us."

"Who would make up this sociable party?" Walker asked, a smile overtaking his features.

"The four of us, of course." Liza picked up the stray cards, stacking and straightening the deck. "We've been courting for several months now, Walker, and we haven't seen much of each other in that time. It would be a good opportunity for proper socialization, with the added benefit of making more room at Swan Walk while your aunt and uncle arrange everything for the move to Spenston Park."

"Why, Liza, that's brilliant!" Mira laughed.

Liza tucked a stray hair behind her ear. "I know. Shall I go and ask Mamma?"

"By all means," Byron said.

"Wish me luck," Liza grinned at them and moved toward the other conversation, discreetly brushing out her skirt.

Walker sighed. "I didn't think I could love her more, but she keeps surprising me."

"And to think, just a few months ago, you couldn't stand her," Mira teased.

"I think the poets were wrong. I think hate is much more blind than love."

Based on the expression on Cyrus' face, Liza's proposition was taking well. The Renaldis were nodding, and soon Liza returned to the group.

"What's the verdict, then?" Walker asked.

"They've agreed! Mamma wants to leave by the end of the week."

THE NIGHT AIR WAS BRISK, THE SLIM bit of moonlight sending silver through the trees as they returned to Swan Walk. Mira and Byron were a step or two behind the rest of the family, practically alone for the first time in weeks.

"Did you get a chance to read the letter?" she asked.

He gave a short nod. "It was illuminating, to say the least. She's given us the full picture of how the Crescent operated within Circe. It always bothered me that for all of Circe's grand plans for war in Europe, a full third of their organization is devoted to petty theft. While money is necessary for a large criminal organization like Circe, surely they'd get enough of it from the smuggling side of things."

"Yes, and it explains why Selene didn't think she could truly be rid of Circe. There was always the looming threat of blackmail." She shivered a little. "I feel so sorry for her. If what she said in the letter is true, she never wanted to betray us."

"And yet, she did." He reached over and took her hand.

"And we were lucky to survive what happened in the catacombs."

"She didn't survive." Mira swallowed. "She did exactly as Durant asked and still . . ."

"Selene shouldn't have trusted him to keep his word. She could have come to us at any time and she chose not to. The fact that she decided to share what she knew in death atones for much, but doesn't negate the fact that she put you in so much danger. A danger that she herself was trying to escape."

"She didn't realize that. People do terrible things when they feel they don't have a choice." Mira bit her lip. "I think she was a good person, deep down. But even good people act wrongfully out of fear."

Byron softened. "You're right. And she did do the right thing in the end by sending us that list. I recognized both gangs and one of the individual names. The Forty Elephants operates in London, for the most part. Primarily made up of women whose husbands are in prison, their main crime is shoplifting. The Lambeth Lads are another London-based gang. They are mostly young men and boys with a more violent streak. I've worked with them in the past to gather information."

"And the name?"

"Terrence Wheeler. He moves around a lot because he's a rag-and-bone man. Easy to recognize him, though, he wears a special pair of shoes made with one sole built up to a platform to compensate for one leg being much shorter than the other.

Her mouth dropped open. "I think I've seen him before! I always wondered who his cobbler was."

"I'm afraid I don't have that name," he teased. "And I don't recognize the other nine on Selene's list." He released her hand and pulled out a small notebook and flicked it open. "Henry Mayhew, Joseph Carney, Norine Askew, Jonathan Wallace . . . I wish she'd given an indication as to what industry they were in or their addresses or something." He tucked the book away. "But we have names, at least, and that's as good a start as any."

She looked away. "I don't think I've properly apologized for earlier. I was so excited about the prospect of new leads, I didn't think of anything else."

Byron laughed a little. "I will say I was surprised. You looked like a fox that escaped from the hunt only to rush headlong into the hounds."

"I felt like one." Her stomach twisted.

"Your transformation between then and the party was incredible," he said. "I didn't have the chance to tell you before, but you are absolutely stunning tonight."

"You would say that no matter what I looked like."

"True. I did like the way your hair fell around your face when you rushed into Palace Court. And I haven't seen your blush in quite some time. Is that why you chose a rose-colored gown for this evening?"

She fidgeted with the buttons on her coat. "It was the first one I found. Truth be told, it's a miracle I made it to the party on time."

"But you did. And with only one hair out of place." He reached over, tucking the strand behind her ear. "There."

They walked a few paces in silence, the gas lamps flickering.

She whispered, "I can't imagine what your family must think of me."

He took her arm, slowing her to a stop. "Does it matter?"

"Of course, it matters. They are your family. If . . . if we are to . . . well, we are courting and that generally, well . . ."

"Leads to marriage? Yes, I have considered the notion."

Her heart raced. They hadn't discussed it candidly yet, but she had hoped she hadn't been wrong about his intentions. Yet, there was still the matter of his family.

"I don't want to be a disappointment," she said, her chest tightening. She looked away.

He stood there, silent for a few moments.

"You will never be a disappointment to me. And if you are to my family, it is only because I was a disappointment first," he said. "I told you how upset they were at my becoming a detective."

"But they are your family." She looked up at him. "I wanted so much to make a good impression."

He took her hand, lacing their fingers together. "You'll have another chance."

They started down the pavement again. A question burned on her tongue, but she was afraid of the answer. As they turned down the street before Swan Walk, she found some courage. "Did . . . did they say anything after I left?"

"Oh, a good deal of things. Are you sure you want to know?"

She wasn't sure if she did, but she nodded just the same.

"There was some question about what sort of girl would run about London in such a state, why you had a key to my rooms. That sort of thing. The main discussion topic was how long we had been courting, what sort of family you had, and what my intentions were."

"Oh."

They reached the steps of Swan Walk and he lifted her hand to his lips.

"You needn't worry," he said, his blue eyes soft. "They'll come around." He tipped his hat, stepping away. She reached out, holding him back.

"And if they don't?"

His smile dipped by a fraction. "I've left the name Sherard behind before."

February 7, 1889

There was nothing so tiresome as trains and stations; the steam, the crowd, the noise of the platform. To say nothing of the cramped little compartments and the rumble beneath one's feet. Perhaps if she had been allowed more time to recuperate from the last trip, there would be a novelty in traveling again. As it was, she stood on the platform waiting for the train with Byron and Walker and she disliked every moment of it.

"I do wish we'd been able to make our own travel arrangements," Walker said, leaning back on his heels. "Why, I'd have gotten us an airship. It'd take twice the time, but think of the views!"

Mira looked up at the two dirigibles gracing the blue above them. It would certainly be more exciting to travel by airship—she could practically feel the exhilaration of flying—but their uncle was the one who arranged for their transportation. Cyrus may have taken an airship to and from France, but that didn't mean he trusted them.

"If we took an airship, we wouldn't make it in time for the music recital," Byron said.

"Oh, I wouldn't mind missing it," Walker said.

Landon returned from speaking with the porters. "I do believe the luggage is all sorted."

"Thank you, Landon," Walker said.

"Of course, sir," he said. "Is there anything else I can help with before I go?"

Walker shook his head, consulting his pocket watch. "Even if there was, you need to be off. Your train leaves from Victoria in two hours."

"I can take the next train if necessary."

"You'll give our love to our uncle when you get there?" Mira said.

"I'll be certain to. Hopefully, he and your aunt have had some time to settle in."

"I wish you could come with us," she said. They'd only been home for a few short days, and she hadn't seen much of the butler in that time.

"As do I. But if your family is to make a successful move to Spenston Park, I need to be there to oversee the new household staff."

"Besides, if he came we'd have two chaperones," Walker laughed a little. "And then, what would we do?"

"Says the man assigned to chaperone us on the way to Bath," Byron teased.

Landon's eyes crinkled at the corners. "The way you carry on about chaperones, Walker, makes me certain that you need one."

Walker sputtered like a gasping fish, but his protestations were drowned out by the train's whistle.

Mira gave the old butler a hug.

"Goodbye, Landon," Mira said. "Take care."

"I will. I'd ask you to stay out of trouble, but I know that's a fool's wish," he teased.

Mira smiled. "I'll try."

"You'll look after her, won't you?" Landon said, turning to Byron.

"Of course, I will."

On the way to Bath, the trio found themselves splitting their time between their own compartment and the dining car. They would be meeting Liza and her family at the station once they arrived, then going on to their lodgings of the next few weeks. Walker was ostensibly acting as chaperone for Byron and Mira during the trip, but said nothing as they held hands beneath the table during tea. They whiled away an hour, consuming pastries, cheese, sandwiches, and jams, talking about this and that amidst the clattering of cutlery and idle conversations from the other occupants of the dining car.

"It's been ages since I attended a musical program," Mira said. "I hope we have enough time to get ready."

"Seems to me that you only need thirty minutes to look presentable, Mouse," Walker said, teasing.

She gave him a glare, though it lacked heat. "I'd rather not rush if I don't have to. Especially as we aren't familiar with the town. We could arrive with hours to spare to get ready, and lose it all in carriage rides to and from our lodgings and Bath proper."

Byron sighed. "I wish I could escort you there, but I believe my family intends to make an entrance."

"You're certain about staying with them in Bath?" Walker

asked between bites of scone. "From what I hear, Davenguard has plenty of room if you change your mind."

"Positive." Byron rubbed the back of Mira's hand with his thumb. "For the purposes of the investigation, it would be best if no one is aware of my work as a detective. Which means I ought to assume the role of Ambrose Sherard, estranged son and brother."

"Must be dashed confusing to keep everything separate," Walker said. "Two names, two personas, two lives."

"One person," Mira whispered.

Byron squeezed her hand. "Seeing as they rarely intersect, it isn't as much trouble as you'd expect."

"And yet, they are intersecting," Walker said. "Are we going to see a new side to you, old boy?"

"Oh, I don't know," Byron said. "There isn't much difference between the way I act with my family and how I act in a professional setting."

"And here I thought one needed to craft an entirely new identity when one had a pseudonym." Walker spread clotted cream across another scone. "Isn't that part of the fun of it?"

"I suppose," Byron said. "But that would add unnecessary complication. Most people who use pseudonyms only need the luxury of a second name."

Walker frowned. "There aren't that many people who use pseudonyms, are there?"

"Oh, more than you would think. Authors, journalists, scientists, and the like often use a nom de plume in order to maintain their privacy. Using a pseudonym wouldn't change much of their actions in the day to day, except, perhaps, in remembering which signature to use."

"Is that why you chose Constantine?" Walker asked. "For privacy?"

Byron paused, selecting a pastry. "In my case, it's a means of separating from my family name. It allows me to do my work without people paying too much attention. Although, as I've made more of a name as a detective, it has become more difficult." He retrieved a petit four and sat back. "The name change also assuages any embarrassment my family might have in my choice of profession."

"Fair enough," Walker said.

They sat in silence for a few moments. Walker's brow furrowed and he worried at his lip, as if considering his next question with great care.

"I've been thinking about our godfather. Ex-godfather, I suppose." As he spoke, Mira's shoulders tightened. She'd been trying not to think about him. Walker continued.

"I don't think he used a pseudonym. At least not with us." His voice was a bit hollow and he averted his gaze. "But I am wondering if the way he acted with us was a persona."

Mira swallowed, thinking back to how Professor Burke acted in the catacombs. How quickly his mask had shattered.

Byron sat forward. "In my experience, when one takes on a persona, it is necessary to build from a place of truth. If you build an entirely new personality and background, you will need to take great pains to remember everything and avoid contradicting yourself over time. If you don't, you'll be liable to act strangely and draw attention to yourself." He took a sip of tea. "However, if you take one aspect of your personality and amplify it, adjusting small details in your history, it becomes much easier to manage."

"It sounds as if you've taken on a persona yourself," Walker said.

"When necessary," Byron said. "I think the most intense one was Elliot Thorne."

"Thorne?" Walker frowned. "I don't believe I've heard this story."

Mira dabbed a napkin where some jam had dribbled down her hand. "It was just before his accident."

"Before and after, to a degree," Byron said. "I still have an issue when I first wake up with remembering what year it is, and whether I ought to head down to the docks for that gunpowder plot."

"It seems this was more than just a nom de plume then?" Walker said.

"I needed to infiltrate Circe. Consequently, I required a tight identity. I took on a different mode of speaking and shabbier dress, and rented rooms on the opposite side of town so that if anyone followed me it would corroborate my new identity. Over a few months, it became more and more natural to be Mr. Thorne." He chuckled a little. "Even when I intended to go to Palace Court, I would often find myself heading to the new rooms out of habit. Still do, sometimes. You see, the longer you are acting within the persona, the more natural it becomes, and there is a risk of blurring the lines between yourself and the act." His tone grew serious. "I wouldn't be surprised if the lines had long been blurred for Professor Burke when it came to his relationships with the two of you and his role as the Charger."

The silence loomed over them again. Mira shifted in her seat. She understood why Walker was asking such questions. She had asked herself the same questions over the past months. It was difficult to reconcile which version of Edward Burke was real. But she'd never considered that both sides could be genuine.

Walker cleared his throat, taking another sandwich. "Is there a reason why an ordinary person would take on a persona?"

Byron thought for a moment before gesturing across the dining car to a couple deep in conversation. "Imagine, if you will, that those two are having an affair. They wish to travel together, but they do not want to be recognized. Their persona, as you put it, is that of a married couple. They might wear different clothes than usual and travel under a different name, but they needn't change anything else so long as they act as if they are meant to be together." He set his teacup down. "If they create a complicated backstory, they are more likely to stumble over their words, trying to remember exactly how to act. That sort of awkwardness is more likely to stick in the memory."

Mira considered the couple across from them. "Do you really think they are having an affair?"

Byron glanced at them. "No. They've been discussing their child's boarding school in great detail. I highly doubt that they would have concocted such a story in advance."

The train whistled, signaling the next stop. Mira set her napkin on the table, ready to escape the conversation altogether. "Only two stops left. We probably ought to get back to our compartment."

THE VILLAGE OF COMBE DOWN SAT ON a ridge just south of Bath, surrounded by ample woodland and pleasant walking paths. Aunt Eleanor's residence, a limestone house called Davenguard, sat within a copse of trees just outside the village. Mira's second-floor room had a beautiful view down to the city. She and Liza were neck deep in petticoats, hairpins, and all the other accoutrement necessary for attending the music recital that evening. Luckily, they had plenty of time to dress at their leisure.

"You see why I need to make a good second impression, don't you?" Mira said, having explained the terrible introduction she'd had with Byron's family.

"I still can't believe you would go out in public without thinking of what you were wearing." Liza fluffed up a rat of false hair and pinned it in place on the back of Mira's head, adding more volume.

"I wasn't thinking at all. Which is why I can't afford for this next meeting to go poorly."

"Isn't the purpose of attending this recital to gain an understanding of society in Bath?" Liza asked. "So that you and Mr. Constantine can determine the most likely suspects for the thefts? Not so you can impress the Sherards?"

"Yes, but the Sherards will be there, and I must recover from that terrible first impression."

"Well, I shall ensure that you look the part. Proper dress and attire is crucial for these sorts of things."

"That won't be enough." Mira turned to face Liza. "Is the etiquette for music programs much different here in Bath? Is there anything I should know?"

Liza laughed a little. "It isn't anything to be worried about. Certainly, your first meeting left much to be desired, but you don't need to overcomplicate things. Why are you so anxious?"

Mira swallowed, taking a moment to consider her words as she turned back to the mirror. She trusted Liza, but it was difficult to determine why this whole affair was so arduous for her.

"I feel like no matter what I do, I never know quite how to do it the right way. I know that there is a correct way to do it, a proper way, and yet no matter how hard I try something goes wrong."

"That's ridiculous. I've been to several parties with you and I don't remember seeing you . . ." Liza stopped halfway through pinning a silk lily into Mira's hair. "Oh, I suppose there was the time I caught you and Mr. Constantine exiting a room alone together at Sutherland's party. But surely, that was due to your chaperone's negligence."

"We didn't have a chaperone then. And we were in the middle of an investigation. But to the outside eye it was entirely indiscreet. Add to that those countless times when my hair has gone unruly, I've tripped over my own skirt, spilled something or said the wrong thing or been in the wrong place . . . you start to see a pattern."

Liza stifled another laugh. "It can't be that bad, surely."

"I assure you that it is. And of course, I have to consider how that looks to my potential future family. The Sherards come from generations of fortune and status. My family's fortune is quite new, and while my uncle cares a good deal about status, we often forget about propriety as it doesn't come naturally to us."

A pit formed in her stomach as the words came out. She hadn't really voiced her insecurities in quite that way before. At least not to someone else. In an attempt to lighten her tone, she held her hand to her forehead and said, theatrically, "I'm a hopeless case! It seems that my years of finishing school were wasted."

"This really is bothering you, isn't it?" Liza set down the brush.

Mira averted her gaze. "I don't want to disappoint them."

Liza set her hands on her shoulders. "And you won't." She picked up another flower to weave into Mira's hair.

"The most important thing to know about music recitals in Bath, and particularly ones held in the Grand Pump Room, is that you are to be silent for the entirety of the performance. Any coughing or whispering is considered a disrespect. There are two parts, with an intermission between, and one is expected to walk for the entirety of the break, discussing the music."

"Is that all?"

Liza nodded. "Most of the recital you will only need to look pretty and stay silent."

Mira let out a breath. "I can do that."

MIRA FELT AS THOUGH THE SHERARDS WERE staring a hole in the back of her head. She, Walker, and the Renaldis were sitting in the third row. Byron and his family in the fifth. And worst of all, the longer they sat listening to some pieces by Mendelssohn, the more a ticklish sensation crept up the back of her throat. By the end of the second piece, the tickle turned into an itch, and halfway through the fifth it felt as if she was going to erupt in a series of raucous coughs. Luckily, as she was considering how to best muffle her impending outburst with a handkerchief, the first part of the program ended and she was able to escape with dignity to an alcove outside the room before commencing her coughing fit.

Unluckily, she was spotted by an old acquaintance.

"Why, Miss Blayse! Is that you?" Maureen Harris said, her red curls bobbing as she cornered Mira who was gasping for breath. "I don't believe I've seen you since, why yes, since you spilled the punch at my gala last year." She fell into a series of tittering giggles.

Mira's lungs recovered, her eyes watering and cheeks red as she forced herself to laugh as well. Maureen was nice enough, and it wasn't her fault that disaster always followed Mira at social events. "Miss Harris, I didn't know you were in Bath."

"Since September." A wistful expression crossed her face as she looked into the crowd. "The society here is much different to London, but I daresay it's lively enough."

Mira nodded. "Is your family only here for the season?"

Maureen looked away. "My Aunt Rosila Callan refused to be too far from the sea because of her health, you understand. Not that it helped her." She sighed. "And now that I'm under the guardianship of Admiral Hoddle, he doesn't want to move. I'm afraid that Bath is where I will stay, at least until my trust is available next year when I turn twenty-one."

Mira's eyes widened. She knew that Maureen's mother had died in childbirth, but she'd spoken with Mr. Harris at the gala the previous February. Had something happened to him? And to her aunt? "Miss Harris, I didn't realize . . ."

"It was a quiet affair," Maureen said. "And I don't wish to speak of it, if you don't mind."

"I understand," Mira said. "I am sorry though."

"Me too." Maureen looped her arm through Mira's and turned towards the crowd. "But enough about that. What about you? What brings you to Bath?"

"I'm here with the Renaldis. My brother is soon to be engaged to Miss Liza Renaldi, and they invited us down."

"How splendid! And when did you arrive?"

"Just this morning."

"Why then, you haven't had the opportunity to scout the society circles. Allow me to help."

She turned, pulling Mira along to a vantage point behind a potted tree that didn't do much to hide them. She made a vague gesture towards an older man in naval uniform with grey mutton chops and a pleasant expression. He held a drink, laughing at something one of the porters had said, slapping him on the back. "That is Admiral Hoddle. He was good friends with my father, which is why my guardianship fell to him. He, unfortunately, has no sense when it comes to good connections, but has at least acquainted himself with the Risewells since coming here." She pointed to a group of four people, two men and two women.

"Mr. Risewell's fortune migh only span a few generations back, but rumor has it that he is one of the richest men in England at the moment." She gestured to the younger woman, who wore a light blue evening dress and had gorgeous honey-colored hair. "Thus, his only daughter, Theresia, is one of the most eligible debutantes in Bath at the moment. She has as many as two to five suitors at any time, though she never shows much interest in them. Currently, there are two in the running. Silas Treadway is the one doting on her now."

The man in question had dark brown hair and light skin. It was hard to tell his age at a distance, but Mira would guess he was around thirty. He smiled as he spoke out of the side of his mouth, obviously feeling clever about whatever it was he was saying. Theresia was unaffected.

"The other," Maureen continued, gesturing to a young man standing off on his own with black hair and a beard, "is Bertie Corbet, of the Shropshire Corbets, you know."

Mira didn't, but she nodded anyway.

"It's unfortunate that your party didn't arrive until this evening. Why, I'm sure if you had come yesterday the Risewells would have offered you an invitation to their ball tomorrow evening. By the way, that's Catherine Meredeth over there. She and her brother—"

Maureen continued after that fashion, pointing out each family she deemed important, from Reverend Knott and his four spinster daughters, to Dr. George Sherbrooke Turpin and his second wife who had recently moved into the neighborhood. The topic of conversation briefly shifted to the construction of the museum for the Roman ruins and how much it had changed social gatherings, before Maureen abruptly changed the topic again.

"Oh, I can hardly believe it. I almost forgot the Sherards! They spend most of the year in Devon, from what I understand, but always winter here in Bath. The father passed away several years ago, and the eldest son is set to be the next Baron Sherard once their uncle passes. You can see him there. I don't recognize the younger gentleman with them. You don't think . . ." Maureen gasped. "There are two younger eligible Sherards. I think that might be one of them!"

Mira suppressed a smile. Byron scanned the room, hopefully looking for her. She took a step away from Maureen and the tree, taking out her fan. Now, what was the proper way to beckon a gentleman to approach? She was always forgetting these things. She would have to ask Liza for a refresher.

Fortunately, he caught sight of her, eyes brightening as he moved over to her, taking her hand.

"Miss Blayse," he said, kissing the back of it.

"Mr. Sherard," she said, her smile breaking free. "How are you enjoying the program?"

"Oh, very well. I understand that the lead violinist, Mr. Heinrich, is in fine form this evening."

Mira nodded and turned towards Maureen, whose wide eyes betrayed her shock, though she wisely kept her mouth shut. "Miss Harris, may I introduce you to Ambrose Sherard?"

"How do you do, Miss Harris," Byron said, dipping his head.

"It is a pleasure to meet you, sir," Maureen said, with a slight curtsy. "Are you staying long in Bath?"

"A few weeks, I believe. Perhaps a bit longer. Are you enjoying the recital?"

"Oh yes," Maureen gushed. "Mendelssohn has always been a favorite of mine. I wish the whole program was only his music."

The crowd began to move back to the main room. Byron held a hand out to Mira. "Might I escort you back?"

"Of course." She bid a still shocked Maureen farewell and walked with him back to the recital room.

"You seemed deep in conversation with her," he whispered.

"She was informing me of the social climate."

"Gossip?" Byron raised an eyebrow.

"That as well."

"Good. You'll have to tell me about it later."

It wasn't until the conclusion of the program that Mira had the opportunity to be reintroduced to Byron's family. The lingering crowd meandered out of the main room to partake of refreshments. The Sherards stood on a raised platform a little away from the tables, observing the scene. Every so often one of them would make a comment to another, but for the most part they remained silent. Like cathedral statues gazing down on the populace. For as much as Byron insisted he didn't take on a persona with his family, he seemed to be standing straighter than usual, and betrayed none of his usual expressiveness.

Somehow, that made her even more nervous.

Liza came to her side. "Are you going to go talk to them?"

"I don't even know what I'll say. Is it appropriate for me to approach without invitation?"

"Mr. Constantine is courting you. Isn't that invitation enough?"

"I suppose."

Liza laughed. "And here I thought that between you and Walker, you were the more level headed one." She looped her arm through Mira's. "I'll come with you."

Mira shook her head, pulling away. "I can do it."

She crossed the floor, weaving her way around the various conversation groups. Upon her approach, Byron stepped away from his family and came to meet her.

"Good evening, Miss Blayse."

She gave a small curtsy. "Good evening, Mr. Con—Mr. Sherard."

Byron gave her a soft smile. "Are you ready to meet my family again?"

"I'm not sure I will ever be ready."

"You'll do splendid."

He offered his arm and they returned to the Sherards. His mother stood between Mary and Castel. She wore a dark blue ensemble with large sleeves and swathes of fabric crisscrossing over her waist. A single strand of pearls adorned her neck.

"Good evening, Mrs. Sherard," Mira said, once again curtsying. "Did you enjoy the performance?"

Byron's mother considered her and gave a short nod. "It

was a good array of pieces. I appreciated the Massenet especially."

"Oh yes, the violin solo was excellent."

"It's unfortunate you had to leave so abruptly after the Mendelssohn section," Mary said. "Are you unwell?"

"No, thank you," Mira said, cheeks heating.

"Oh, good. I was so worried that you had consumption after I heard that coughing fit in the hall. That wasn't you, then?"

"I-it was."

Byron stepped closer. "It doesn't particularly matter, Mary. As you can see, she is perfectly fine now."

Castel smirked. "Yes, I suppose if it was tuberculosis, she wouldn't be so flushed."

Mira's shoulders tightened as she attempted to retain what little grace she had. "Thank you for asking after my health. I am well. I simply had a tickle in my throat during the performance. And you know how difficult it is when you ought not to do something, and feel inclined to do it anyway." She turned back to Mrs. Sherard. "I wish to apologize for my conduct earlier this week. I assure you, that is not my usual state."

"We shall see, won't we? One's true character tends to show itself over time." Mrs. Sherard opened her purse, removed a card from it and handed it to Mira. "You will come to brunch tomorrow."

Mira took the card, glancing at the swirling calligraphy. "Thank you. I will."

Mrs. Sherard snapped the purse closed. "Good evening, Miss Blayse."

Byron lingered for a moment after his family started to leave. He took her hand, giving it a squeeze. "You did well."

She let out a shuddery breath. "It didn't feel like it."

"Yes, well, Mary can be a bit difficult at first." He kissed her hand. “I wish we could talk more, but I think I had better keep up appearances.”

“We can talk tomorrow.”

He smiled and turned away, following after his family. Liza came to her side.

“That seemed to go well.”

“I’ve been invited to brunch tomorrow.”

“Oh, that’s good isn’t it?” Liza grinned.

Mira shook her head and whispered, “You didn’t see how she looked at me.”

February 8, 1889: Morning

The Royal Crescent was a curved set of connected buildings with Palladian columns and grand windows that overlooked a large green space with sheep grazing upon it. The Sherards had taken up residence in number eighteen for the duration of their stay in Bath. Mira's stomach turned itself into knots as her carriage followed the curve of the road in front of the Crescent and came to a stop.

A footman strode out of the house, opening the carriage door before she had even reached for the handle. She took his offered hand, stepping out onto the pavement, her breath clouding the air. The footman gave half a glance to the interior of the carriage, closed the door, and paid the driver before Mira could take out her purse.

"Is it only you today, Miss?" the man asked.

"Yes. Did I misunderstand the invitation?" She tried to keep her words even as her anxiety spiked. Could she do nothing right?

"It's not my place to say. The Sherards are waiting for you in the parlor. If you'll come this way."

She gave a short nod and followed the footman into the house. He announced her arrival and left her at the mercy of Byron's family.

The first things she noticed about this particular parlor were the chairs. It appeared as if the Sherards kept with the accepted style of armchairs for gentlemen and chairs with deeper seats and no armrests for the ladies. Miss Penistone, Mira's etiquette teacher at finishing school, had never elaborated on the "whys" so Mira wasn't exactly certain what the point of it was. Perhaps it was a ploy for better posture.

In yet another social blunder, Mira's family preferred armchairs as a general rule. Mira in particular enjoyed reading a book near the fire with her legs over one arm and her back resting against the other.

Castel occupied one of the two armchairs in the room, albeit with a much more appropriate posture, but he stood when she entered. Byron was standing by the mantle. His mother and sister had arranged themselves on the only two wide, armless chairs with their skirts splayed out like china dolls. A tea tray sat on a low, Japanese-style table in the center of the room.

"You came alone?" Mrs. Sherard said, the statement bearing only the slightest resemblance to a question.

"I did, ma'am. The invitation did not indicate whether my brother or the Renaldis would be welcome."

A crease appeared on the older woman's forehead. "I see."

Byron stepped forward. "Won't you have a seat?"

Mira nodded. At least she was aware of the rules in this circumstance. She avoided the unoccupied armchair and took a seat on the only sofa in the room. Mary wrinkled her nose, but Mira couldn't decide if she had made the wrong decision or if that was Mary's way of acknowledging her presence. Once she was seated, Byron poured her a cup of tea and took up residence in the other armchair.

"I trust, from what Ambrose has told me, that you too had a pleasant trip from London?" Mrs. Sherard asked.

"Yes. It was enjoyable enough." She glanced at Byron. What was she supposed to say? What were they even supposed to talk about? She fell back on the safe, albeit boring, topic. "I'm glad the weather has kept."

"The weather is almost always amiable in Bath," Mary said. "Why, it hasn't snowed all winter and the rain has been fairly warm for the season."

"That is fortunate," Mira said. "When did you come down?"

"Just after Christmas," Mrs. Sherard said, then changed the subject entirely. "I have come to understand that you have been in my son's employ since September. Is that correct?"

"As his secretary, yes."

"And this is why you have a key to his rooms?"

"Yes." Mira tried to ignore the way her cheeks heated. She took a sip of tea. "Initially, it was so I could more easily help him with his memory loss."

"Yes, well," Mrs. Sherard lifted her chin, "I understand that his memory has improved in recent months. Although, not well enough for him to remember to inform me of it himself."

Byron shook his head. "As I told you before, I was on a case. Several cases, actually."

"With how much you rely on writing things down, I would think you would be more familiar with paper and pen," Mrs. Sherard said. A small smile came to her face as she raised her teacup to her lips. "Or is it the envelope that eludes you?"

Mira inhaled some of her tea, looking up at Byron's mother, trying not to choke. Had that been . . . a joke?

Mrs. Sherard turned her full attention back to Mira abruptly, and it was as if the smile had never existed. "Now then. I am told that your uncle is a merchant, is that correct?"

The conversation carried on in similar fashion until they were called to the dining room. Mira took solace in the fact that she was seated next to Byron, but then the onslaught of questions continued. Who were her parents? How long had she been in the care of her uncle? Where did her brother go to school? Where did she go to school? She had been expecting questions about her family, but she was surprised by the sheer number and rapid pace.

Towards the end of the meal, Mary said, "It is curious to me why a woman in your position would take up a secretarial job. Surely your uncle was against it."

"He was. It was more of an accident that led me to the job. I had come to By—Ambrose for help to solve a mystery of my own. And my uncle, well," she looked at Byron and couldn't help the smile that suffused to her face, "he couldn't have made his position clearer."

Byron's eyes crinkled at the corners. "I still remember how shocked he was when he realized I wasn't a charlatan after all."

The two of them fell into a bout of laughter, silenced the moment Mira realized that none of his family were joining them. Mrs. Sherard had an expression on her face that Mira couldn't decipher.

Mira dabbed at her mouth with a napkin, deciding to take the conversation in an entirely new direction. "I hear that you have a mystery that needs solving. Thefts?"

"It will be sorted soon enough," Mary said, but it was abundantly clear what she meant to say was, *We don't want you involved.* Surprisingly, Mrs. Sherard offered more information.

"It happened last week on the twenty-eighth. We were hosting a dinner party that lasted about four hours. The guest list included the Risewells, Admiral Hoddle and Miss Harris.

After we bid them goodnight, I came to my room and found my jewelry box open. The police determined that the window lock had been picked but haven't been helpful in any other regard."

Mira turned to Byron. "Have you started your investigation?"

"I wanted to wait for you."

Warmth blossomed in her chest and she turned back to Mrs. Sherard. "Might we see your room after brunch?"

"Certainly."

THE SPACIOUS ROOM HAD BLUE-GREEN WALLPAPER IN the style of William Morris and an oriental rug covering a dark wooden floor. Mira and Byron started their investigation at the vanity which stood against a wall adjacent to the bed.

"I don't keep much of my jewelry on hand. Most of it is in the safe in Gurrington House or in the bank," Mrs. Sherard said.

Byron picked up the box, examined the lock, and removed a strand of pearls. "I gather you were wearing these during the dinner party?"

"Yes. They took everything else."

"And left the box. That's curious. One would expect them to take the box and pick the lock at a safer location." Byron set the box back down. Mira looked out the window. Behind the Royal Crescent was a row of walled off courtyards and gardens and then a procession of houses on the opposite side.

"The police think they came through the window?" she asked.

"Where else would they have come from?" Mary asked from where she stood at the threshold of the room. "Surely we would have heard them if they had come through the house."

"It was merely a question, Mary." Byron came to Mira's

side. "The window was locked the evening in question?" he asked.

"Of course," Mrs. Sherard said. "It is not my habit to leave things unlocked that needn't be. The inspector had the audacity to suggest I had left it unlocked in a moment of 'feebleness.' As if my age is the only indicator of my state of mind." She grimaced at the notion.

"He is ill informed in regards to our familial faculties, in that case," Byron said, testing the lock himself and opening the window. He stuck his head out for a brief moment and came in again. "I think we'd better see how they got up."

The party was soon in the courtyard looking up at Mrs. Sherard's bedroom. There was no ivy or trellises that would allow for an easy climb. Byron moved to the garden bed beneath the window.

"Have you had your windows cleaned recently?" he asked.

"Heavens no," Mrs. Sherard said. "We're in the wet season."

"These indentations suggest the use of a ladder. I doubt the thief brought it with him. Do you have one?"

"The gardener might," Mary said. "In the shed."

"Is it kept locked?"

"How am I supposed to know?"

Byron rubbed his temples. "Show me."

Mary sighed and picked up her skirts, walking towards the back of the garden. Byron and Castel followed after.

Mira turned back to the window and the ladder indentations. The lock had been on the inside of the window, so how could a thief have picked it from the outside? She searched along the ground for any sign of a tool being dropped. Instead, she found two circular holes on either side of the doorway to the kitchen, about a halfpenny in size. Ignoring Mrs. Sherard's sharp gaze, she removed one of her gloves and measured the depth with her finger. She didn't touch the bottom of it.

"Perhaps this would be of some use." Mrs. Sherard offered her cane, which was about the same width as the hole.

Mira nodded and used the cane to measure the depth—about six inches. The other hole measured the same.

She stood, handed the cane back to Mrs. Sherard and rubbed the dirt from her hand with a handkerchief. "Thank you. You don't happen to remember making these holes with your cane, do you?"

"No. I haven't been in this courtyard since early January, and it has rained some since then."

Silence settled between the two of them and Mira wasn't sure what to do with it. The garden was quiet, with the exception of a few birds chittering away as they feasted at a porcelain bird feeder.

"There is something I've always wondered, if you don't mind me asking," Mira said, testing the waters.

Mrs. Sherard inclined her head, but didn't look in Mira's direction. She took that as invitation to continue.

"You named him Byron Ambrose Sherard, with Byron as the first name. Yet you all call him Ambrose. I know it's a family name, but then, why not use Ambrose as the first given name?"

Mrs. Sherard smiled a little, her gaze growing distant and unfocused. "When I was a girl, I loved to read poetry. Lord Byron was a particular favorite of mine. As I grew older, I thought it would make a fine name for a son. Little did I know, I would marry a reverend."

Mira was surprised at the warmth in her voice and her candor. It didn't match her earlier demeanor whatsoever. She was so forthright.

"My husband didn't care much for Lord Byron. Said he was overdramatic and his lifestyle scandalous. I suppose that was true, but his poetry was beautiful, and he died a hero in Greece. After Castel, Philip, and Simon, rest his soul, then Ralph, all family names, my husband agreed that if we had another son,

I could name him Byron. When the time came, he wasn't as agreeable to the idea, so we compromised. His middle name would be Ambrose, after the saint, and we called him that."

"You mean, Ambrose isn't a family name at all?" Mira asked.

Mrs. Sherard shook her head. "Whenever someone would ask, we would say it was. All the rest of the boys were named from the ancestral line."

Byron, Castel, and Mary were making the trek back across the lawn. Mira lowered her voice.

"Does he know?"

Mrs. Sherard glanced her way for the first time, a twinkle in her eye. "I'm not sure that he does."

Once her children were within hearing distance, it was as if a wall came up between them again.

"The shed was unlocked," Byron said, and Mira couldn't help but make the comparison between him and the famous poet. Perhaps not quite so brooding, but certainly as handsome. "Did you find anything else here?"

Mira pointed out the holes on either side of the door. "I'm not sure if these are related, but they are too uniform to have happened accidentally."

Byron crouched to the ground. "I'd agree. If I'm not mistaken, these holes were made by a couple stakes, driven into the ground, likely with a wire across them."

"Why would the gardener do that?" Mary asked.

Byron looked up at his sister. "The gardener didn't. The thieves did, to ensure their escape should anyone in the house notice them. Tripwires."

"I've heard of that," Castel said. "The burglaries at Bournemouth and Ascot last month used the same method."

Byron stood, stretching his back. "I really ought to find time to catch up on my newspapers. What was stolen in those cases?"

"Jewelry," Castel said. "I only paid attention to it because the first happened to the Austrian-Hungarian ambassador and the second to the Secretary of American Legation. The Foreign Office likes to keep track of those sorts of things. Almost ten thousand pounds worth of jewels between the two of them."

Byron whistled. "That is quite a sum."

"Could the burglaries be connected?" Mary asked.

"It's possible," Byron said. "You mentioned on Monday that there had been more burglaries here in Bath, yes?"

"Three. One being within our circle. The Meredeths had a necklace stolen a week before our robbery," Mary said.

"Shall we take the conversation inside?" Mrs. Sherard stated, already moving.

Once they were seated in the parlor again, Byron said to Mira, "You seem to be deep in thought. What's your view?"

The whole company of Sherards turned to her and her stomach twisted.

"The window bothers me," she said, trying to focus only on Byron. "If we extrapolate from the discernible facts, the thieves set up a wire to trip anyone, should they be discovered. They borrowed a ladder from the shed and accessed the window with it. But the latch is on the inside. The thief wouldn't have been able to pick the lock and the window wasn't forced." She straightened her shoulders, finally looking at the rest of the family. "So someone had to have unlocked it from the inside."

"I've been wondering that too." Byron pulled out his notebook and flipped to a new page. "Did any of your guests leave the group at any time?"

"Surely you aren't suggesting that it's someone in our circle," Mary said, incredulous.

"We can't rule anything out yet," Byron said, raising an eyebrow. "Well?"

"Mrs. Risewell and Miss Risewell both left to freshen up between courses," Mrs. Sherard said. "And Miss Harris stepped outside for some air before joining the ladies in the drawing room."

Castel frowned. "Admiral Hoddle asked for directions to the WC after the women left the dining room."

Byron hummed. "That doesn't narrow it down much." He looked up at Mira. "We'll need to make some inquiries." After a disapproving look from his sister, he said, "Discreetly, of course."

Mrs. Sherard stood and pulled a cord near the fireplace. A faint ringing sounded, and a few moments later, the butler appeared.

"Greerson, I need you to send a note to the Risewells asking if they might allow for some additional guests for the ball this evening." She turned to Mira. "How many were in your party with the Renaldis?"

Mira blinked. "One gentleman and four ladies, counting myself."

Mrs. Sherard nodded, speaking to Greerson again. "You'll want to verify that Ambrose is invited as well. Send one of the footmen in the carriage and make sure that he doesn't return without the response."

"Yes, madam," Greerson said, leaving the room.

"There. That's settled," Mrs. Sherard said. "You best let your friends know, Miss Blayse, as I doubt the Risewells will refuse."

February 8, 1889: Evening

In deed, the Risewells did not refuse, and neither did the Blayses nor the Renaldis. As such, Mira entered Wynmar Park on Ambrose Sherard's arm at precisely nine o'clock. A footman greeted them and directed them down the hallway, where another footman received them.

"The ballroom is just through here," the man said, his voice a little shaky. He ducked his head and extended an arm towards the open door.

The Risewell estate was west of Pucklechurch, a good hour from the city, but that didn't preclude half the society of Bath from attending. Perhaps that was an exaggerated estimate, but there were at least a hundred people from what Mira could see. The Georgian-style ballroom was breathtaking with ceiling roses, decorative plasterwork, columns, and cornices.

Mira adjusted the sleeves of her blue silk evening gown. The gathering was more akin to a soirée than a ball. The guests flitted about between the refreshment tables and conversations. A few tables were set up for cards and there was a young lady playing the piano in the corner.

For the case of the stolen Sherard jewelry, Mira and Byron determined there were five main points of inquiry. The first was the servants at number eighteen, Royal Crescent. They had already exhausted that line of questioning earlier in the day and determined it to be unlikely that any of the staff had been an accomplice, due to their long history of service and loyalty. That left the dinner guests. Specifically the ones who left the group for a period of time: Mrs. Risewell, Miss Risewell, Miss Harris, and Admiral Hoddle. Any of the four could have slipped up to Mrs. Sherard's bedroom and unlocked the window.

Mrs. Risewell and her daughter, Theresia, stood greeting guests at the entrance of the ballroom. Admiral Hoddle was gesticulating widely, his drink sloshing around, as he told a story to a group of men near the fireplace. Maureen Harris stood by the refreshment table talking to a young man.

Another footman, standing just inside the ballroom, directed them towards the Risewells.

"—this is my youngest son." Mrs. Sherard said, making the introductions. "And this is Mrs. Davidson," she pointed to Aunt Eleanor, "Mrs. Renaldi and her daughter, and Mr. and Miss Blayse."

Mira nodded. "Thank you for extending the invitation to include us."

"Oh, we were happy to do so," Mrs. Risewell said, her eyes crinkling at the corners. She wore a blue dress with a frilly bodice and enormous sleeves with a dark choker around her neck.

Theresia stepped forward. She was willowy and wore a red and pink dress with lace detailing and roses along the sleeves.

Her honey-brown hair was piled on her head with ringlets and roses placed around the crown. She fluttered her fan just beneath her chin. "I was wondering when we would have the pleasure of meeting you, Mr. Sherard. Your sister has told us so much about you."

"Has she?" Byron chuckled. "I certainly hope you've been saying good things about me, Mary."

"Of course," Mary said.

"Do you shoot, Ambrose?" Mr. Risewell asked.

"A little," Byron said. "I'm afraid I haven't had much time to perfect the sport."

"I was just talking with Castel. We're putting together a party to go shooting sometime this week, if you're up to it." He gestured to Walker. "You as well, if you'd like."

"We'd be happy to," Byron said.

It didn't seem proper to question the Risewells about the thefts with so many people in line behind them, so after exchanging a few more pleasantries, the group moved on.

"That was advantageous," Byron whispered to her. "I might find it easier to question him in a more casual setting."

"I'll see about talking more with Theresia. Maybe Liza can help with that. They are about the same age."

Byron nodded. "I believe we'll need an introduction to speak with Admiral Hoddle. Would you rather we use my family or Maureen?"

"Why not both? He may act differently in front of your family. You and your family can approach him first while I talk with Maureen. Then she can introduce me and we can compare afterwards."

"Splendid thought. And you can scout out the refreshment table at the same time." He glanced in that direction. "Although, I believe Walker will be the better informant on that front."

With that, they separated, each on their own mission. As Mira wound her way through the crowd towards the refreshment table, a bit of conversation piqued her interest. A circle of women she didn't recognize stood together, gossiping.

". . . and every year they come back, like birds to nest," one of the ladies said.

Mira stood far enough away as to not draw attention to herself and half-pretended to admire a painting on the wall. Romantic era. Perhaps Turner.

The same lady continued, "I wonder why the Estfields dislike wintering here so much."

"In comparison to Italy, my dear, I see their reasoning."

"No, no," a third chimed in. "I thought they were in the French Riviera this year."

"They could be staying in as foreign a place as Chipping Sodbury and it wouldn't matter to me," the oldest of the group said. "What I find more curious is how the Risewells are handling the staff situation." She took a sip of her drink.

"Oh yes," said the second again. "Didn't they bring only two servants with them and hired the rest once they arrived?"

"That isn't so unusual, is it?" the first asked.

"No. But it is unusual for one of the two to be a gardener," the oldest said. "It is much harder to find good butlers and footmen than it is to find gardeners."

"Very strange with it being winter too. I would have thought the Estfields would leave their own gardener to take care of the general maintenance."

"Oh, they did," the oldest said.

"Why then, what need do the Risewells have for a gardener?"

The third looked towards the piano and wrinkled her nose. "Oh, someone ought to stop Miss Meredeth. She's so heavy handed with the high notes."

"At least she plays better than Miss Harris. That piece she exhibited a few weeks ago was simply dreadful."

Mira frowned. Maureen played the piano rather well—her

father had taught her. Perhaps it was a different Miss Harris they were talking about. She stepped away from the conversation as it continued in a more musical direction.

Could the Risewells be working with a thief? A gardener would have better knowledge of where to find a ladder and the use of stakes and gardening wire. They would have to look into it later. For now, she focused on tracking down Maureen Harris.

It was an easy enough prospect, as Maureen hadn't moved from her conversation with the young gentleman, although a second gentleman had joined their circle. As she approached, Maureen lit up and beckoned her over, her yellow taffeta skirt making a rustling scroop noise as she moved.

"Why, Miss Blayse! I didn't realize you were invited. It is so good to see you again." She pulled Mira closer and gestured to the gentlemen. "I don't believe you've met Silas Treadway."

Silas grinned and some of his brown hair fell into his face.

"And this is Bertie Corbet," Maureen said.

Bertie gave a slight bow, his dark beard masking his expression. "It's a pleasure to meet you, Miss..?"

"Samira Blayse," Maureen answered for her. "We ran in similar circles in London."

"It's nice to meet you too," Mira said.

"Now, Miss Blayse, what brings you to Bath?" Silas said.

"I'm visiting the Sherards," Mira said, deciding that was the least complicated way of explaining her stay. "Ambrose Sherard and I are courting, you see."

"Ah. I haven't had the pleasure of meeting him yet."

"We just arrived from London yesterday."

Bertie pursed his lips. "He's the detective, isn't he?"

Mira's eyes widened. They'd been so careful to keep his professional and personal lives separate.

"Detective?" Silas straightened.

"I saw him coming in," Bertie said, "Doesn't he work under the name Constantine?"

"I think I know who you're talking about," Mira said, mind racing for a way to maintain their story. "They do have a remarkable resemblance to one another." She lowered her voice. "Though you ought to know the Sherards dislike the comparison. They hate publicity and I can't think of a more conspicuous profession."

"Can you imagine?" Maureen said.

"I am sorry for interrupting your conversation," Mira said, hoping to change the subject. "I only meant to stop in for a moment."

"We were only talking of Mr. Treadway's service in the Sudan," Maureen said.

"You are in the army, Mr. Treadway?" Mira asked.

"I was honorably discharged last year due to an injury."

"And he won't tell me anything about what it was like," Maureen said.

"It wouldn't be appropriate for a lady to hear." Silas smiled apologetically.

"The least you can tell me is what General Gordon was like."

Silas shook his head. "I'm afraid I never had the opportunity to meet him."

Maureen looked off towards the window, sobering considerably. "I remember hearing the news when he was killed." She turned back to Silas, eyes brightening. "Did you know, my father was invited to take a trip to interview him about the conflict?"

"He was a journalist?" Silas asked. "I don't believe I knew that."

"One of the best," Maureen said. "He worked with the Foreign Office, you know."

"Is that so?" Silas said.

Mira picked up a plate, considering the various refreshments. "I'm sure the society in Bath is much more pleasant than the Sudan."

"Quite different," Silas said.

Bertie scoffed.

Silas raised an eyebrow. "You disagree?"

"I know nothing of the society you experienced in the Sudan, but I've found society here to be its own kind of warfare."

"Oh?" Mira said.

"Underneath the trappings of polite society, there is a calculated ruthlessness," he said. "For instance, one could describe the conversations here as idle gossip or one could liken it to a type of reconnaissance. The socialites who know the most are the most dangerous, and there is a strategy in knowing when to speak and when to remain silent."

"I've never thought of it that way," Mira said.

Silas clapped Bertie on the shoulder. "And there's always the rivalry that comes from pursuing the same debutante, eh?"

"I wouldn't put it that way." Bertie's demeanor chilled and he stepped away from Silas. "If you'll excuse me." He gave a short bow and left the group.

"An odd duck, that one," Silas said.

"He hasn't been the same since his brother died," Maureen said with a sigh. "Killed in the war last year, poor man."

"Yes, quite sad," Silas said, pulling out his pocket watch. "I think I'll pop out for a bit of fresh air, if you ladies don't mind. It's getting a bit stuffy in here."

The room was warm, although less so now that the numbers had dwindled some. It appeared the families with younger children had left.

"Oh, of course. Please do," Maureen said.

Silas tucked his watch away and left their company.

"He's so interesting," Maureen said. "I can't imagine why Theresia doesn't like him."

"You mean, in a courting sense or generally?" Mira asked.

"Both. I mean, if you don't like someone generally, how would you ever withstand a courtship with them? Of course, I've never been courted myself, and likely never will, so who am I to say anything."

"Don't say that. You're not even twenty yet."

"Oh, I don't mean because of my age or looks or anything like that. No. I simply don't think Admiral Hoddle is over-keen on my meeting any eligible men."

"Why do you say that?" Mira lowered her voice. "He isn't misusing your estate, is he?"

"Heavens, no. He doesn't have any real access to the trust at all. That's all handled by my father's solicitor. No, it's just a feeling I get whenever we talk about my getting married or moving. I think he may just be attached to my aunt's house here in Bath. Which is strange, since he's only been living there a month or so."

"That reminds me," Mira said. "I had meant to ask you to introduce him to me."

"I'd be happy to." Maureen linked her arm with Mira's and looked about the room. "I'm not sure where I saw him last."

"He was near the fireplace earlier."

"Oh, that's right. On his third whiskey, if I remember correctly. He's not there now." Maureen picked up a plate from the table. "Perhaps we should bring him a peace offering."

They took a few minutes to sample and comment on the refreshments before making their way around the room. They passed Theresia and the Risewells as they walked.

"Why do you think she dislikes him?"

"Who?" Maureen asked.

"Theresia and Silas. You said it was a general dislike. I wondered why."

"Clash of personalities, I suppose. Although, I think I already told you that Theresia doesn't really like any of her suitors. We aren't close enough for me to ask why, and even if we were, I don't know if she'd tell me."

They searched the whole ballroom, passing in and out of conversations with no sign of Admiral Hoddle. After the better part of an hour, Maureen said, "Does it seem to you that there aren't quite so many people as before?"

Mira glanced about the room. Sure enough, the numbers had dwindled significantly. Only about thirty or so people left and Admiral Hoddle wasn't among them.

"It is getting late," Mira said.

"Not for the Risewells. They keep all hours. There's a side door along that hall there, maybe Hoddle went out on the veranda," Maureen said, pulling Mira along.

The hallway was dimmer than the ballroom, which surprised Mira as it was lined with windows on the west side and the moon was half full. It was also quite a bit colder. The grandfather clock in the hallway chimed eleven.

"I do hope he hasn't left me here. I didn't think the carriage would be coming until after midnight."

"If he has, there's enough room in ours."

Maureen opened the side door and a chill wind rushed around them, sharp bits of ice stinging their cheeks. A heavy snowfall was descending, with several inches already on the ground. Mira helped Maureen push the door closed again.

"I certainly hope Admiral Hoddle didn't go out in that," Mira said.

They returned to the ballroom and found Byron, Walker, and the Renaldis standing together.

"Why, Liza Renaldi!" Maureen said. "It is so good to see you."

"You as well," Liza said, giving Maureen a hug. "I haven't seen you since your—"

"Yes. I know," Maureen said, too quickly.

Mira shared a glance with Byron. She'd have to ask Liza

what she knew about Miss Harris, but now was not the time. Instead, she covered for Maureen. "Have you seen the snow?"

Byron nodded. "Someone noticed it worsening about thirty minutes ago, hence the mass exodus. I only heard about it five minutes ago, but with the way it is coming down, I doubt anyone got ahead of it."

"I hope no one gets stuck on the road," Liza said. "That would be dreadful."

"Did the Admiral go too?" Maureen asked.

"I haven't seen him since ten or so," Byron said.

The Sherards joined their group, Mrs. Sherard looking particularly drawn.

"Mamma, do you need to sit down?" Byron asked, coming to her side.

"No, no. I need you to hire another carriage," Mrs. Sherard said.

Byron frowned.

Mary said, "Benson has informed us that the carriage became stuck in the mud as he brought it around. When he and one of the staff here tried to free it, the horses moved too fast and the axle snapped."

"Which is why we must call for another carriage. If we are going to leave, we ought to do so in short order," Mrs. Sherard said.

"Mamma, the weather is bad enough, I don't think it would be wise for us to travel, regardless of the carriage." Byron said.

"I agree," Mary said. "It wouldn't do for you to catch your death of cold. And how are we to hire a carriage all the way out here?"

Mr. Risewell approached. "I am so sorry for the inconvenience."

"You couldn't have foreseen the weather changing so abruptly," Mrs. Sherard said.

"If I had known an hour ago how much it would snow, I

never would have let anyone attempt the journey." Mr. Risewell said. "I have already informed my staff that our guests will be staying the night. I'm afraid we only have six extra rooms, but if everyone is game, I think we'll manage." After a moment, he added, with a laugh, "And if the weather clears up well enough, we might even have a good hunt tomorrow! Just give us a few minutes to sort things out, and in the meantime, if you can divide yourselves into proper sleeping arrangements, I'd be much obliged."

Mira looked at the remaining group: Dr. Turpin and his wife were there, Bertie Corbet stood off on his own, and there was Admiral Hoddle. She hadn't seen him come in. She nudged Maureen.

"I think, considering the circumstances, the introduction can wait until tomorrow," she said.

"Oh yes, that's probably best."

MIRA HOPED THAT THE ACCOMMODATIONS WOULD ALLOW her to glean information one-on-one from Theresia, Maureen, or Liza. Unfortunately, due to the lack of rooms, she wouldn't have the opportunity.

"It was incredibly generous of the Risewells to put us up like this," Liza said, running her fingers through her hair.

"Oh, they couldn't very well throw us into the storm," Maureen said.

A knock came at the door and Mira stood to open it. The same footman that had gestured them into the ballroom stood there with a stack of clothes in his hands.

"Miss Risewell asked for these to be sent over," he said, his head turned to the side.

Something about his voice was vaguely familiar. He was fairly short and stocky, but in the dim light it was difficult to see his face. "Thank you," she said, stepping aside. "Can you put them on the dresser, please?"

He seemed surprised, hesitating for a moment before entering. A gas lamp was on the wall above the door and as he passed beneath it Mira caught sight of a small scar on his cheek.

"What was your name?" she asked, hoping to hear more of his voice.

"Fitzwilliam, miss," he said, still avoiding her gaze.

She nodded. "You don't happen to know where my brother's room is, do you?"

"Brother, miss?"

"Walker Blayse. I believe he's with two other gentlemen."

"Oh, yes, miss. He's in the Blue Room. On the far end of this landing with Mr. Constantine and Mr. Sherard. Would you like me to take you to him?"

"No, that's alright," Mira said. "I just wanted to know. Thank you, Fitzwilliam."

The footman nodded and left the room. Mira drummed her fingers on the top of the dresser.

"What was that about?" Liza asked. "You already knew which room was Walker's."

"I was just testing something," Mira said.

Maureen paused in braiding her hair. "Your Mr. Sherard must really bear a resemblance to this Constantine fellow. First Bertie and then the footman? Any chance they are secretly twins?"

"It's strange, isn't it?" Mira said, changing into the borrowed nightclothes and wrapping herself in a dressing gown. The more she thought about it, the more she was certain that her hypothesis was correct. Though she didn't want to give anything away to the footman.

After fifteen minutes of idle conversation, she cited a need for the WC and left their room, heading for the Blue Room.

She tiptoed across the carpet, hoping that the footman wasn't keeping an ear out.

She knocked on the door and Castel opened it, his brow furrowing.

"Dare I ask what you are doing here in such a state?"

Mira's cheeks burned. "It is perfectly acceptable for this time of night. May I come in?"

"Who is it?" Walker called from inside the room.

"Your sister, who I hope is here for you and not my brother."

"May I come in?" Mira repeated.

Castel stood aside, and Mira stepped in. Walker sat on the edge of the bed. Byron looked up from where he was writing at the desk, his hair rumpled and shirt half unbuttoned. He left his writing, evidently not noticing his own state of undress. Castel closed the door behind her.

Before anyone could ask her what was wrong, she asked, "Did you notice the footman?"

Byron frowned. "Which one?"

"The one helping us with our rooms. I recognized him. I'm almost positive that he's Charles Montague."

Byron's frown deepened. "I'm afraid I'm a bit fuzzy on that name."

Walker spoke up. "Wasn't he the one you met with in Reading?"

"Yes. Monty."

"The thief." Byron's eyes sparkled.

"Reading?" Castel said. "This wasn't that business with the sheep, was it?"

"You heard about that?" Byron asked.

Castel shrugged. "I keep in touch with Wensley. How else am I to know anything about your work?"

"But don't you see," Mira said, "if he's here, then he must be involved with the thefts."

"We don't know that for certain." Byron tapped his finger on his chin. "And we don't know for certain if it is Monty."

"He referred to you as Mr. Constantine, even though I didn't mention you at all, and he has a scar on his cheek."

"From the parrot," Byron said, clicking his tongue. "Does he know that you recognized him?"

"I don't think so. I tried to be discreet."

"In some aspects, certainly," Castel said, tone dry.

"That was quick thinking on your part," Byron said, ignoring his brother and opening the door again. "You'd best get back before anyone notices. We can question him tomorrow."

February 9, 1889: Early Morning

Wynmar Park sat at the top of a hill with a gradual incline on the east side and a steep drop on the west. The Rose Room, where Mira, Liza, and Maureen had been put up, had a view of the fields beyond the drop. The snow had let up during the night, leaving a pristine blanket of white all the way to a line of trees at the far end of the property. Mira sat in the window seat and looked out over the quiet, winter morning. The other women were still asleep.

She traced the edge of each window pane, the cold seeping into her fingertips. Dark horses with red-clad riders moved across the snow towards the woods. Dogs ran beside them. It seemed Mr. Risewell had his hunting party after all. She had heard some movement in the house—that was what had woken her.

She knew she probably ought to be thinking over the case. If Byron had gone on the hunt, when would they confront Monty and what questions would they ask? Had the Risewells brought their footman with them to the dinner party at the Royal Crescent? Was he the accomplice who unlocked the window in Mrs. Sherard's room?

No matter how much she tried to focus on the case, her thoughts kept returning to Byron and his family.

On her first meeting with Castel Sherard, she found him cold, disagreeable, and calculating. He certainly placed a greater importance on status, hierarchy, and propriety than even her uncle did. But he seemed to truly care about his brother, despite the age difference between them and despite Castel's clear disdain for Byron's career choice. When they had spoken at Sutherland's party all those months ago, she could tell he held real guilt over Byron's memory loss. He felt as if it were his fault for bringing the case to him. At this point, it seemed as if they were on friendlier terms.

If Castel was cold on their first meeting, his sister, Mary, was frigid and openly hostile. Mira closed her eyes, letting her head fall against the window frame, as the memory of their first meeting, less than a week ago, flooded her mind again. Why had she been so careless? She wasn't sure how she would ever overcome that embarrassing first impression.

It shouldn't matter. Byron loved her. He was willing to give it all up, and she loved him for it. But she didn't want to force him to choose.

And then, there was Byron's mother. Mira didn't know what to think of Mrs. Sherard. She held the same tenets as her two eldest children when it came to status and family standing. And yet, Mira felt as if something had shifted when they spoke in the garden about Byron's name. Some warmth had shone through for a moment before that icy exterior slid into place.

Why would a mother hide her warmth from her own children?

Or had Mira imagined the warmth, hoping for some maternal connection that wasn't there at all?

A knock sounded at the door, rousing Liza and Maureen from their slumber. Mira opened the door. This time it was Theresia Risewell, laden with more clothes.

"My apologies," she said. "I didn't realize you weren't all up."

"I've been up for nearly an hour," Mira said, opening the door farther so that Theresia could come in.

Liza pulled a blanket around her shoulders. "It's no bother."

Maureen stifled a yawn. "Has the snow stopped?"

Theresia nodded, setting the clothes on the bed. "Most of the men have headed out to hunt. I thought we could have some breakfast and then walk to the bottom of the ridge to meet them when they return."

"Did Mr. Blayse go?" Liza asked. When Theresia nodded again, Liza said, "Oh, I've always wondered what he would look like in hunting pinks."

"All the men went, except for Admiral Hoddle," Theresia elaborated. "He couldn't be roused this morning."

"I'm not surprised," Maureen said. "He never was an early riser, especially after a party."

After breakfast, the walking company set out along the snowy paths. They took a long route down a switchback to the west of the estate in order to avoid the steeper sections. A few flurries flew around them, but it was pleasant enough. The group was comprised of Mira, Liza, Maureen, Theresia, and Aunt Eleanor who insisted on coming as soon as she discovered their object.

"So many young men, all with their blood up after a hunt," Aunt Eleanor muttered under her breath, though Mira was certain she wasn't the only one who heard it. Eleanor said a bit louder, "And to drag an old woman through the chill and snow."

"You didn't have to come," Liza said. "You could have stayed up at the house with my mother."

"It isn't right for you young ladies to be unaccompanied."

They came to the base of the hill with the steep slope to their right and continued down the path, boots crunching over the snow. Mira increased her pace so she could walk next to Theresia. She wasn't exactly certain how to ask the question she wanted in a way that wouldn't cause suspicion. If the Risewells were working with the thieves, it wouldn't do to put them on their guard. But she was so curious about that bit of gossip she overheard the night before, and, if Byron was questioning Mr. Risewell during the hunt, she ought to do her part.

"I heard that your family leases this estate every year, is that right?"

Theresia inclined her head. "My father is an avid hunter, as you probably noticed, but we don't have the land to raise birds and deer and still have enough pasture for the horses. We split our time between our home outside of London in the summer and here in the winter. The Estfields have an annual holiday, and my father doesn't have to maintain the game."

"That's reasonable enough. Does Wynmar take much upkeep, then?"

"Oh, not really. The Estfields leave their gardeners and stewards."

"Then you really only have to worry about the manor staff. And I'm sure you bring your staff with you from London, so that isn't much of a change."

"Oh, no. We always hire most of the staff here new each winter. My father prefers the house in London to remain open while we're gone. You see, he returns to London a few times during the winter to check on his business assets. We only bring our grooms along to take care of the horses. I wouldn't trust my horse, Verona, with anyone else."

"That's funny," Maureen said. "I've heard tell that you brought gardeners with you."

Theresia laughed. "People fixate on the strangest things, don't they? Mr. Sharpe was our gardener years ago, but he proved to do better with horses than horticulture. And he's an excellent gamekeeper too."

They came around a bend and Mira froze in place. There, up ahead, was a dark mass just off the path.

"What is that?" Maureen asked, her voice shaky.

"I think it's a body," Mira said, picking up her skirts. "I say!" she called as she approached, praying that whoever it was was still alive.

There was no answer, and as she came closer she discovered it was the body of a man, face down and half covered in snow.

She swallowed and crouched beside him, turning him over. His face was blue with cold, cloudy eyes staring at the grey sky, blood coating his forehead and coloring the snow beneath him.

Maureen screamed, taking several steps back. "No. Not again. No."

"Why . . ." Theresia said. "That's Silas."

Hands shaky, Mira removed one of her gloves, pushed the collar of his coat back, and pressed her fingers to his neck.

Nothing.

Her heart and mind were racing. Was it murder? An accident? Suicide? She looked up the side of the slope. If he had fallen, whatever the cause, the snow had covered any mark of his descent. There were no other footprints aside from theirs. Theresia was frozen beside her. Aunt Eleanor had a hand over her mouth in a state of shock. Maureen was pale as a sheet, staring at the blood in the snow.

Liza put her arm around her. "Shh. It's going to be all right."

"There's so much blood," Maureen cried.

Mira took off her coat, draping it over the body to hide it from view. "Liza, will you and your aunt take Miss Harris back to the house?"

"Of course. Come along, Maureen. We'll get some tea made for everyone."

"But . . . the blood."

"I know. You'll be all right."

Mira turned to Theresia. "Miss Risewell, did Dr. Turpin join the hunt this morning?"

"Y-yes. He did."

"Do you think you—" she stopped mid-sentence. She was going to ask if Theresia would be up to fetching the doctor and Byron from the hunt, but the poor woman was shaking like a leaf. "Would you mind if I borrowed your horse?"

Theresia shook her head, pointing. "The stables are on the north side. T-there's a path up ahead."

"Good. Does Wynmar have a telephone?"

"In the study."

"Go and call the police, then. Even if it is an accident, they will want to make sure."

Theresia dragged her gaze away from Silas for the first time since they discovered the body and locked eyes with Mira. After a moment she took a sharp breath and turned, hurrying after the other women.

Mira hated to leave the body, but she needed to fetch Byron and the doctor. She turned in the opposite direction, running towards the path Theresia had pointed out.

As she rounded the bend she ran headlong into Admiral Hoddle. He stabilized them both with hands on her shoulders, sideburns thick with snowflakes, as if he had been outside for some time.

"Why, my dear girl, what's happened?" he asked, voice lilting and warm. "You'll catch a chill running in such a state!"

Mira caught her breath, heart rate skyrocketing. He had been one of the suspects for the thefts, and her mind rang with the word "murderer!" But she shouldn't jump to conclusions. They didn't know how Silas had died, yet. More likely to be an accident than anything. But if it was murder, was it wise to leave the body with a possible suspect?

"I forgot my coat," she said, trying to think up a lie. "And I thought a good sprint might warm me up a bit."

"Yes, but what in the heavens are you doing out of doors in the first place?" He looked back the way he came. "I don't suppose you are a guest at Wynmar, are you?"

"Actually, I am," she said. "I'm Samira Blayse. I came with the Renaldis. You're Admiral Hoddle, aren't you?"

"Of course I am, who else would I be?" he said, eyes twinkling. "Are you one of Maureen's friends? I do believe I saw you talking with her yesterday evening. Ah, to be a gleeful youth, smiling upon the old and decrepit generation. The stories I could tell you of times past. And here I am talking you to death, doing you no good, no good at all. You ought to come back to the house at once." He linked his arm with hers and turned them back towards the path that led up to the house.

Mira blinked. She had not expected him to be so . . . exuberant. "Well, sir, I was actually looking for you because Miss Harris has had quite the shock."

His wiry brow furrowed. "Oh that poor girl. What's upset her this time? It wasn't one of those lads who's after Miss Risewell, is it? They are always saying things that upset her. Not in public, mind you, but I know it pains her, still grieving her aunt and her father not buried a year."

"You'd better talk to her about it," Mira said. She wasn't sure if she should be worried or grateful that she'd picked up a penchant for deception. "She wasn't exactly forthcoming."

"Yes, she takes after her father in that regard. Always tight lipped he was. That's what you get when you've got a friend working in the Foreign Office. How long did you say you've known Maureen?"

"Oh, we've run in the same circles since we were little," Mira said. "Though we haven't kept in contact as we ought to have."

"Yes, it is tragic how friendships fizzle out like a wet matchstick when you don't tend to them."

When they came to the top of the ridge Mira extracted her arm from his and stepped away.

"Miss Risewell also wanted me to give a message to the grooms. I think Maureen will likely be in the sitting room with some tea by now."

"You'll be blue before you get back, a regular Lucy Gray, 'the storm coming on before its time.' Better get a coat before going to the stables."

"Oh, no. I like the cold," Mira said, using all her might to prevent her teeth from chattering as she turned and hurried off to the stables. She hadn't been lying about hoping the run would warm her up, but it was still dashed cold. She'd been so focused on shielding Maureen from the body and the blood that she hadn't thought about the consequences. And it wasn't as if she could just take the coat up again. Oh, she hoped it hadn't gotten blood on it. It was a strange thing to focus on when one just discovered a corpse, yet she couldn't help it.

It was much warmer in the stables and she rubbed her hands together after she closed the heavy door behind her. A man was humming a jaunty ditty from within one of the stalls, singing the occasional phrase.

"Excuse me?" she called.

"Yes, miss?" The young man stepped out from the third stall, a pitchfork in hand. "Can I help you with something?" He was tall and broad-shouldered, with dark black hair, brown eyes, and handsome features. He had his sleeves rolled up, but his arms were wrapped with cloth and he wore dusty gloves.

"Can you saddle Verona?" she asked.

The man set the pitchfork aside. "That's Miss Risewell's horse, miss. I couldn't—"

"She's given her permission. We just found a man and, well, I need to fetch the doctor back immediately from the hunt."

His eyes widened and he stepped back. "Of course, miss. Seeing as it's an emergency." He rolled his sleeves down and opened one of the stalls where a beautiful chestnut Welsh Cob stood.

"Poor devil. Reckon he froze dead from the cold?"

"I think he fell from the drop-off. We found him near the path." She rubbed at her arms.

"Oh, the West Ledge?" He tutted. "Should have been a fence there long ago."

He worked quickly with the tack clearly knowing his work.

"What was your name?" she asked.

"Rudy Foster, miss."

She nodded. "Thank you for your help, Mr. Foster."

"Of course. You do know how to ride, don't you, miss?"

"Since I was six."

He nodded. "Ol' Verona is gentle as anything, but if you'd never galloped before I wouldn't want you falling off."

He secured the saddle in place and pulled a tub of grease from the shelf. "This'll stop the snow from getting stuck in her hooves," he told Mira as he spread the thick paste along the horseshoes and soles of Verona's hooves. "But mind you don't keep her out long. This only protects her for an hour or two."

Once he was done, he took off his gloves and helped Mira onto Verona's back. She settled into the side saddle and arranged her skirts the best she could. Rudy led the horse out of the stable, the chill wind passing over her coatless back again.

"Where do you think the party would be by now?" she asked, scanning the horizon.

"They are likely coming back. They usually take the path on the north side of the trees there." Rudy pointed.

"Thank you." She picked up the reins and started the horse at a trot.

She hadn't been lying when she said she'd been riding since she was six. But she had omitted the fact that she really only rode while on holiday, once or twice a year. There had been more opportunities while she attended finishing school, but that didn't mean she was proficient.

With her stomach twisting, she pushed Verona to a gallop and headed off towards the woods. The wind chilled her to the bone, ice biting her cheeks. The rhythmic pace of the horse's hooves kept her focused on maintaining her balance. One, two, three, four. Mira's hair fell from its style, flying in the wind behind her. All the while, her mind was transfixed on the image of Silas Treadway's staring face. Of Liza and Theresia. Maureen, had been so focused on the blood. There hadn't been that much. Not in comparison to Mr. Sutherland. Not as much as Selene. Mira swallowed, the taste of iron on her tongue, the smell of smoke overtaking her. Why had Maureen been so overcome by the blood?

They approached the tree line and Verona veered towards a wider path, slowing to a canter and then to a trot. One two, one two.

Crack.

Mira jolted as a gunshot rang out through the trees. Barks followed and Verona turned in the direction of the sound, speeding up. She clung to the reins as Verona's breaths clouded like smoke in the air.

They came to a clearing in the woods and stopped just shy of running into the hunting party: seven men on horseback and a gamekeeper on the ground with the hounds.

"Mira!" Walker said, eyes wide. "What are you—"

"You need to come right away," she said, out of breath.

The gamekeeper stepped forward, taking Verona's reins.

Byron steered his horse to her side. He removed his coat and placed it around her shoulders. She hadn't realized how cold she was until the warm fabric touched her skin.

"What's happened?" he said, voice calm and steady.

"Silas Treadway is dead," she said, teeth chattering. "I sent Miss Risewell to call the police, but I thought I'd better fetch you, erm, fetch Dr. Turpin back."

"Dead?" Mr. Risewell said, paling. "What do you mean? What's happened?"

"We need to get back to the house." Byron brought his horse about. "She can explain on the way."

February 9, 1889: Morning

"He's right along here," Mira said. They had brought the horses to the fence line adjacent to the path. Byron dismounted and handed the reins to the gamekeeper.

"We ought to avoid disrupting the scene as much as possible," he said, helping Mira down from her horse. "Dr. Turpin, if you'll come with me."

The good doctor was soon on his own feet and the three of them crossed the stile to the other side of the fence. The body hadn't been disturbed, thank goodness, though there was some fresh powder on top of Mira's coat. There weren't any new footprints to or from the body either. Byron removed the coat from where it was draped over the body, shook out the snow, and hung it over his arm.

"You moved him?" he asked.

"I turned him over. I-I thought he might just be unconscious. But I didn't find a pulse."

Dr. Turpin crouched beside the body, lifting one of the hands. "Rigor mortis is just setting in, though the cold would delay that. Poor fellow." He looked up the face of the slope and called back to the others. "He must not have seen the drop-off."

"When do you think he died?" Mr. Risewell called back.

Dr. Turpin stood and brushed the snow from his clothes. "Midnight or thereabouts. Best to leave specifics to the coroner."

The three of them crossed over the stile again. Byron helped her over, frowning as he took her hand. "We ought to get you warmed up."

"Shouldn't we look for—"

"The doctor is right," Byron interrupted, catching her gaze. "We should leave it to the professionals once they get here. Though, the body ought to be guarded until then."

"I'll stay," Walker said.

"As will I," said Bertie Corbet.

"That's settled," Mr. Risewell said. "Mr. Sharpe, if you'll take care of the dogs and the horses?"

The gamekeeper nodded.

They started the trek back up to the house, Byron with an arm around Mira.

"Shouldn't we stay to investigate?" Mira whispered.

"I think it's best, for the time being, if I remain a civilian, rather than a detective," Byron said, voice gentle. "And I'm a little more concerned about you at the moment."

"I'm f-fine."

"Of course you're fine. I can tell by the way your teeth are chattering," he said, his tone good-humored. "We can discuss our next steps after you are in some dry clothes and have a cup of tea in hand. Was there a reason you left your coat behind?"

"Maureen was in hysterics. I thought covering the body would help."

They entered the house together and the glorious warmth rushed over them. Mira's fingers and toes tingled as Byron closed the door behind them.

"Let me check on Maureen before I head up," Mira said, moving to the sitting room. Sobs reached her ears before she reached the open doorway.

Mrs. Renaldi sat with Maureen on the sofa, trying to calm the poor woman down. Mrs. Turpin sat on the opposite side, doing the same. Aunt Eleanor sat near the fire, incredibly still and pale. Admiral Hoddle was behind the sofa, pacing back and forth in a show of worry. Every so often he opened his mouth to say something, then closed it again.

Mrs. Sherard sat in one of the wide, wing-backed chairs and Mary stood by the window. Both turned their attention to Byron and Mira the moment they entered the room.

She was certain she looked a mess. Her wet, stringy hair was plastered to her neck and face. Her skirts were sodden, her skin red from the cold. And, of course, she had Byron's coat draped around her shoulders. It was much worse than her first impression, but frankly, she couldn't bring herself to care.

She walked across the room, ignoring haughty stares and curious looks, and crouched next to Maureen.

"Are you all right?"

"No. No. That . . . the blood."

"I've been trying to convince her to go rest," Mrs. Renaldi said.

Maureen's gaze was unfocused. She was looking at Mira, but it was as if she couldn't see her.

"Do you know where you are, Maureen? Can you feel my hand?"

"She's hysterical," Mary said, stepping away from the window. "Gone weak from the shock."

"Hysteria?" Admiral Hoddle said, stopping in place. "Why, I hadn't considered it before . . ."

Mira looked back at Maureen. She wasn't certain it was hysteria in this case.

Byron helped her to stand. "You really ought to go rest yourself."

"I'm fine, really," Mira said. "Just a little damp."

"Here's the tea," Liza said, coming through the door. She paused, taking in Mira's state of dress, and set the tray on the table. "Why, you look positively frozen, Mira."

Byron gave Mira a pointed look.

"I'm warming up," Mira said. She glanced back at Maureen and lowered her voice. "Maureen seems to be taking this rather badly."

"I'm not surprised," Liza said. "It is rather a shock to her, after her father, you know."

Mira frowned. "I had heard he had died but . . . what happened?"

"I'll tell you later," Liza whispered. "It isn't the time or the place for it."

Byron cleared his throat. "Where are the Risewells?"

"I'm not sure. Mrs. Risewell left when we came in, and I haven't seen Theresia since . . . since we found Mr. Treadway."

"What are you all whispering about?" Mrs. Sherard said. "Are the police here?"

"Not yet, Mamma," Byron said. "Likely won't be for another hour or so with all the snow."

Liza took Mira's hand. "We ought to get you out of those wet things. Come on."

ONCE IN THE SAFETY OF THE ROSE Room, Liza helped her peel

off the wet, sweaty layers and set Mira in front of the fire with a blanket wrapped around her.

"I'll take these down to the kitchen to dry," she said, gathering Mira's clothes in her arms. "Will you be all right for a little while?"

Mira nodded.

"I ought to check on Maureen again too." Liza headed for the door. "Is there anything else you need?"

Mira opened her mouth to say no, but a question popped out instead. "What happened to Mr. Harris?"

Liza stilled. "There was an attempted burglary back in August. He was shot and . . . well, from what I understand, Maureen is the one who found him."

"Oh." Mira pulled the blanket tighter around her shoulders. "I didn't know."

"There wasn't much publicity about it, thank goodness. But that means she didn't have as much support as she ought to have had."

"Did they ever catch the burglar?"

"I don't know. We wrote one another after she moved here to live with her aunt, Mrs. Callan, but she never mentioned it. And then her aunt passed away in January."

"Was it natural?"

Liza frowned. "As far as I know. Heart attack, from what I remember. She was always in bad health. That was why she didn't want to leave Bath when she became Maureen's guardian. She thought the waters were keeping her alive."

"Poor Maureen," Mira said. "No wonder she is so upset."

"I'd better get back to her," Liza said.

"One more thing," Mira said. "Will you ask if I can borrow another dress from the Risewells? I'm sure when the police come they won't want to wait to question me and who knows how long it will take for my things to dry."

"I'll see what I can do." The door clicked behind Liza as she left.

All that remained was quiet. Too much quiet. It made the silence in Mira's mind all the louder. She tried to string thoughts together, but they dissipated like smoke. Like Verona's breath in the cold air. Now that there wasn't anything to do, no rush, no explanation, she felt—

Numb.

She looked at her hands, feeling oddly detached from her body. Perhaps she should have been more concerned about it, but the concerns she had were distant and fuzzy. There was a wall in her mind between where she was and where all her emotions were crashing together like waves. The heat from the fire was almost too much, but she didn't care to move.

She sat there, unaware of the passage of time, when another knock came at the door.

"Come in," she said, her voice sounding strange to her ears.

To her surprise, Mary Sherard entered, arms laden with fabric.

"Here are your clothes. Or your undergarments at least. The dress is Miss Risewell's."

"Thank you," Mira said, voice shaking, though she didn't know why.

Mary set the clothing on the bed. "They say it was an accident, so there's no need for you, or my brother, to cause a scene. That is, not more than you already have."

Mira pulled the blanket tighter around her, a burst of indignation breaking through the numbness. "A man was found dead. What would you have had me do?"

Mary fell silent, slowly tracing the bed frame with her finger, stopping her hand on the brass knob at the end. It seemed to Mira that the action wasn't hesitation or a lack of response, but rather an intimidation tactic. She hated that it was working.

"I take it you have some affection for my brother, do you not?"

"I do."

"Then you should know better than to pull him into another case." She looked Mira up and down, the corner of her lip lifting in disgust. "You ought to have left the whole thing alone. So what if a corpse falls into your path? You have no business meddling in such things. Leave it to the police." Mary turned toward the door.

Mira fisted her hands in the blanket, trying to keep her temper at bay. "Miss Sherard?"

"Yes?" Mary stopped on the threshold.

"How well did you know Mr. Treadway?"

Mary looked back at her with that scrutinizing stare and a forced smile. "I didn't."

The door clicked closed again. It took longer than Mira expected to calm down while she dressed. She kept losing focus, and her hands were still shaky. It didn't make sense. It wasn't as if this was her first time discovering a body.

She hoped it was the last.

As she came down the stairs, Mary's voice echoed up from the lower landing. She pressed herself against the wall, hoping to avoid another confrontation. Unfortunately, what she heard was worse.

"She is wild, has no sense of propriety, and no understanding of what it means to be gentry," Mary said. "Honestly, I don't know what Ambrose is thinking. Do you think it is some residual effect of his accident? Some abnormality of the brain?"

Mira's chest tightened. How dare she say such things about her own brother?

"He has always been headstrong," Mrs. Sherard said. "The accident didn't change that."

"Yes, but remember when she walked into his rooms at Palace Court? Bedraggled, hair loose, shouting out his name as if she were calling for a dog. And my impression of her hasn't improved on further study. Tripping over corpses and rushing about in the cold. You should have seen her in there just now."

Mrs. Sherard hummed.

Tears burned in the corners of Mira's eyes. She could barely breathe.

Mary kept talking. "Surely, he can't be in love with a woman like that. Does he feel some sense of duty because she helped him with his memory troubles?"

"It seems to me that the very reasons why you dislike her are the reasons he likes her so much."

"We cannot allow this to continue, Mamma. She will only bring him and the Sherard name down."

"Perhaps you are right," Mrs. Sherard said. "By the way, the Risewells have agreed to let us borrow their carriage to return to Bath. Benson will stay here to receive the wheelwright . . ."

Their voices petered out as they moved away. Mira swallowed, throat thick. She closed her eyes, one hand clutching her mother's cameo.

Since she was little, she had dreamt about what it would be like to marry into a large family. She could never replace her parents, but she thought that, perhaps, her husband's parents would accept her as their own. Her husband's siblings would become hers.

She had her brother for a sibling, but she always wanted a sister. Back in December, she rejoiced to have a sister in Emilie. Someone to confide in. But now Emilie was dead. She had her Uncle Cyrus and Landon as father figures. Once, she counted Professor Burke as family as well, though the man he was when she was a child was long dead.

What she never had was a mother. She longed for a woman who could offer a mother's love, show her maternal care once more. And while Loretta might someday fill that space, she was rightfully occupied with her own children.

Tears were falling now and she couldn't stop them. Her body shook with anger, shock, and grief. There was too much to feel. A sob wracked through her and she muffled it with the back of her hand.

Someone cleared his throat and Mira jolted, opening her eyes. Castel Sherard stood on the landing above her, presumably coming from his own room.

"Are you quite well, Miss Blayse?" He arched one eyebrow.

She stood there, unable to speak, unable to move. Yet another strike against her. Yet another improper display of feeling on her part. She wiped her eyes and looked desperately for a place to hide away.

"You're shaking," he said in a matter-of-fact sort of way. "I think you ought to sit down."

"I—"

Castel moved down the stairs and took her arm. She let herself be led, like a lamb to slaughter, into the unoccupied library.

He helped her to a chair. The fire crackled. She managed to hold her tears at bay, but she couldn't stop herself from shaking.

"I would think by this point you would be used to this sort of thing," Castel said.

Her jaw tightened. "What sort of thing?"

"Finding corpses. Detective work. You've done enough of it by now, I shouldn't wonder."

Her anger sprung to the surface, outweighing every other emotion. "Yes, well, I still have some proper feeling. Unlike—" she stopped herself before saying anything she would regret.

Castel was unaffected. "My sister, I presume?"

Mira averted her gaze.

"Wood isn't the best at dampening shrill voices," he continued. "I heard the end of what she was saying about you."

Mira stood, not wanting to hear another round of abuse.

"Thank you for your help. I was actually coming down to see if the police had arrived. They'll want my statement."

"She's wrong, you know," Castel said as she reached the door.

Mira froze.

"Byron isn't one to do something merely out of a sense of duty. If he was, then he wouldn't have started up this detective business in the first place."

There he was, disparaging his brother once again, after everything Byron had done to prove himself. She clenched her fists and turned, but he spoke before she could.

"That isn't to say he doesn't do anything out of duty. But when it comes to tradition for tradition's sake . . ." he clicked his tongue, moving over to the bookshelf. "He tends to make his own path. Much like you."

Her brow furrowed. His tone was almost kind. Completely different than the usual cold, clipped conversation she had come to expect from him and the rest of Byron's family.

"Mr. Sherard, that almost sounded as if you approve of me."

Castel's mouth ticked up. "From what I know about you, Miss Blayse, I don't think you need anyone's approval." He took a book from the shelf and settled in one of the armchairs. "I do believe that Byron is in the sitting room, if you wanted to find him."

She paused a moment more on the threshold. "You called him Byron."

"I have many times before now." His gaze flicked up to hers. "Is it so surprising to call one's kin by their first name, Mira?"

She smiled and stepped back towards the door. "I suppose not, Castel."

"Good. Now, weren't you going to go do some investigating?"

She left him there, gently closing the door to the library behind her. Though her emotions were still swirling within her, she found that the shaking had finally subsided.

❧

When she came to the sitting room, Mira found most of the original occupants still there. The notable exceptions were Maureen and Liza, who Mira assumed had left to find a quiet room for consolation. Mr. and Mrs. Risewell, Dr. Turpin, Bertie Corbet, and Walker had rejoined the group. A tall man in a tweed suit stood in the midst of them with a police constable in blue. Mrs. Sherard and Mary were sitting in their own little corner, and Mira's stomach twisted remembering their earlier conversation.

Byron made his way through the crowded room to her. "How are you feeling?"

"Much better, thank you."

He nodded and turned, gesturing to the unknown man in tweed and the constable. "This is Inspector Rutledge and Constable McGuire of the Bath City Police. Inspector, this is Miss Samira Blayse."

"How do you do?" The inspector inclined his head. "I understand you were the one to discover the body?"

"Yes."

"In that case, I'm afraid I have a few questions."

"I'll try my best to answer them."

Rutledge looked around the room, then stepped to the side. "Why don't we move to the parlor?"

She followed him and the constable down the hall. The inspector gestured for her to take a seat. McGuire pulled out a notebook as the interview commenced. After the general questions of what she was doing in Bath and how she knew the Risewells, the inspector moved onto the meat of the business.

"What time would you say you discovered the body?"

"It's difficult to say. We started our walk around nine o'clock this morning. Perhaps quarter past nine?"

"Would you describe what you saw and how you reacted?"

"There was something on the path ahead. When we got closer, I realized it was a man. I moved to his side, and I'm sorry to say that I turned him over. I wanted to see if he was alive."

"Was he?" McGuire asked.

"No. He didn't have a pulse and his eyes were cloudy. I draped my coat over him and sent the other women back to the house to call the police. I knew Dr. Turpin was with the hunt, so I went to fetch him." As she spoke, her nerves evened out.

"I see," the inspector said. "And you also informed Detective Constantine at that point?"

Mira frowned. "Detective Constantine?" Had Byron said something?

Rutledge gave a small laugh. "Oh, I meant to say 'Mr. Sherard.'" He tapped the side of his nose. "He informed us of the true nature of your visit to Bath, so there's no need to keep up the act with us. We've been investigating the burglaries ourselves, but I suppose a detective that works with Scotland Yard is a mite bit more impressive." There was a sarcastic tinge to his voice.

"Not just any detective," Constable McGuire said, entirely in earnest. "Byron Constantine."

Rutledge blustered. "Yes, well, erm. Back to the question at hand."

She nodded. "Yes, I informed him at the same time that I found Dr. Turpin."

McGuire licked the end of his pen and Rutledge continued the questions. "Now, did you know Mr. Treadway?"

"I only met him yesterday. We spoke briefly before he excused himself for some fresh air."

"Did anyone else witness him leave?"

"Miss Harris was with us."

Inspector Rutledge nodded. "Is there anything else you think relevant?"

Mira considered the events of the morning and previous evening and shook her head. "No, I can't think of anything."

"That'll be all for now, then." Rutledge gestured towards McGuire who flipped his notebook closed.

The three of them returned to the sitting room where the occupants waited with rapt attention. Mira sat next to Byron on the sofa.

"Any of you may be asked to give testimony at the inquest. The coroner should send notice of the date by tomorrow afternoon. And don't none of you worry. This case is as open and shut as I've ever seen. Pure accident. Though . . ." he pulled something from his pocket and held it out to them. "Do any of you recognize this?"

A gold work necklace dripped over his fingers, clusters of pearls separating the jeweled settings.

Mrs. Risewell brought a hand to her chest. "May I see it?"

Inspector Rutledge obliged. Mrs. Risewell turned the necklace over in her hands.

"Why, this is mine," she said. "From my jewelry box upstairs."

"Yes, I thought it might be. It was found in the pocket of his coat. And there were a few more pieces." He gave a smug smile to Byron. "Seems we found our burglar."

"So it seems," Byron said.

Rutledge extended a hand. "I'll need to hold onto it as evidence, if you don't mind, Mrs. Risewell."

"Oh. Yes, of course." She handed the necklace back and the inspector pocketed it again.

"I'll send a man to get your statement on the theft in a few hours. I believe we had best get the body to the morgue. A good day to you all." The inspector tipped his hat and left the room.

"I never would have guessed it," Admiral Hoddle said, dabbing at his face with a handkerchief. "A thief, all this time. 'Do not lay up for yourselves treasures on earth,' and all that."

"These treasures were laid up by my grandfather," Mr. Risewell said, standing. "And I intend to determine what was stolen."

"Oh yes," Mrs. Risewell said. "We had better. The inspector did say he would send a man for our statement."

Mira strained to think up an excuse to go with them. A glance at Byron told her that he was doing the same.

"Would you like someone to make a list of what was taken as you look?" Byron said, pulling out his notebook. "It would make it easier when the constable comes."

Mary Sherard rolled her eyes at the suggestion, clearly upset by Byron's insistence on meddling, but Mr. Risewell easily agreed. "Capital idea," he said. "I'd be much obliged to you."

"Do you think that anything was stolen from Miss Risewell?" Mira asked.

"Oh, I hope not," Mrs. Risewell said. "I lent her one of my grandmother's necklaces day before yesterday."

"I'll find her and we can check together," Mira said.

"Yes, please do," Mrs. Risewell said. "Though I'm not sure where she's run off to now. Perhaps she's with Miss Renaldi and Miss Harris. I directed them to the conservatory. Thought the light would do her some good."

"I'll check there first, then," Mira said, standing.

Admiral Hoddle stood as well. "I'll come with you. I ought to bring Maureen home. After all, she's had quite the trying morning, poor thing, and is probably is in need of some peace and quiet."

"You don't happen to know the way to the conservatory, do you?" Mira asked, halfway down the hall. "I'm afraid I'm not particularly acquainted with the house."

"I've visited a few times since I came to Bath," Hoddle said.

"A striking house, though I'd say it could do with some trellises and ivy to cover up some of the old-fashioned brickwork. I think the turn is here."

"It was kind of you to become Maureen's guardian," Mira said. "You and Mr. Harris must have been close."

"We were like brothers," Hoddle said. "I'd do anything for him. Wish I could turn back time and stop the blaggard who shot 'im. This way, I think."

"Yes, I had heard about that," Mira said, turning down a new hall with him. "A burglar, wasn't it? Do we know what was stolen?"

"Nothing at all. The coward ran."

"No wonder Miss Harris is so upset at all this," Mira said. "It must have brought back so many painful memories."

"She'll be better in a few days, after some rest and time alone."

Mira frowned. Knowing her own experience, she couldn't imagine it would do Maureen much good to be alone for too long. "Might we come visit her tomorrow to see how she's getting on? Perhaps we could bring her with us to church. I'm sure the atmosphere could only do her good."

He screwed his face up a moment in thought. "I'm sure she would like that, yes. Though I think we ought to avoid too much excitement."

"Of course."

They reached the conservatory and found all three women within, huddled on a bench, plants all around them. The midday sun shone through the glass paneled walls.

"Maureen, dear, how are you doing?" Hoddle said, moving to his ward.

"Better." Maureen's voice cracked.

"I'll see about getting more tea." Theresia stood, making to leave the room, and Mira followed her.

"I'm afraid I have some news for you," Mira said.

"Me?" Theresia frowned.

"It seems that some of your mother's jewelry was found on Mr. Treadway's body."

Theresia's eyes widened. "Really?"

Mira nodded. "After you arrange for the tea, I think it would be prudent to check your room as well to see if anything is missing."

"Of course," Theresia said, quickening her pace. "This is rather exciting, isn't it? I don't think we've ever been burgled before."

Mira kept pace with her. "Aren't you worried at all? He may have stolen your great-grandmother's necklace."

"I hope he did," Theresia said. "It was ghastly."

February 9, 1889: Afternoon

Sure enough, the necklace was missing from Theresia's room. There didn't seem to be anything else missing, so they joined her parents and Byron in Mrs. Risewell's room.

"Do you generally keep the box unlocked?" Byron was asking as they came in.

"Heavens no, there's a key. I keep it in the drawer here." Mrs. Risewell moved to the vanity, but Mr. Risewell stopped her.

"There's a hidden compartment," Mr. Risewell said. "And though I trust you, Mr. Sherard, I think it would be best if it stayed hidden."

"Certainly," Byron said. "Do you keep all of your jewelry here, or do you store some elsewhere?"

"She keeps most of her jewelry in the safe," Theresia said from where she and Mira stood in the doorway.

Mrs. Risewell whirled towards them. "Did that thief steal anything from you?"

"Yes, Mamma," Theresia said, crossing the room to sit on the bed. "He took great-grandmother's necklace. It's terribly exciting, isn't it?"

"Theresia," Mr. Risewell said, a warning in his tone.

"The police have already found it all, haven't they? We haven't lost anything, not really, so it doesn't matter if he stole it or not. He's dead, anyhow."

Mira fought to keep her mouth from falling open. At the party the night before, Theresia had such an air of decorum. It was surprising to see her being so openly flippant—even defiant—with her parents.

"It's the principle of the thing," Mrs. Risewell said. "And we don't know whether they found everything."

Theresia rolled her eyes. "Yes, well let me know if anything else interesting happens." She stood and headed towards the door.

"Where are you going?" Mr. Risewell asked.

"The stable. Verona ought to be rewarded for having to gallop through the snow."

"That girl." Mrs. Risewell shook her head. "I don't know what to do with her."

After fetching Walker from the sitting room to act as chaperone, Byron and Mira retreated to the study to talk in peace.

"At least it was an accident," Mira said, adjusting her skirts as she took a seat. "After all, if it were murder, they wouldn't have found the jewels."

"Not necessarily," Byron said, pacing.

"You mean, you think he was murdered?" Walker asked, considering the books on the shelf.

"I'm only saying that we ought not to rule it out just yet. We ought to consider all four possible scenarios for this little mystery."

"I only count two," Mira said. "Whether Mr. Treadway was murdered or whether he fell by accident."

"Add in the additional variable of the jewels. Was Mr. Treadway the thief, or was he not? Therein lies the additional scenarios. For instance, it is possible that Mr. Treadway was not the thief and he fell by accident."

"Then why would he have the jewels?" Walker asked.

"You don't think the real thief planted them, do you?" Mira said.

"It is something to consider. Now, let's examine the possibility of Mr. Treadway being our burglar, as it would be quite a tidy explanation. Regardless of whether it was an accident or not, why might he feel the need to steal? Was it a compulsion? Debts to be paid?" Byron spun on his heel, facing her. "Did he strike you as a gambler?"

"No. Though I only spoke with him for a few minutes."

"An opportunity I did not receive. Think. Did anything stand out to you?"

She furrowed her brow. "Well, he was rather vague."

"About what?"

"His military service in Sudan. Maureen kept asking him questions about it, and he kept avoiding an answer. Though, perhaps he didn't want to bring up any memories. He was injured, you see."

Byron sat in the armchair across from her. "What sort of injury?"

"He didn't say."

Walker sighed, pulling a book from the shelf and slumping into one of the chairs. "He wasn't limping was he?"

"Not that I remember," Mira said.

"That gives us a line of questioning," Byron said. "In speaking with the Risewells, I discovered that he and Mr. Corbet have been staying here at the house for the past two months. We might ask any of them if they know more about the injury. Although it seems unlikely that a burglar would be able to work around a leg injury, especially where ladders might be involved. We will need to check with the coroner to see if there was any sign of a wound there."

"Under what pretense?" Mira asked. "Or will you be announcing your occupation to everyone now?"

"Inspector Rutledge mentioned that, did he?" Byron chuckled. "I should have warned you. I find it best, in most circumstances, to be as frank as possible with the police. Besides, I think he's pleased that he 'solved' the burglary case before I could."

Mira sat up. "You don't think the case is solved, then?"

"Too many unanswered questions. We know that he had the jewels on his person. But, assuming he was the thief, why did he have them with him that night? Had he just nipped outside and up to Mrs. Risewell's room, nicked the goods, then on his way back to the party got stuck in the snow?"

"There wasn't a way for him to get up from the outside." Mira remembered what Admiral Hoddle had said. "There isn't any ivy or trellising, and I don't recall seeing any outbuildings near that side of the house where he could have found a ladder."

"And so he would have no choice but to cut through the house during the party," Byron said. "Then, why did he go outside? To corroborate his story about getting some air? Or was he bringing the jewelry to another person so that when it was found missing, it wasn't in the house?"

"He wasn't wearing a coat when we spoke to him last night.

But when we found him this morning he was," Mira said. "He must have known he would be outside for some time and fetched it after leaving the ballroom."

Byron nodded. "Usually in cases like these, there's a partner. Someone who can bring the jewelry to a third party to be sold, or has the expertise to dismantle the pieces and sell the gemstones individually." He drummed his fingers on the armrest of his chair. "We'll need to talk to the jewelers in town and see if any of them have had an influx of inventory."

"We already know the thief has a partner," Mira said. "Someone had to have opened the window in your mother's room."

"I'd forgotten about that," Byron said. "Hoddle, Miss Harris, or any of the Risewells."

Walker gave up on reading his book. "Say, you don't think the Risewells are framing Treadway for this, do you?"

Byron hummed. "Could be. This could be a ploy to push suspicion off themselves, if they are involved with the burglaries. But would any of them have killed Mr. Treadway, or was his death an accident and they took advantage of the situation?"

Mira frowned. Could Theresia have gotten up to the house, taken the jewelry, and planted it on the body in the time it took her to ride Verona, find the hunt, and return? It seemed unlikely.

"Let's continue exploring the more nefarious angle. Who else might wish Mr. Treadway ill?" Byron asked.

Mira said, "I don't know anyone here well enough to say for certain."

"Oh, Corbet has been obvious enough in his dislike for the man," Walker said. "Their rivalry when it came to Theresia was clear, at least."

"Theresia doesn't care for either of them, though," Mira said.

A knock came at the library door. Mira moved to answer it and to her surprise, "Fitzwilliam" Montague stood on the threshold.

"I know it isn't my place, miss," he said, glancing behind himself. "But may I come in?"

She nodded, stepping aside so he could enter. She closed the door behind him and he removed his cap.

"I know you may not have recognized me," he said, twisting his poor cap near to death. "But my good conscience knows that you'll find out soon enough who I am and what I've left."

"Charles Montague, yes?" Byron said, sitting back at his leisure.

"Oh, yes, sir. I'm sorry to say it, but it's me," Monty said, words all a jumble. "Course you recognized me. Yer a detective, a right knowing one, and I should have come to you as soon as I noticed you."

"It was Miss Blayse who remembered you, not I."

"Is that right? Well, you fooled me last night. You're a regular actress, begging your pardon, miss."

Mira smiled, moving back to her seat by the fire. "Won't you sit down?"

"No, I'd rather stand. If the missus or master was to enter, they wouldn't take kindly to a footman sitting in good company."

"What did you want to talk about?" Mira said.

"It's about the thefts. I knew there'd been all these burglaries about, but it didn't have nothing to do with me so I didn't pay them much attention. But when I saw you come in with all the other swells, I couldn't help but squirm. I thought you were here to investigate, but maybe, I thought, maybe you wouldn't give me no notice. But then the tittle-tattle below stairs is that there's been a corpse found, that Mr. Treadway is dead. And then I thought to myself that you'd be questioning the staff, and soon enough you'd come to me, so I'd better get it over with and come to you first."

"A reasonable thought," Byron said, pulling out his journal and flipping through it. "I take it you are innocent?"

"Yes, sir. I didn't do it. Not the thefts, not the murder, nothing. I never liked being on the dub lay. And I ask you, why would I foul my own nest by filching my mistress's baubles or doing in a guest?"

"Didn't you escape from the prison in Reading?" Mira said.

Monty's face took on a reddish hue. "Oh, well, I did do that. No use in gamming you, seeing as I stand before you now." He turned to Byron. "And I know you must do your duty, sir, and send me back there again. But I swear, on my grandmother's grave even, that I'm done with the criminal life. I've come here to make a fresh start. I'm even getting used to this footman's toggery." Monty brushed his sleeves and looked sheepish.

Byron stopped on a particular page, scanning it. After a moment he snapped the journal shut and sat forward, steepling his fingers. He looked up at Monty, his scrutinizing stare on full display. Monty took a step back, obviously not used to that kind of intensity.

"You'd best get back to work," Byron said. "We wouldn't want the butler to worry about where you wandered off to."

Monty gaped like a fish. "You mean, you aren't going to turn me in, sir?"

"Not at the moment, no. If you really aren't involved, there isn't a reason to turn the police suspicion onto you. And if you are involved, well," Byron smiled. "We'll find out, won't we?"

Monty paled considerably. "I didn't do it. None of it. Really I didn't, sir."

"Off you go, then. Might we come talk to you later? I may have some questions about the staff."

"Oh, of course. Anything you need. Just let me know."

"Thank you, er . . . what name are you going by?"

"Fitzwilliam, sir."

"Very good, Fitzwilliam."

Monty gave a nod to each of them and moved to leave the room. But just as he reached the door, Byron called out again, "Actually, I think I do have a quick favor."

Monty slowly turned back towards them. "Yes, sir?"

"We need to see Mr. Treadway's room. Do you think you could arrange that for us? Discreetly?"

"I'm sure I could manage, sir."

WALKER TOOK IT UPON HIMSELF TO DISTRACT the Risewells and their guests so that Byron and Mira could search Treadway's room without interruption. Monty stood guard at the door, polishing the same stretch of wood over and over again as an excuse.

Mira started by looking through the wardrobe while Byron went through the desk.

"He has an excellent tailor," Mira said, examining the stitching on a jacket. "And good taste."

Byron hummed.

"Do you really think he was going to meet someone?" Mira asked. "In that terrible weather?"

Byron ran a hand through his hair, leaning back in the chair. "If I'm right, his partner would have met him somewhere close to the estate. He wouldn't have wanted to leave his partner waiting and would have braved the snow to meet him. But, we are assuming the weather was bad when he left. It hadn't turned when he left your company, had it?"

"I don't think so."

"So, it depends on whether he had stolen the jewels before or after his conversation with you and Miss Harris. If they were already in his possession, he would have had more time to meet up with his mysterious partner before the weather changed." He closed the drawer of the desk. "Nothing of interest there. And I'm afraid the blotting paper has nothing of note on it."

"Oh, it wouldn't," Bertie Corbet said from the doorway.

Mira and Byron both jolted, turning towards him.

"You may want a new watchdog. Fitzwilliam is too easily distractible. I sent him down to the servant's quarters under the threat of an angry butler." He moved over and offered a hand to Byron. "I'm Bertie Corbet. I take it that you are Detective Constantine?"

Byron shook his hand. "Yes, though I'm surprised to be recognized."

"I've followed your cases for a while now. Recognized you from your picture in the newspaper."

"Ah, that explains it. What were you saying about the blotting paper?"

"Silas wrote all of his letters in pencil. He was worried about people reading them, so he'd go directly to the post office in town to mail them instead of putting them in the mail bag like anyone else would."

"Fascinating," Byron said. "Did you know him well?"

"Evidently, none of us knew him well. Though I'm not surprised he was a thief."

"Why do you say that?" Mira asked.

Bertie chewed on the inside of his cheek. "My brother knew him. Or at least, he mentioned a Lieutenant Silas Treadway in his letters. When I learned he would be staying at Wynmar, I was looking forward to meeting the man my brother wrote about. He was one of the last people to see my brother alive."

"Did Mr. Treadway not live up to expectations?" Byron asked.

"My brother described a brave and honorable gentleman. I do not wish to speak ill of the dead, but I found Mr. Treadway to be an obsequious, wheedling fellow. One would ask him a question and he'd dance around the answer more times than not. I always thought he was hiding something—though I assumed he was a deserter. Thieving is cowardly enough, I suppose."

"Forgive my asking," Byron said. "But is your opinion of him colored at all by your shared interest in Miss Risewell?"

"You've been listening to gossip, but I suppose you must, as a detective." Bertie's mouth ticked up at the corner. "You have my word, as a gentleman, that my opinion of Silas has nothing to do with our rivalry. In fact, can you call it a rivalry if neither of us are in the running?"

"You mean, you aren't courting her?" Mira asked.

"It is difficult to court someone who isn't interested in being courted. Miss Risewell hasn't given any indication that she will ever consider me."

"Then why do you stay?" Mira asked.

"My parents think it would be a good match." Bertie shrugged. "I enjoy hunting with Mr. Risewell, and there are more opportunities for socialization in Bath than in Shropshire at this time of year."

Mira frowned. "I thought you disliked the ruthlessness of society here."

Bertie chuckled. "I may hate the games, but the *brave monde* demands that I play them. So, every year I come back, hoping perhaps she has changed her mind and when she inevitably hasn't, I make the most of it." He stepped back towards the door. "By the way, the police constable is downstairs taking the Risewells' statement on the thefts. I expect he'll make his way here next. You may want to leave if you intended to remain inconspicuous."

"Thank you for the warning," Byron said, tucking his notebook into his jacket pocket.

"By all means." He turned to leave the room. "Oh, and if you were wondering, your secret is safe with me, 'Mr. Sherard.'"

THEY REJOINED WALKER IN THE HALL DOWNSTAIRS.

"Sorry about Bertie. I couldn't think of an excuse to keep him down here."

"Thank you for trying," Byron said, leading the way back to the study.

"Did you find anything?"

"We didn't have much of a chance," Mira said with a sigh. "Though I'm not sure there was anything to find."

"I doubt we'll have another opportunity to search," Byron said. "It's dashed difficult to work as a civilian. So much sneaking and subterfuge, excuses and lies."

"Now you know how I felt when I first started working with you," Mira said. "Do you think we could ask Monty to search the room for us?"

"Perhaps . . ."

"It was awfully decent of you to let him off like that," Walker said.

Byron shook his head. "He's already proved that he's more useful here than behind prison bars. Besides, based on what I wrote in my journal, the mastermind of the duo was Aaron Dennis. Monty only went along with it because it was convenient. If he really has left the criminal life behind, I'd hate to put an end to that."

The door opened again, this time with Liza coming in. Walker stood.

"You look positively exhausted."

Liza sighed. "I just don't know what to do to help Maureen. She's calmed down, finally, but it really has been a shock to her."

Mira fidgeted with her hands. "Reliving the past is always difficult."

"Yes, well," Liza said. "Admiral Hoddle took her home."

"He mentioned that he would. I asked if we could bring her with us to church tomorrow, and he agreed," Mira said. "Do you think she's all right for the moment?"

"Much better than before," Liza said. "Earlier it was as if she couldn't hear me at all. Like she was in an entirely different place."

Mira caught Byron's gaze. They both knew what that was like.

February 10, 1889

"I really didn't mean to cause a scene," Maureen said, taking a sip from her teacup. She was still incredibly pale and a little shaky, but overall, she seemed to be doing better. She, Mira, and Liza sat at a little table in a nook at Number Five Henrietta Street, a tea tray shared between them.

"It's entirely understandable," Liza said. "Considering the circumstances."

"Truth be told, I hardly remember it." Maureen set the cup down, averting her eyes from the group. "I am sorry to hear that your aunt is unwell, Liza."

"Oh, she'll rally soon enough. Especially with Mother looking after her."

What Liza didn't say was that Aunt Eleanor was still reeling from the discovery of the body, felt as if it were a harbinger of doom, and refused to leave the house. Which left Mira and Liza in the awkward position of being unable to go anywhere with their suitors. At least until they came to some compromise with Mrs. Renaldi or found another chaperone.

"That window lets in such good light," Mira said, changing the subject. "This room would be a joy to paint in."

"You're an artist, Miss Blayse?" Maureen asked. "I don't believe I knew that."

Liza laughed. "She has graphite on her hands more often than not. Haven't you noticed?"

"I suppose I haven't," Maureen said. "I'm not much of an artist myself."

"Yes, but you play the piano," Mira said. "And much better than I ever could."

Maureen smiled. "I'm not as good as I once was. I haven't had as much time to practice since . . . well, since moving to Bath."

"Why not?" Mira asked.

"My aunt didn't like me to practice when she was sleeping. And as she slept most of the time, it was rather a difficult prospect. I've been playing a little more in the last month."

"Can you play for us?" Liza asked.

Maureen ducked her head in a rare show of shyness. "I suppose I could, if you really wanted me to."

They finished their teacakes and withdrew to the music room on the second floor. A lovely pianoforte stood in the center, glowing in the light filtering through the thin, delicate curtains covering the window. Near the door stood a credenza displaying *objets d'art*.

"What a lovely little carousel," Liza said, admiring one of the curios. It was a delicate thing with gold work and tiny, porcelain horses with different colored saddles and bridles. It stood on a heavy base engraved with swirls and flowers.

"It's a musical box," Maureen said, pausing next to it. She opened a drawer in the credenza and pulled out a key, slotted it into the base of the carousel, and turned it. The springs creaked before a delicate tinkling sound rang out.

"It's beautiful," Mira said.

"Isn't it? It's one of Mendelssohn's Songs Without Words. I find it incredible that the little box is able to play both the harmony and the melody at once. Although I find the tempo a little faster than it ought to be."

Mira smiled. "That suggests you know how to play it."

Maureen's eyes sparkled and she opened one of the doors on the credenza, pulling out two folders of sheet music. "I've dabbled."

"Are you a Mendelssohn enthusiast, then?" Liza asked.

"Oh yes. My father was partial to him." She sighed. "He actually gave the box to me a few weeks before he died."

The musical box filled the silence, before slowly coming to a stop.

"I'm so sorry," Mira said.

Maureen blinked rapidly and stepped towards the piano. "I'm fine. I'm still surprised when the sorrow overcomes me." She lifted the sheet music. "I'll play the Mendelssohn first."

Mira and Liza took their seats on a low-backed velvet sofa while Maureen opened the piano.

"You know, he wrote these songs without any titles or suggestions as to how one ought to feel when listening to or performing them. He felt that music could communicate so much more than words ever could. Poetry in music alone." She set the sheet music on the rest above the piano keys and arranged her skirts over the bench. "Of course, since he died people have given most of them names, which defeats the whole purpose."

"Does this one have a name?" Liza asked.

Maureen smiled. "I'll tell you after I play." She took a breath and started with her left hand playing the lower keys.

The notes were warm and bright, the melody joining the bass line and washing over them. It hadn't occurred to Mira before how much she relied on the programs at musical reviews to tell her what to think and feel about a piece. The history behind it, the reasons why the composer might have written it, secrets hidden within the notes. And, of course, the title.

She closed her eyes and let the music envelop her. The high notes spoke and the lower register responded, a call and response. The general tone of the piece was happy, but beneath it all the harmony was tinged with sorrow. Nostalgic, though Mira didn't believe she had ever heard the piece before. What was Mendelssohn trying to communicate? Some hidden message tucked between the rests and quarter notes? The full piece was deep and rich in a way the musical box would never achieve.

Maureen lightened her touch as she finished the piece. Liza's clapping brought Mira back from her revelry.

"Oh, that was wonderful, Maureen," Liza said.

"I'm a little out of practice." A blush rose to Maureen's cheeks.

"I never would have known," Mira said.

Liza sat straighter. "Did it have a name?"

"'Sweet Remembrance,'" Maureen said. "Although, I don't think the title fully encompasses the feeling."

"I agree," Mira said.

Maureen switched out the sheet music. "This is the piece I've been working on. I haven't quite been able to figure it out, so forgive me if it sounds a little strange."

Unlike the previous piece, the notes that sprang from the strings of the piano were chaotic and indecipherable. A phrase of musicality surfaced every so often, but just when Mira thought she knew the direction it would go, the notes would change drastically. It was haunting and dissonant. The piece was mostly in the upper register, so there was not much of a second hand line. If this was the piece Maureen had exhibited, it was no wonder those women at the party thought she didn't play well.

Halfway through she stopped abruptly. "It's just a jumble of notes. I don't understand why it doesn't sound like anything."

Mira stood and moved to the piano, looking over Maureen's shoulder. The sheet music was handwritten, the ink blotchy in places. "Where did you get this?"

"It was my father's," she said, morose.

"Your father composed that?" Liza said.

Maureen shook her head. "My great-uncle sent it, I think. Father had been practicing it for weeks, but he never made it sound any better than I have. It has just about every conceivable flat and sharp. But no matter how I play it, it never sounds right."

Mira furrowed her brow. "How strange . . ."

Maureen shrugged and stacked the sheet music up again, placing it back in the folder. "Would either of you like to play?"

They spent the rest of the afternoon in the music room, listening to each other play, and discussing the difficulties of playing the works of different composers. Maureen seemed in much better spirits. Mira was stumbling through her third piece when Hoddle stepped in.

"I do hate to interrupt, but I'm afraid I must steal Miss Harris away. Dr. Turpin is here."

Maureen frowned. "I didn't realize he was coming today."

"I thought after yesterday, shock as it was, it would be prudent to have the good doctor look in on you."

"I suppose . . ." Maureen looked at Liza and Mira.

"We probably ought to get home as it is," Liza said. Mira looked at the clock for the first time in several hours. It was already half past four. She nodded.

"I left the doctor in the front parlor," Admiral Hoddle said.

Maureen stood, taking Liza's hands in hers. "It was so good of you to come. Thank you for a wonderful afternoon."

"Oh, we were happy to."

"I'll see them out," Admiral Hoddle said. "Best not to keep the doctor waiting."

Maureen nodded and left the room.

"I can't tell you what good it has done my soul to have the two of you come visit today," Hoddle said as he escorted them to the door. "So very kind and thoughtful. Miss Harris has gone through such a trying time this past year. It is so very good for her to have friends such as yourselves."

"It's the very least we could do," Liza said. "I'm glad to have her company again. We've missed her in London."

"I'm sure you have, yes," Hoddle said, wiping his forehead with a handkerchief. "She is such a joy, in spite of the earthly sorrows she has endured. This isn't the first time she's been affected by a bout of hysteria, poor girl. I do hope the doctor has some suggestion of what to do to help her endure it."

"She seemed much recovered today," Mira said. "It was upsetting for all of us to discover poor Mr. Treadway in such a fashion."

He cleared his throat. "Yes, yes. It is such a tragedy. Poor man. Must have not seen the drop-off with the fog and snow. Such a full life ahead of him, too." They reached the door and he opened it. "I do hope that you come again. Good day to you both!"

THEY REACHED DAVENGUARD AS THE SUN WAS starting to set. Mira handed her coat to the butler and followed Liza into the sitting room. Walker and Byron stood as they entered.

Mrs. Renaldi turned. "Oh good, you're back. How was Miss Harris? I feel so sorry for her, poor thing."

"She is much improved since yesterday," Liza said, sitting next to her mother. "I hope to visit her tomorrow, as well."

Mrs. Renaldi frowned, turning to Byron. "Will there be time with the inquest?"

"It's tomorrow?" Mira asked, taking up one of the deep, armless chairs. "I thought it wouldn't be scheduled until later this week."

"The county coroner happened to finish up another case and is in town still," Byron said. "We received the message a little while ago. As it is only the preliminary investigative inquest, it should only take an hour. However, that entirely depends on how much evidence the police have to bring forward."

"Must we all go?" Liza asked.

"I'm afraid we're all witnesses, before or after Mr. Treadway's death," Byron said.

"This is all a bad omen," Aunt Eleanor said, wringing her hands. "A very bad omen."

February 11, 1889: Morning

THE CORONER, A MR. W. J. ENGLISH of Bathampton, was a short, bespectacled gentleman with graying sandy hair and a round face. He sat on a stool much too tall for him at a table near the front of the guildhall. Another man sat next to him with pen and paper, waiting to record the proceedings. An additional table was set up perpendicular to theirs, near a tall south-facing window. A few clerks had set up thirty-odd chairs in rows along the back wall, most of which were occupied, whether by those directly related to the incident of Silas Treadway or by those whose curiosity brought them snooping.

Mira sat in the front row as a principal witness in the discovery of the corpse. Byron, Mr. Risewell, Dr. Turpin, and Inspector Rutledge shared the row with her. The rest of the party-goers from Wynmar Park took up the better part of two rows behind.

Mr. English removed his pocket watch, consulted the time, and cleared his throat. A police constable standing near the front table gave a low whistle and shouted, "Hear ye, hear ye. The Inquest held the Eleventh of February, in the year of our Lord eighteen hundred and eighty-nine, shall come to order. Mr. W. J. English, coroner, presiding over reception of evidence."

The guildhall quieted down and Mr. English adjusted his spectacles. "Very good, Bronson. Now, as the police have deemed the case as likely being an accidental death, we shall proceed without a jury. First, I should like to acquaint all here with the particulars of the death."

He gave a short summary of the events leading up to the discovery of the body and all persons involved before calling Mr. Risewell to witness.

Mr. Risewell took his position at the table beneath the window and adjusted his cravat.

"Now, Mr. Risewell, how long have you been leasing Wynmar Park from the Estfields?" Mr. English asked.

"We've leased it for three of the last four winters. This year we came in November. I believe it was November the fifteenth."

"Would you say you are well acquainted with the landscape?"

"Yes, sir. Very well acquainted."

"Would you describe the area where the deceased was found?"

Mr. Risewell sat back in his chair. "We call it the West Ledge, as it's to the west of the property. Mr. Treadway was found at the base of the drop-off, near a path that runs along the front of it and back to either side of the house. The path splits off at the northern side to head across the pasture to a wooded area. The ledge is quite steep, and thirty or so feet from the house."

"How tall is the ledge by your estimate?"

"Oh, about fifteen feet, sir."

The coroner gestured for his clerk to take a note. "About where is the West Ledge in relation to the ballroom?"

"The ballroom is at the center of the house, but there are several hallways attached to it, one of which leads to a side door to the west."

"And how long had Mr. Treadway been staying with your family?"

"Since the middle of December. He and Mr. Corbet came the same week, so I'm not certain who came on which day. We've made a grand hunting party up to now."

"Do you have any notion as to why Mr. Treadway left the ballroom during your soiree?"

"It was rather hot. I heard that he left for some air, poor man. Not sure why he wandered so far. Maybe he saw something."

"Saw something?" The coroner stopped writing and looked at him over his spectacles.

"Never met someone with better vision. Could spot a rabbit or sparrow in the dark of the thicket. Any kind of movement."

"From my understanding, Mr. Risewell, the night in question was rather snowy. Do you remember the visibility?"

Mr. Risewell scratched his chin. "You could see down to the gamekeeper's lodge at ten. I know as much, as I pointed out its direction, and the wood, to Dr. Turpin in discussing a future hunt, and I wound my pocket watch to the time of the grandfather clock around that time. The weather didn't worsen until about ten-thirty, I'd say."

"Thank you, Mr. Risewell. Now, Miss Blayse? Will you come forward?"

Mira took the witness stand, trying not to let her nerves overcome her.

"Miss Blayse, you are in the unique position of being one of the last people to see Mr. Treadway alive and also being in the party that found him. First, when did you last speak with Mr. Treadway?"

"Sometime before eleven. Maybe ten?" She glanced at Byron. He gave her the slightest smile and her anxiety lessened. She only needed to relay the facts. Taking a breath and sitting a little straighter, she continued. "He, Mr. Corbet, Miss Harris, and I were talking near the refreshment table. Mr. Corbet left us, and shortly afterwards Mr. Treadway mentioned needing some air. Miss Harris and I went looking for her guardian, Admiral Hoddle, but couldn't find him anywhere. After about an hour, we thought he might have gone outside. That's when we discovered that it was snowing and I remember the clock in the hallway struck eleven."

"Make a note of that time," Mr. English said to the clerk before turning back to Mira. "Now, will you please inform those present as to the circumstances that led to the discovery of the body?"

"Yes. That morning, the men went out on a hunt. Miss Risewell thought it would be good to walk out to meet them, so after breakfast we left the house and walked down to the path at the south end of the drop-off—the West Ledge, I suppose. There's a gentler slope there that the path takes, you see. And when we came to the base of the ledge, there was something dark on the path ahead of us."

"You did not immediately recognize it as a body?"

"No. But when we got a little closer, it was unmistakable. I approached first. I thought maybe he was unconscious and needed help. I turned him over—"

"The deceased had fallen on his face, then?"

"Yes. When I moved the body, I saw the blood. There wasn't a lot of it, but it was clear he had hit his head. It rather upset Miss Harris, so I sent her and Miss Renaldi and Mrs. Davidson back to the house. I checked for a pulse and when I found none, I sent Miss Risewell to telephone the police from the house."

"You didn't send her for a doctor the moment you found the body?"

"No. Dr. Turpin was with the hunt, so I thought it would be faster if I sent her to call for the police while I fetched him on horseback."

"I see. Thank you very much, Miss Blayse. Dr. Turpin would you please come forward?"

Mira passed the doctor on the way back to her seat, her body absolutely buzzing. Somehow it felt as though she'd done something wrong, even though she'd relayed the events exactly as she remembered them.

"Dr. Turpin, how long have you been practicing medicine?"

"We are approaching eighteen years, sir."

"Very good. Would you describe the state of the body as you found it?"

"At the time that I first examined the body, it was lying on its back. The eyes were cloudy. The body was just beginning to show the signs of rigor mortis. I estimated the time of death to have been around midnight, based on the temperature. The only major injury I could see was to the head. Blunt force, consistent with a fall. There had been some bleeding, but the cold would have slowed the bleeding considerably and much of it had been absorbed by the earth and snow."

"Thank you." He turned to the audience. "For the knowledge of those present, and the recorder, Dr. Turpin assisted me with the post mortem. We found a few scrapes and bruises that likely occurred during the fall. A fall from a height of fifteen feet is not always lethal, but the angle at which the deceased hit the ground broke his neck. He would have fallen unconscious immediately. Death would have occurred within a few minutes to an hour, as his respiratory system failed. My estimate for the time of death based on when he was last seen alive and his injuries would be between eleven and midnight the night before his body was discovered. Based on the evidence given—"

Inspector Rutledge stood, clearing his throat and Mr. English turned to him, looking over his spectacles again.

"Inspector, was there something you wished to add to these proceedings?"

Rutledge nodded and removed his hat, turning to address the room.

"My investigations corroborate what has been said here. But I do wish to inform those present that several pieces of jewelry were found on the deceased, which suggests that he is the culprit in the recent burglaries. We are still making inquiries at this time. Also, if anyone has any knowledge as to how to communicate with the family of the deceased, I would be much obliged."

"Thank you, you may take your seat."

The inspector gave a nod and returned to sit beside Byron. Mr. English removed his spectacles and placed them in front of him on the table.

"As I was saying, the evidence heard this morning has answered the questions of the inquest. First, that the body discovered was Silas Treadway. Second, that the death occurred at the bottom of the West Ledge at Wynmar Park. Third, that the death occurred between eleven and twelve the night of February the eighth. And fourth, that the cause of death was cessation of respiratory function due to a spinal injury from a fall. With all that put forward, and considering that by all accounts the deceased chose to venture into the inclement weather of his own volition, my conclusion is that Silas Treadway met his death by misadventure. We thank the police for their efforts in investigating. The body shall remain in custody of the coroner's office until the family retrieves it, or two weeks have lapsed, thereafter the body shall be buried in proper fashion."

"I KNOW THE CORONER WAS SIMPLY DOING his job, but it all feels so clinical," Liza said over lunch. The Renaldis, Miss Harris, Admiral Hoddle, and the Sherards had adjourned to Davenguard after the inquest, and Mira was grateful for the extra buffer her friends provided with Byron's family.

"I agree," Maureen said. "They didn't talk about Mr. Treadway's character or anything about him really, other than how his corpse looked. There was much more to him than that."

"Well, it was an inquest, not a funeral," Walker said. "They are meant to focus on the aspects of the death, not the life of the person."

"I wonder why they weren't able to contact his family," Mrs. Renaldi said. "It was short notice, but surely they should have been able to send a telegram and receive a response?"

"Oh, Mr. Treadway didn't keep close contact with his family," Maureen said. "He told me that they didn't agree with him joining the army. He didn't even tell them that he had returned. Though if I remember, he was from York, so even if the police did get ahold of them, they wouldn't have been able to come in time."

Castel dabbed at his mouth with a napkin. "York?" He glanced at his sister. "Mary, you don't suppose he was related to your Mr. Treadway, do you?"

Mary's face tightened. "Certainly not."

Byron tipped his head to the side. "There can't be that many Treadway families from York, can there?"

"If he is related, he must be a nephew or something of the sort," Mary said.

"Well then," Byron said, "I'm sure the police would be gratified to have some lead, even if there isn't a direct relation."

"Yes," Mrs. Sherard said. "You ought to send him a letter."

Mary's eyes widened. "But . . ."

"Your brothers are right. We ought to help the police as best we can." She gave Byron a pointed look. "Within reason."

"I've actually heard of several different Treadways from that part of the country," Admiral Hoddle said. "One set in York, another in Leeds, and another in Fangfoss, if my memory serves. Why, one of the Treadways from Leeds was commander under me on the *Serapis*. Fine fellow, that, and a good commander. And the *Serapis* was a fine ship. I hated to leave her after so many decades, but one must retire at some point."

Castel took a sip of wine. "When did you retire?"

"At the beginning of last year. I miss the sea something terrible. Sometimes I wake and can almost feel the salty breeze on my face, and then it's gone in the same instant. But I suppose an old salt like me will always have the sea in me. And the stories, why, the stories and memories, they keep me well enough."

AFTER LUNCH WAS OVER AND ADMIRAL HODDLE had finished a lengthy bout of storytelling, he and Miss Harris returned to Henrietta Street. The remaining members of the party moved to the sitting room. While everyone else settled into idle conversation, Byron paced the room in an agitated state. After excusing herself from a discussion of sleep remedies with Aunt Eleanor, Mira met him by the window.

"Does the pacing actually help?" she teased.

He gave her a small smile. "A little. Moving helps me think."

"Is something wrong?" she asked.

He ran a hand through his hair, keeping his voice pitched low. "I just can't shake the feeling that something is off about this situation. The case seems straightforward enough and yet . . ."

"You think it was something more than 'death by misadventure?'"

He tipped his head to the side. "There's no evidence to refute that verdict."

"You both seem rather pensive," Castel called from where he sat. "I had meant to ask what your thoughts were on the inquest, Byron."

Byron let out a long breath, turning towards his brother. "I don't want to besmirch the good name of Inspector Rutledge . . ."

"But?" Mira said.

"It seems to me that a man with good eyesight, who knows the landscape well from going on hunting parties with Mr. Risewell, would remember the location of the drop-off. Furthermore, at the time he left Miss Blayse and Miss Harris, the weather was still clear. Even if he had ventured thirty feet into the freezing weather to find more suitable air to breathe, I doubt that he would have fallen."

"He did have that injury from the war," Walker said. "Perhaps he walked out a bit farther for the view, lost his footing, and slipped."

"Perhaps," Byron said, rubbing his chin. "But the coroner said nothing to indicate a past injury to the leg."

"Could it be that the injury was fully healed but the cold aggravated it?" Liza asked.

"That could be it," Byron said. "But there is still something strange about it all."

"Oh, leave it alone, Ambrose," Mary said. "Can't you leave it to the professionals?"

Byron bristled, opening his mouth to say something, but Mira put a hand on his arm.

"I wonder if the Risewells wouldn't mind a visit," she said. "This has been such an ordeal for them, and I'd like to thank them for their hospitality."

He softened, looking down at her. "That's not a bad idea."

"I'm sure Miss Risewell is feeling the loss particularly," Mira continued. "We should bring her some flowers."

"I'm afraid I won't be up to it," Aunt Eleanor said. "After all that excitement, I need to lie down."

"You certainly can't go without a chaperone," Mary said.

Byron froze for a moment, before breaking out in a smile. "Thank you for offering, Mary. We can wait to go until after you write your letter."

"Offering? But—"

"I shall come too," Mrs. Sherard said. "I should also like to give the Risewells my gratitude." She looked Mira over with one of her indecipherable expressions. "And it would be good to see how Benson and the wheelwright are faring with the repairs to the carriage."

"But—" Mary spluttered.

"Good," Byron said, turning to Aunt Eleanor and changing the subject. "I meant to tell you earlier, Mrs. Davidsoni, but lunch was a triumph. You really ought to congratulate Mrs. Pettigrew."

February 11, 1889: Late Afternoon

The hired carriage rumbled up the drive towards Wynmar Park, with Mira, Byron, Mary, and Mrs. Sherard all bundled up inside. Castel cited a need to catch up on some letters and Walker chose to stay behind with Liza and the Renaldis.

The flowers in Mira's hands, a bouquet of pink sowbread, white hellebore, purple monkshood, and yellow daffodils, bowed with each bump in the road. She sat next to Mrs. Sherard and across from Byron. The atmosphere was thick with tension, silent as a grave. Mira knew her every move was being studied and judged. If a tickle started up in her throat again, she wasn't sure what she would do. Luckily, they reached Wynmar Park before anything too grievous occurred. Mira stepped out onto the gravel, looking up at the estate.

"I do hope they are at home," Mrs. Sherard said. "It would be a shame to drive all this way to discover they are back in Bath."

"Perhaps we can go for a walk if they aren't in," Byron said, his eyes twinkling.

"Would you like me to wait here, ma'am?" the carriage driver asked, voice rough and deep, as if he had a cold. His coat was pulled tight around his neck and a grey muffler covered his mouth and nose.

"Yes, please do," Mrs. Sherard said. "We shouldn't be too long."

The group moved up the path to the front step where Byron rang the bell. A few moments later, the butler opened the door.

"How may I help you?"

"We are here to visit Mrs. Risewell and her daughter. Are they in?" Mrs. Sherard asked.

"Certainly. If you will wait a moment, I shall fetch them directly." He ushered them through the door and into the parlor.

Mrs. Sherard took the most prominent chair for herself, Mary the one next to her. Mira didn't know what to do with herself, or the bouquet, but ended up on the sofa next to Byron.

No sooner than they had all sat down, Mrs. Risewell swept into the room, her purple walking dress swishing behind her.

"What a surprise!" Mrs. Risewell said. "To what do I owe the pleasure?"

Mrs. Sherard gave a slight bow of her head. "We wanted to thank you for your hospitality this past weekend. It really was too kind of you to offer your home at short notice and to let Benson stay on with the carriage."

"Oh, we couldn't possibly have done otherwise. I'm only sorry it meant you were all wrapped up in that unfortunate business with Mr. Treadway." She turned to Mira. "You handled it all very well, my dear. I don't know if I would have been as quick thinking in the same situation."

"Thank you," Mira said. "But I wouldn't have been able to do it without Theresia. She telephoned the police and gave me directions to the stable. And she was as shocked as any of us about Mr. Treadway."

"I'm so glad that she didn't lose her head or anything like that." Mrs. Risewell laughed a little. "Why, I'm sure I would have."

"She must be having the most beastly time with all of this." Mira adjusted the bouquet in her hands. "I hoped to give her this to lift her spirits. Might I see her, or is she keeping to her room?"

"Sometimes I wish she would keep to her room," Mrs. Risewell said. "No, she's been out riding this afternoon. However, it's almost time for tea, so she may be coming back now. If you wanted to go out to the stable, you might find her there."

Mira stood. "Thank you, I think I will."

"Would all of you like to stay for tea?" Mrs. Risewell asked as Mira left the room and headed down the hall towards the side door.

The weather was sunny and clear, warm enough that Mira almost didn't need a coat. Her breath didn't cloud the air and there were only a few spots of snow here and there, with clumps of ice in an oddly regular pattern, especially around the stable.

The door to the stable opened as she approached and the stable hand, Rudy Foster, walked out. His face was flushed from his work, his arms still wrapped, though the fabric looked new, and he carried his gloves in his hand. He tipped his cap to her, a little flustered.

"Good morning, Miss. I didn't realize you were still staying at Wynmar."

"I'm just visiting with the Sherards today."

"Are you looking for their Mr. Benson? He's still working on that axle of theirs over in the carriage house."

"No, I'm actually here for Miss Risewell. Is she still out riding?"

"No, she's just come inside with Verona." He opened the stable door to let her go through.

The door closed with a soft shush behind her, the stable quiet save for some whispering coming from Verona's stall.

"That's a good girl," Theresia said. "I might be able to bring you some sugar after tea."

"Miss Risewell?" Mira called out as she came near the stall.

Theresia jolted, looking up. Strands of her hair had fallen out to frame her face, and her eyes were wide.

"Why, Miss Blayse! You've scared me to death. What are you doing here?"

"I came with the Sherards to thank your family for their hospitality. And I wanted to bring you this." She lifted the bouquet. "This whole situation with Mr. Treadway has been terrible, and I wanted to make sure you were all right."

"You barely know me," Theresia said, but she stepped closer and took the flowers from her, smelling them. "And I'm coming to believe that I don't know you all that well either."

"Oh?"

Theresia's mouth twisted. "I'm going to ask you something, and I want you to tell me the truth. Is Bertie right about your Mr. Sherard? Is he actually a detective?"

Mira froze, at the unexpected question. Byron was still acting under the name Sherard, but if Bertie had broken their confidence it wouldn't do to lie to Theresia.

"He is."

"Then this visit isn't just for pleasantries." Theresia fussed with the bouquet, pulling some flowers forward and others back. "You think that Silas didn't die accidentally."

"We don't know yet."

Theresia cocked her head to the side. "I'm terrible with the language of flowers. Do they mean anything?"

Mira blinked, the abrupt change in conversation blindsiding her once again. "I'm afraid that I'm not fluent either. Byron is, but—"

"Byron?"

Mira flushed. "I mean, Ambrose. Mr. Sherard."

"Ah. I see. Is he actually a Sherard, or is he just masquerading as one for his work?"

"He was born a Sherard. But as a detective he goes by Byron Constantine."

Theresia's eyes widened. "Bertie said he was a detective, but I didn't know he meant Detective Constantine!"

Mira smiled. "You've heard of him, then?"

"Oh yes. My father works with Ambassador White. We heard all about the debacle back in October. Did you know about it?"

"I was the one who found Mr. Sutherland."

Theresia gasped, eyes sparkling. "No wonder you weren't shocked by the body. I had wondered. Do you know, we would have been at Sutherland's party that night, but we had another engagement. To think we might have met sooner."

"What small circles we run in," Mira laughed.

Theresia turned her attention back to the bouquet. "So did he choose these? Detective Constantine, I mean."

"No. He stayed in the carriage with his mother and sister. I had to have the owner of the flower shop help me. The pink ones are sowbread, they signify a parting of ways. The white is hellebore, representing hope in adversity. The purple is monkshood and is a protection from evil. And—"

"I know the daffodils. Something to do with spring and new beginnings." She slumped down on one of the hay bales. "To be honest, Miss Blayse—"

"You can call me Mira, if you like."

"Well then, Mira, I'll tell you a secret." She lowered her voice to a whisper. "I never really liked Silas Treadway."

Mira sat beside her. "I know. Maureen told me."

"You've been thorough in your questioning then."

"Not really. I just remember her mentioning offhand at the party that you never like any of your suitors."

Theresia tucked a strand of hair behind her ear. "That isn't exactly true."

They sat in silence for a few moments.

"I didn't like him, but I wouldn't have wanted him dead," Theresia said at last. "He was self-aggrandizing one moment and disappearing off to who knows where the next. Perfectly charismatic and quite the gentleman, but it all felt like a false front. Like the real Silas Treadway was buried beneath everything else. Have you ever met someone like that before?"

Mira swallowed, thinking of her godfather. "I wish I hadn't, but yes."

"I don't even know where he came from. Usually one is introduced by a mutual acquaintance. I've known Bertie Corbet since before he wore breeches. But Silas just showed up in Bath one day, and for whatever reason, my father saw him fit to be a potential match. I suppose that was novel, in a way. And so is the fact that he was a burglar."

"If he was the burglar," Mira said, "and wasn't framed by the actual thief."

Theresia's mouth dropped open. "I hadn't considered that . . ."

Mira hesitated. Maybe she shouldn't have mentioned Byron's theory. But, then again, the conversation was turning in a quite useful direction for the investigation, if she could only ask the right questions. Though, with Theresia knowing their true purpose and identity, she would need to be careful not to push too far.

"Would you mind if I asked a few questions?"

"I expected as much with you courting a detective. Or is that a ruse too and you're his assistant or something?"

"I was his secretary at first."

Theresia turned on the hay bale so she was facing her. "I'm sure that's quite the story."

"Another time, perhaps," Mira said. "First, the questions."

Theresia sat back. "I know the first one. When did I last see Silas Treadway alive? Just before the party. He was in the upstairs hall, just coming out of his room. We talked for a moment and then I came down. I didn't see him again until we found him." She grimaced. "He usually followed after me like a dog at parties and those sorts of things, so I can't imagine what he was up to. Other than talking to you and Maureen, of course. You said that at the inquest, didn't you?"

Mira nodded. "He mentioned he was in the war in Sudan but was sent home because of an injury. Do you know what injury it was?"

"I think it was his leg, but I never saw any sign of it. He didn't have a limp at all and the weather never affected it."

Mira frowned. "That's odd."

"That's Silas for you."

"Has your family had anything stolen before this?"

"Not that I know of," Theresia said. "And Silas would have had plenty of opportunity. It's strange that he waited until the party to do it, when he could have done it any time he wanted."

"Yes, he was staying with you, wasn't he?"

Theresia sighed. "Unfortunately. It happens every year. We come to Bath, father wants hunting companions, and inevitably they want to court me."

Mira pulled a strand of hay out of the bale and wrapped it around her finger. "You said there was at least one suitor you liked."

"Just one. And he isn't even a proper suitor, so it doesn't

matter." She stood. "Thank you for the flowers, although I really am all right. I'm more worried for poor Maureen."

"She's doing better."

"I'm glad. It's been positively awful for her, one thing after another. She was so withdrawn when she first came to Bath. I'd just managed to get her to open up to me when Mrs. Callan died."

"That was her aunt, right?"

"Yes. She was such a kind old sort. A hypochondriac for certain, but I imagine anyone would manifest illnesses to explain away aches and pains when you're at that age."

"I had heard that she was frequently ill," Mira said, brushing the hay from her skirts and following Theresia outside the stables.

"Ill enough she didn't leave the house. We'd invite her over time and time again, but she never took us up on the offer. Speaking of which, do you think the Sherards are staying for tea?"

"I'm not certain."

"We'd better go in and see."

Mira looked out towards the West Ledge. "I'll catch up in a minute. I think I'd like to get a little exercise in."

Theresia followed her line of sight. "I'll leave you to your sleuthing then." She winked.

They parted ways at the upper juncture and Mira followed the path she had taken away from the body the previous Saturday. It was much easier to navigate without all the snow. When she came to the place where the body had lain, she found Byron coming from the opposite direction.

"I thought you were with your family," Mira said.

He smiled. "They think I am talking with Mr. Risewell in his study."

As they spoke, they turned their attention to the steep slope that rose before them. It started out almost at a ninety degree angle at the top, then lessened towards the bottom where they stood. If someone were to fall, one would hit the rocky outcrop quickly and then roll down the incline. Even though the snow had melted, it was impossible to tell if Silas had followed that path due to how rocky it was. At the base there were some scrubby grasses and a few scabby bushes.

"How was Miss Risewell?" Byron asked.

"Surprisingly open. I discovered why she hasn't considered Bertie Corbet as a suitor. I think she's in love with someone else."

"Who?"

"I don't know. She was vague on that point. She just went up to the house," Mira kicked at one of the bushes with her boot. "By the way, she knows you're a detective. It seems Bertie Corbet is telling everyone. So much for him keeping a secret."

Byron sighed dramatically. "That's the trouble with having a reputation."

"She's very impressed with your record," Mira said. "And she seems entirely oblivious to your memory loss."

"I don't advertise that. Nor will I, now that I have such a beautiful memory keeper beside me."

"Flatterer."

"I only speak the truth."

Mira laughed. "You are an incorrigible flirt. Which reminds me—we ought to come up with a plan for how we will rejoin the others."

"How so?"

"Can't you see how it will look? I go off to find Miss Risewell, and she returns from the stable without me. You go to find Mr. Risewell in his study, but never arrive. If we return together, your family and the Risewells will only imagine the worst."

"Oh, my family is dealt with easily enough. I shall just tell them we were investigating the scene of the crime, and they are certain to be more disappointed and outraged than before. As for the Risewells . . ." he looked over at her. "I can't think of an excuse, but I suppose we could prove their fears right."

"Oh? And what shall we do?"

Byron grinned. "Hold hands? Share a chaste kiss? Certainly both are scandalous enough with our not being engaged. Though, we have broken the rules enough by now, perhaps we don't need to orchestrate it."

She laughed again, stepping away. "Yes, and the coachman is watching."

"Who cares about the coachman?"

"Well, I thought we—" She stopped, feeling something flat under her foot. She stepped away and the sun caught a flash of silver. Though the day was warm, a chill came over her.

"Byron . . . you had better have a look at this."

He crouched beside her, pulled a handkerchief from his pocket, and picked up a dagger with an inlaid handle. Half of the blade was covered in rust-colored splotches.

Byron looked up at her. "Seems murder is becoming more likely all the time. It's impossible to know whose it is—the blood or the dagger, for that matter." He wrapped the knife in the handkerchief and tucked the bundle into his coat pocket. He looked about and found a few sticks, inserting them into the ground in a triangular pattern around where the knife had lain. "There. Now we'll remember where we found it. We'll need to bring this to the police, but first I'd like to take a better look from where he likely fell." He took her hand and they headed up the southern path.

"Surely the blood couldn't be his, could it? You and I both saw the head wound."

"We'll have to talk with the coroner about it. Or Dr. Turpin. The whole thing is a bit strange."

When they came to the top of the ridge, Byron let go of her hand and stepped closer to the edge.

"Be careful," Mira said. "There are still some icy spots."

"I find that curious," Byron said, crouching. He measured several patches of ice with his hand. "Almost uniform in size too. I would think they were footprints, left behind by compressed snow, but these are too large and there weren't any on the southern paths. Yet here, and to the north . . ." he clicked his tongue.

"There were more by the stable. Could these prints belong to a horse?"

Byron stood. "That is a possibility. The weight of a horse would provide more compression, and therefore, a more solid bit of ice." He turned in place. "If these do belong to a horse, the creature must have stopped here, turned around, and headed back to the stable. The ice is all a jumble here, but see there," he moved along the path and pointed out two separate bits of ice. "We have a steady gait with tracks heading to that point and then back again." He followed the path a few more paces away. "And here we have more definite proof—horse dung."

Mira frowned. "But the hunting party left their horses with the gamekeeper after we looked at the body, and surely he brought them straight back to the stable. The horses wouldn't have come this way at all."

Byron tipped his head to the side. "Unless a horse was brought to this point on the night of the party. We discussed the possibility of Mr. Treadway going to meet a partner. However, I would have expected them to choose a more secluded location than this." He gestured to the slope. "Suppose Mr. Treadway took a horse in order to ride out to meet his partner. Then, when he arrived here, the horse was spooked and Mr. Treadway fell. The horse, being well trained and not wanting to be out in the inclement weather, trotted back to the stable. The new snow hid the tracks and fecal matter the morning after."

"What about the knife?" Mira asked.

A twinkle came to Byron's eye. "You always ask the right

questions. I believe we have an additional item to add to the agenda. Would you be so kind as to escort me to the stables?"

They followed the icy tracks from whence they came and Byron pulled open the heavy stable door. "I say, is there anyone in here?" he called out.

Some rustling came from one of the stalls and Rudy Foster poked his head out. "Yes, sir? How might I help you, sir?" He approached them, wiping his hands with a cloth.

"We have some questions about the night of the eighth," Byron said.

Rudy's eyes widened. "You mean when the poor man fell from the ledge?"

"Yes, that's the one. Were you working that night?"

"N-no sir. The Risewells gave the outside staff the night off, on account of the party."

"So you wouldn't know if anyone had come for a horse, say, around ten o'clock?"

"If it were the family wanting a horse, they would have come found me in the lodge. I stay there with Mr. Sharpe, the gamekeeper."

"But someone might have been able to take a horse without you knowing?"

Rudy frowned. "All the horses are accounted for now, sir. And they were the morning of the hunt."

"We noticed some dung near the top of the West Ledge," Byron said. "Are horses often taken over the ridge by that path?"

"N-no sir. The Risewells usually only take the horses into the woods for hunting or riding."

"Is there anything on that side of the property that can't be accessed from the lower paths?" Mira asked.

"There's a gate there in the wall surrounding the estate, but I don't remember the Risewells ever using it. Some of the staff that live in Doynton use it to come and go."

"Thank you," Mira said. "Do you know where we can find Mr. Sharpe?"

"I just left him in the gun room. Today's polishing day. I can take you there."

The sun was veering to the west as he led them back up the hill to the house and through a side door that led directly to the gun room. Wood paneled walls and the smell of oak greeted them. A large, leather-topped table sat in the center. Most of the guns were displayed on racks lined with velvet, save a few on the table in front of Mr. Sharpe. He looked up as Rudy came in.

"Lad, shouldn't you be cleaning the—" he stopped as he noticed Byron and Mira. "Begging your pardon."

"They wanted to speak with you about the eighth," Rudy said.

Sharpe set down his polishing cloth and lay the rifle across his lap. "You've shown 'em here. Now back to your work."

Rudy nodded and left. The cool air rushed around them, replaced with warmth as he closed the door.

"Terrible accident," Sharpe said. "The Estfields ought to put fencing along that there West Ledge. I've told Grantham, their gamekeeper, as much when the Risewells switch houses."

"Do you remember anything odd about that night?" Byron asked.

"Why are you concerned with it? The police have already come and gone. Inquest is over, ain't it?"

"Yes," Byron drew the word out, glancing at Mira as if he needed permission for something. "But you see, we are trying to settle a bet."

She nodded, ready to go along with this new lie.

"A bet?" Sharpe raised an eyebrow.

"Miss Blayse here has a brother. And at the party last Friday, he said he would be able to take a horse from the stable and return it without anyone noticing. He says that he did it, but didn't bring any proof. We were hoping that maybe you could tell us if any of the horses were missing or in the wrong stall or anything like that."

Sharpe laughed. "You youngsters and your practical jokes. No, sir. There weren't any horses in the wrong place or nothing of the sort. Though the horses are more of young Mr. Foster's domain these days. You spoke with him, I take it?"

"Yes. Just before coming to see you," Mira said.

"He'd know better than I. He's in the stable often enough. Spends his free time in the hayloft, pining after that girl of his. Writes poetry, he does. So I doubt your brother managed to get past him."

"Girl?" Mira asked.

"Oh, one of the shopkeep's daughters in Pucklechurch. I'm certain from the way they make eyes at each other. I've told him to approach her, but he's too nervous to even talk to her."

"Thank you very much, Mr. Sharpe," Byron said.

"Happy to help."

"I suppose we'd better get back," Mira said. "What is the best way to return to the parlor?"

"Just through that door there, down the hall, and to the right."

"Thank you."

They stepped into the hall and Byron closed the door behind them.

"Either one of them is lying," Mira said. "Or both of them are."

"Most definitely. What are you seeing?"

"There had to be a horse on the ridge either that night or the morning after. Otherwise there wouldn't have been any snow on the ground to make the icy tracks. We know it couldn't be the morning after, so it had to have been the night of the party. If Treadway took a horse to that location and fell, the horse surely had to make its way back to the stable and wouldn't be able to open the stable door on its own."

"Or the door to its own stall, for that matter." Byron clucked his tongue. "Someone had to have brought the horse back. The question is, why would Foster and Sharpe lie? Is someone paying them off, or are they involved in the murder?"

"I don't know. But I do know that your sister is liable to murder me if we take much longer."

"Mary doesn't have the imagination," Byron said, but began the trek across the house to the parlor. "Do you think it is better for us to enter together or separately?"

"I think together. If we arrive separately we will be guilty of both indiscretion and deception."

They entered the parlor, and Mira pointedly avoided facing the two Sherards, though she could feel their sharp gazes upon her. A tea tray, the pot of which was likely cold, sat on the table at the center of the room.

"I'm so sorry for the delay," Mira said. "You have such lovely grounds, I felt the need to explore a little."

"Oh, it is no trouble at all," Mrs. Risewell said.

"And what is your excuse?" Mary asked Byron.

"I don't believe I need an excuse." He pulled the handkerchief from his pocket. "I stepped out for a bit of air and found this." He unfolded the fabric and revealed the dagger.

"Heavens, is that . . ." Mrs. Risewell brought a hand to her neck.

"Blood? Yes." He folded the handkerchief up again. "I found this near where Mr. Treadway fell."

Theresia frowned. "But, I thought he died from the fall!"

"That is what the coroner said." Mary adjusted her skirts. "Surely he would know the difference between a blow to the head and a knife wound."

"Certainly." Byron tucked the bundle back into his jacket pocket. "But I believe the police ought to have a look at it, just the same."

"Then we should deliver it before it gets too late. Thank

you so much once again for your hospitality, Mrs. Risewell. And you are certain it isn't an inconvenience to have Benson staying on a little longer? The wheelwright said it would be a few days yet."

"Not at all. We are happy to oblige for as long as you need."

"You really are too kind." Mrs. Sherard stood. "We must do this again sometime."

"Oh yes!" Mrs. Risewell said. "Are you coming to our little Valentine's Party on Thursday? You are all invited." She turned to Mira. "The Renaldis too, if they wish."

"We'd be delighted," Mrs. Sherard said.

February 11, 1889: Evening

By the time they reached Bath, it was far too late to catch Inspector Rutledge. Not wanting to hand the dagger over to just any police constable, Byron and Mira thought it wise to keep the weapon in their possession for the time being. Since they had some questions about the post-mortem, they decided to pay a visit to Dr. Turpin. They would have preferred to speak with Mr. English, the coroner, but he had returned home to Bathampton after the inquest.

"This is all highly irregular, Ambrose," Mrs. Sherard said, as the hired carriage stopped in front of the doctor's rooms in Brock Street. "Is this how you spend all your days? Flitting from one place to the next in search of clues?"

"When I'm on a case, yes," Byron said. The group exited the

carriage, asked the poor driver to stay once more, and moved up the front steps.

"It's quite exhausting. Why couldn't we leave the dagger with the constable at the desk?" Mary said.

"This is the sort of evidence best given to the head inspector." He gave three raps with the large brass door knocker.

Dr. Turpin's wife opened the door. "Oh, good evening. My husband didn't mention we were expecting company."

"He doesn't know," Byron said. "You see, we're here for, erm . . ." He paused and it occurred to Mira that they hadn't discussed whether or not to tell Dr. Turpin the truth about their investigative purposes.

"It's my head," she said. "I've had a pounding ache in it since this morning and, as we were passing your house, I wondered if Dr. Turpin might suggest a treatment for it."

Mrs. Turpin gave her a soft smile. "I'm sure he'll be able to do something. He's just finishing up dinner now, but if you'll wait in the surgery, I'll fetch him."

She directed them into a set of rooms off to the right and left to find her husband. There were enough seats for the women, and Byron stood near the door.

"I'm quite surprised that you are able to lie so easily," Mary sniffed. "Perhaps I shouldn't be."

Mira steadied her breathing. "I thought you would prefer to keep your brother's profession secret from your acquaintances, seeing as you find it so distasteful. But if you'd rather I confess my deception to Dr. Turpin, I can certainly oblige you."

Mary shook her head. "No. At this point it would be far more disgraceful to reveal the truth. And it certainly isn't the worst breach of decorum you've committed today."

"Mary—" Byron started.

Mira interrupted him. "You may think what you will about what Byron and I were up to in the garden, but I can assure you it was nothing untoward."

"Knowing my brother I can believe that. I'm sure he's much more focused on solving this crime, if there is one, than on your attractions. But the Risewells certainly don't know that. And on top of that, you had the gall to give Miss Risewell that frightful bouquet."

Mira bit back a retort, curiosity and embarrassment overtaking her ire. She hadn't made a mistake, had she? The florist had been incredibly specific in the meaning. She looked over at Byron, her voice uncertain. "Was there something wrong with the bouquet?"

"Well—" Byron was once again interrupted by his sister.

"You didn't mean it?" Mary laughed. "Of course not. You don't even know what you said, do you?"

Mira's stomach dropped. "The florist said that—"

"You ought never to trust a florist. Half the time they are only trying to sell you the more expensive flowers. No, dear, you just gave Theresia Risewell a bouquet that says she should be warned because a dangerous scandal is in her future. And that someone close to her will never see her again."

A real headache began at the base of Mira's neck. "I didn't know."

"I might be able to respect the choice if it was intentional, but to send such an awful message on accident?"

"That's enough, Mary," Byron said. "There is more than one way to interpret flowers."

"And Theresia didn't know," Mira said. "I had to translate it for her."

"Thank goodness for that," Mrs. Sherard said. "We can only hope that her mother is also ignorant of the unintended meaning."

"I doubt that she is," Mary said. "She's far too cultured to miss such an obvious insult."

Mira's chest tightened. She hadn't meant it as an insult at

all. She turned away from the others, the corners of her eyes burning.

Footsteps sounded down the hall and Dr. Turpin stepped in, his spectacles slightly askew. "Good evening. I usually close up shop by now, but when I heard the Sherards were on my doorstep, I knew I had to make an exception."

"I am sorry that we have come so late," Mrs. Sherard said. "Usually I wouldn't dare to impose, but Miss Blayse has quite the headache."

Mira swallowed, nodding.

"Any other symptoms? Nausea? Spots in the vision?"

"No. Just a pounding at the back of my neck."

Dr. Turpin nodded. "How long has it been aching?"

The truth was about five minutes. Or perhaps from the moment she met Mary Sherard.

"Since the inquest," she said instead. "I'm wondering if it is from the stress."

"A fair assumption. Do you often get headaches?"

"Not as a rule, no. Though I also haven't been sleeping well since . . . well, since we found Mr. Treadway."

"Is that so?"

Mira nodded, continuing the lie. "I keep dreaming that he was stabbed."

Byron stepped forward. "I've told her that is quite impossible. You would have known when you looked at the body, wouldn't you?"

"Yes, and if I had, it would have come up at the inquest. A head wound like the one found on the body is consistent with what one might expect from a fall."

"And the scratches on him? That couldn't have come from a knife?" Byron asked.

"No. They weren't deep enough."

"See, there isn't anything to worry about, Miss Blayse," Byron said. "It was only an accident."

"Hysteria is only natural after having such a beastly experience," Dr. Turpin said. He moved over to one of the cabinets and pulled out a bottle. "It is likely that all the stress has built up and caused your headache and the nightmares. If you can release the stress, both should go away." He poured some purplish liquid into a little cup and handed it to her. "This syrup of figs should help move the process along."

Mira drank it down. It had a sickly-sweet taste and coated her tongue.

"Thank you," she said. "I feel quite silly about the whole thing."

"Nonsense. As I said, it is only natural for you to have an adverse reaction to such dreadful things. And you certainly don't have the worst case of hysteria I've seen, even this week."

"You mean Miss Harris?" Mary asked.

"Why, yes. From what Admiral Hoddle has told me of her symptoms, if she doesn't improve soon, I may have to recommend her to an asylum."

"Surely it isn't that bad," Mira said, real nausea coming over her at the thought of Maureen in an asylum.

"It would be for a very short time, just to rehabilitate her. The Mendip hospital in Wells is very nice, so I've heard, and I'm personal friends with Dr. Wade, the superintendent. Maureen has so many bad memories. This whole ordeal with Mr. Treadway has only made things worse."

"I still can't believe it myself," Byron said. "From what I understand, he had survived so much in the Sudan. Sent home because of a leg injury. Then to die from a fall like that, by pure accident. Poor fellow."

Dr. Turpin frowned. "A leg injury?"

"You seem surprised."

"A little, yes. He never complained of his leg when hunting, and surely the motion of a horse aggravates leg injuries. And I don't recall seeing any damage or scarring on the leg during the post mortem."

"Perhaps I was mistaken," Byron said. "I never talked to the man myself."

"Could be." Dr. Turpin returned the bottle to the cabinet. "Is there anything else I can do for you?"

"No, I think my head is already starting to feel better," Mira said, truthfully.

"I'll see you out then." Dr. Turpin opened the door to the surgery and the group filed out. "Give it a few weeks and you'll be right as rain. If you keep having the headaches and nightmares past the end of the month, you ought to see someone about it." They reached the front door and pleasantries were exchanged on both sides. Just as they were about to leave, Dr. Turpin said, "A moment, Mr. Sherard? I have a question for you."

Byron lingered at the door while the women moved down to the carriage.

Mrs. Sherard walked next to Mira. "That was quite the performance."

Mira didn't know whether that was a compliment or an insult. "Thank you?"

"Yes, it takes so much talent to deceive others," Mary said. "Did your family teach you?"

Mira stepped up into the carriage. "I learned it from your brother, actually."

Before Mary could respond in outrage, Byron came to meet them, brow furrowed.

"What's wrong?" Mira asked.

"Nothing," he said, though he clenched his jaw. "He asked whether or not we had laudanum at home."

"Laudanum?"

"He suggested I tell Mrs. Renaldi to administer some to help you sleep."

"We have a bottle if the Renaldis do not," Mary said.

"Why wouldn't he have suggested that when we all were together?" Mira asked.

"He thinks it would be better to do it without your knowledge, lest you get upset about it." Byron shook his head in disgust.

Mira's stomach twisted, though not from the medicine. "I certainly hope that isn't the treatment he suggested for Miss Harris."

AFTER A TENSE DRIVE, THE GROUP ARRIVED back at Davenguard and were welcomed by the Renaldis and Walker, who were playing cards in the drawing room.

"Have you eaten?" Mrs. Renaldi asked.

"I'm afraid we haven't," Mrs. Sherard said.

Mrs. Renaldi stood, leaving the room. "I'll get some supper sent up for you then."

"How were the Risewells?" Liza asked, looking up from her cards.

"Quite well," Mira said.

"Did Castel return to Royal Crescent?" Byron asked.

Walker shook his head. "He left for London, a little after you left for the Risewell's."

"London?" Mira asked.

"He said something about needing to pop into the Foreign Office, I think."

Byron frowned. "How strange . . ."

February 12, 1889

"I NEVER THOUGHT I WOULD SAY THIS, BUT I wish Aunt Eleanor would take over her chaperone duties again," Walker said as they approached the police station.

"It is getting rather taxing for you, isn't it?" Mira said. "Tell you what, tomorrow I promise to chaperone you and Liza. You can do whatever you'd like."

"Whatever we like?" Walker teased.

"Within reason, of course. Otherwise, I'll be banned from being your chaperone."

"This errand shouldn't take too long," Byron said. "We simply need to hand over the dagger and be done with things. Although, I wouldn't mind taking a look at the other objects found on his person."

"The jewels, you mean?" Walker said.

"And anything else that might give us some insight into his character."

They marched up the steps of the constabulary and up to the front desk where Constable McGuire sat.

"Why, hullo, Mr. Constantine, Miss Blayse! And you are?"

"Walker Blayse. Chaperone and brother."

"Of course. Can I help you all with something?"

"Yes, I believe you might," Byron said. "I've—"

"Anything I can do to help, I'd be happy to do so. It really is a pleasure sir, if you don't mind me saying. I've read so much about your work and your cases."

Byron blinked. "Well, at the moment, I just need to speak with Inspector Rutledge."

"Is it to do with the burglary case?" McGuire's eyes twinkled. "I knew there was something more to it."

"Is the inspector in?"

"You're in luck. He's just in his office. End of the hall, there."

"Thank you very much."

A short walk, a quick knock, and a soft 'come in' brought them into Rutledge's office.

"Why, Mr. Constantine. To what do we owe the pleasure?"

Byron pulled the handkerchief-wrapped bundle from his coat. "Found something on a walk at Wynmar Park and thought you might want to see it."

"Oh?" Rutledge took the package and opened it up, frowning. "Where did you find this?"

"Around where Treadway fell. I marked the location with some sticks, in case you wanted to take a look at it."

Rutledge picked up the dagger, turning it over. "This couldn't be Treadway's blood. But . . ." He reluctantly continued. "It would be quite the coincidence if it was unrelated to his death."

"That was my thought, sir," Byron said. "I wanted to take a look at Mr. Treadway's personal effects, if you didn't mind."

"Certainly. We have them in a box in the back, waiting to be collected by his next of kin." He stepped into the hall.

"He's taking it well," Walker said. "We may have just broken open the entire investigation."

"Possibly," Byron said.

Inspector Rutledge returned. "I've sent McGuire to fetch the box." He tipped his head to the side looking over the dagger again, a glint of confidence coming to his eye. "Come to think of it, this could very well have belonged to the deceased. I wouldn't be surprised if it dropped from his pocket when he fell."

"And the blood?" Byron asked.

"He often hunted with Mr. Risewell," Rutledge said, straightening. "He might have not wiped it thoroughly the last time he caught a rabbit or something."

"Or something," Mira said, annoyed. The inspector was grasping at straws to maintain his clean "death by misadventure."

McGuire came in with a box and began laying everything out on the table. "There's everything we found."

Mira scanned the items. Pencil. Handkerchief. Pocket watch. Leather gloves. Cigarette case. Matchbook. A few foreign coins. And then the stolen jewels.

Byron pulled out his journal and a pen. "Let's see . . . there's the emerald bracelet. The diamond ring. The gold work necklace. The diamond brooch." He made a tick mark as he checked each one off. "I do believe that's all of it."

"No," Mira said. "We're missing a necklace."

"Are we?" Inspector Rutledge said.

"Mrs. Risewell's grandmother's necklace. It was made of amethyst and jade. Theresia described it to me when she discovered it was missing."

The five of them turned back to the assortment on the table.

"What do you make of it, Inspector?" Byron asked.

"Erm. Well. Perhaps Miss Risewell only misplaced it. Or the necklace is hidden somewhere in his room at Wynmar."

"There is one other piece of evidence that we found at Wynmar yesterday," Byron said. "Rounds of ice, uniform in size, that suggest a horse was taken to the top of the ridge and then returned to the stable. My prevailing thought is that Mr. Treadway intended to hand the stolen goods off to a partner. I doubt he would forget such a significant piece of jewelry."

"Do you have a theory, then?" Rutledge said, lips pressed together in a thin white line.

"I do. Though I currently lack the proof to ratify it. Would you, and some of your constables, be so kind as to accompany us to Wynmar Park?"

"Well . . ."

McGuire perked up. "We really ought to account for the location of the necklace, sir."

Inspector Rutledge sighed. "Very well, then."

"Excellent." Byron turned to Walker, writing something down in his journal and tearing the page out. "Would you follow us there after completing these instructions?"

Walker's brow furrowed as he read the page. "I'm meant to be chaperoning you, Constantine."

"Right you are," Byron turned to the inspector. "You wouldn't mind if one of your constables took on that role, would you Inspector?"

"I suppose not."

Byron nodded, heading for the door. He stopped on the threshold and spun around. "Oh, and incidentally, you may want to bring two carriages, because I believe we'll be making an arrest."

After some negotiation, the police headed out to

Wynmar Park. By some stroke of luck, Mira and Byron were assigned to a carriage with only one policeman—Constable Welter. It wasn't exactly private, but he was better than some of the chaperones they had had as of late, especially when, with an hour left in the drive, the rocking sensation of the wheels lulled the man to sleep.

"And what is the grand mastermind up to now?" Mira asked, keeping her voice pitched low.

"Hm?"

"With Walker. You have a plan."

"I have a theory. Though part of me hopes that I'm incorrect. I sent him to the only jeweler in town."

"You think someone has already sold the necklace?" Mira frowned. "But if Mr. Treadway had passed the necklace to his partner, why did he have the other jewelry on him?"

"I never said that Mr. Treadway took the necklace."

Mira's eyes widened. "You don't think . . . you don't think it was Theresia, do you?"

"Now, why would I think that?" Byron's eyes smiled.

"She's the one who said it was stolen. But why would she have taken it?"

"I have a theory about that too. I'm surprised you haven't thought of it yet."

"Can't you give me a little hint?"

"You'll see soon enough."

Mira tipped her head to the side. "I thought we weren't going to have secrets between us."

He held out for about two seconds. "All right. I suppose it is only fair. Consider what Miss Risewell told you yesterday."

"About her dislike of her suitors?" Mira looked down, mulling over the conversation. "Except for one." She turned to him, the pieces falling into place. "She said he wasn't a proper suitor. Which means her family either doesn't know about him or doesn't approve."

"In which case," Byron said, "she would need money to elope."

"That explains the necklace."

"If her paramour is who I think it is, it explains quite a bit."

Mira worried at her lip. "It would have to be someone below her station. But the only person I can think—"

The constable snorted in his sleep and the two fell silent until it was clear he wouldn't be waking.

"Could it be Rudy Foster?" Mira whispered.

"That's the conclusion I've come to. I don't have all the details sorted yet. One scenario is they were going to run away together that night. Hence the horse. But Silas Treadway caught them. There was a bit of a scuffle, one of them drew a knife, and Silas fell. Not wanting to draw suspicion to themselves by disappearing or being found with the jewels, they stashed most of the ill-gotten goods on his person and pretended like nothing had happened."

Mira shook her head. "No, that can't be right. Otherwise, Theresia wouldn't have been so shocked that morning. And she certainly wouldn't have been so open with me when we spoke in the stables. And what about the other burglaries? Were they stealing jewelry from other houses in order to fund their escape?"

"Good questions, all of them. The only thing I know is the answers lie with Rudy Foster, and so to Rudy Foster we must go."

Mira averted her gaze. "If it is true, I feel sorry for them. It is hard enough gaining familial approval without a class divide."

He looked over at her. "You know that from experience now, don't you?"

She nodded.

"Is it just Mary, or the lot of them?"

Mira traced the floral pattern on her skirt. "Castel seems

to have come around. Your mother is a mystery. But I have no idea what I've done to make Mary hate me so."

"She doesn't hate you." He caught her hand with his and gave it a squeeze.

"Well, she certainly doesn't like me. Will you concede to that?"

He sighed. "I witnessed your verbal sparring last evening. I imagine if she's willing to speak that way in front of me, it's even worse when I'm not around. What has she been saying?"

"That I'm not good enough for your family. I feel as if I'm Elizabeth Bennet facing down Lady Catherine. But falling short no matter what I do."

"Does that make me the brooding Mr. Darcy?" he teased.

She slid her gaze over his face, considering. "No. Because I've never hated you."

A rare blush rose to his cheeks and she looked away before it spread to her, continuing. "Everything with her is about position and societal standing, what others think. And now I'm finding myself caring about that too, and I wish I could go back." She drew in a long breath. "I can't help but feel sorry for her. Because it is exhausting to be so preoccupied with how everyone else thinks."

"She wasn't always that way." Byron said, voice hesitant. "When I was little, I even remember her having fun."

"What changed?"

He remained silent for a few moments.

"A few things. I think it started with Wilburn Treadway."

"The Treadway that Castel mentioned?"

"The very one. He courted Mary for several years. I don't remember all the specifics, as I was only six when they parted ways. What I do know is, my father did not approve of the match and Mary was devastated."

"Then why would she do the same thing to you?"

Byron ran a hand through his hair. "Just two years after

that, she lost one of her closest friends and confidants." He looked away, his voice going hoarse. "Our sister Catherine."

Mira's mouth went dry. "I didn't know you had any other sisters."

"There were three others, actually. Catherine, Edith, and Alice. And each of them died when they turned twenty-one." Byron swallowed. "It felt like a curse. One after another, a few years apart. And then father died. With each funeral, Mary became more and more protective of the rest of us."

"Oh."

"As I'm the youngest, and younger than her by sixteen years, she's all the more protective of me."

Mira laid her head on his shoulder. "Then no one will ever be good enough for her."

He brought her hand up to his lips. "Thank goodness she's not the one who gets to decide."

They fell into silence for the rest of the ride, Byron running his thumb over the back of her hand.

IF THE RISEWELLS WERE SURPRISED TO HAVE the police on their doorstep again, they hid it well. They spoke briefly to Mr. and Mrs. Risewell, learned that Theresia was out riding again, and headed out to the top of the West Ledge.

Byron crouched by the edge. "The ice has melted some since yesterday, but you can see the tracks well enough, can't you inspector?"

"Yes. I can." Rutledge folded his arms, puffing on a cigarette. "But I don't see how this changes anything. He stole a horse and fell from it."

"If I'm right, it's a bit more complicated than that." Byron stood, brushing himself off. "Come down to where we found the dagger."

They trekked along the path and found the place marked with sticks. "Miss Blayse, would you refresh our memory on where you found the body?" Byron asked.

Mira frowned, looking up the slope and then out past the fence line, determining where it had been. She moved to stand a few feet away from where they found the dagger.

"About here, I'd say."

"I'd agree to that," Inspector Rutledge said.

"If the dagger had merely fallen from his pocket, surely it would have been found closer to the body, or underneath it," Byron said. "But if the knife was in his hand at the time, the distance can be accounted for. And what reason would he have to draw his knife, unless there was an assailant?"

"You think it was murder?" Constable Welter asked.

"I think there is more to the story than meets the eye. Whether it was murder or not does not preclude the necessity of discovering the truth."

"Ho there!" Walker called from the top of the ledge.

The whole group looked up at him.

Byron waved, calling back. "Was I right?"

"Down to the letter!"

Byron let out a satisfied sigh. "I thought I would be." Louder, he said. "Meet us by the stable!"

Walker nodded and disappeared from view.

"What's this all about, Constantine?" Rutledge asked.

"The missing necklace. We've found it."

"Oh?"

They hurried up the path, meeting Walker at the entrance to the stable. Walker handed the inspector a piece of paper.

"Here's a statement, signed by the jeweler," he said, a little out of breath. "A woman matching the description of Theresia Risewell sold a jade and amethyst necklace yesterday after the inquest."

Rutledge scanned the paper, frowning. "Why would she do that, I wonder?"

"Why don't we find out?" Byron said, moving to the stable door. "After you, Inspector."

Soft light filtered through the dust of the stable, the musk of horses and stench of manure dulled by the cold. Rudy Foster's voice cut through the air, singing a quiet melody in time with the sound of a pitchfork in hay.

"—with steps, solemn, mournful and slow. Had I the wings of a little dove, far, far away would I fly, I'd fly—"

He was up in the hayloft, sending hay raining down into the stalls.

"—Straight for the arms of my true love. And there I would lay me and—"

"Mr. Foster?" Byron called out.

The singing stopped and Rudy looked down from the edge of the loft. "Aye, that's me." His shoulders slumped as he cast his gaze across Byron, Mira, Walker, and the police.

"We have some questions for you."

Rudy let out a long breath and set the pitchfork into a bale of hay. "I thought you might."

He sat on the edge, bracing himself for the fall before dropping down in front of them.

"I suppose you know then," he said. "Miss Risewell mentioned you were a detective."

Byron inclined his head. "I don't have the entire story. I thought you might be willing to fill in the gaps." He gestured for Rudy to take a seat on one of the stools.

"I knew it would come out, one way or another," he said. "I don't think I done nothing wrong, 'cept keeping quiet about it. But the guilt I've felt has been something terrible. So if I can be rid of that now, I'll tell you anything you want to know."

"First," Byron said. "Might we see what you're hiding beneath those wrappings?"

Rudy averted his gaze, but gave a small nod and began the process of unwrapping the fabric from around his arms. With a sigh, he lifted his left arm, revealing a jagged, raw, red mark running up the side. Mira grimaced.

"There's the missing piece," Byron said.

"I didn't mean to," Rudy said. "And I know I ought to have told someone, but I didn't want to lose my position here. It's a good job."

"And if you lost it, you'd lose Miss Risewell too?" Mira asked.

Rudy's eyes widened. "How . . . I mean . . ."

Byron set a hand on the man's shoulder. "What is your relationship to Miss Risewell, Rudy?"

He worried his lip. "I suppose there's no use hiding it. I love her. But that's no crime. And I've known all along it would never work. The two of us are too different. I don't have the money to give her the life she deserves. I've told her as much in the past. Told her to find a good man. Which is why . . ."

"You didn't like Silas Treadway?" Constable McGuire offered.

Rudy rubbed the back of his neck, avoiding looking at any of them. "I had no real opinion of the man. Thought he might be a good match. But then . . . well, I saw him a few weeks ago meeting with a woman at the southern gate."

"Is that why you killed him?" Rutledge asked.

Rudy's eyes flew wide. "I didn't kill him, sir! Or leastways, I didn't mean to. It was an accident, I swear it was."

Byron nodded. "You don't need to admit to anything at this time, but considering the knife and your injury, it might be in your best interest to tell us what happened that night."

Rudy swallowed heavily, fidgeting with his hands.

"Mr. Treadway came into the stables. He didn't know I was in the loft, didn't notice me any. I'd been asleep, so it weren't until he was leaving with Fortinbras, that's Mr. Risewell's horse, that I knew anything.

"It wasn't unusual for him to take a horse for a ride, but he had only ever done it during the day before, not at night, and never in such bad weather." He hesitated, running a hand through his hair. "And, well, the last time he went out, I was exercising Seneca in the pasture and I saw him meeting with that other woman."

He fisted his hands in his lap. "So for him to be leaving at such a time as that, with the weather, I thought perhaps he was making another rendezvous." He looked up at them. "I'll admit, I was angry when I followed him. But what happened afterwards was an accident."

"What happened?" Byron asked, voice gentle.

"I caught up to him on the West Ledge. He dismounted and made the weak excuse that he felt the need to go for a ride. I asked him if he were going to meet with that woman again, and his whole attitude changed. He asked me how much I knew and if I'd told anyone. I told him I knew he'd been meeting a lady and I'd seen him giving her jewelry." He shook his head. "I didn't know he was the burglar everyone had been speaking of. I thought he was being unfaithful to Miss Risewell. And seeing as . . . seeing as we couldn't be together, I thought she'd be able to at least find an honest man."

"Was the knife yours or his?" Byron asked.

"His. He drew it on me when I said I'd tell Miss Risewell what he was up to. We fought and when he cut my arm here, I threw him off of me with all my strength. And, well, that was enough for him to lose his balance."

"Did you check to see if he survived?" McGuire asked.

"No sir. I hate to say it, but the way he was acting seemed downright murderous. I thought he might recover and follow me. The snow was coming down something awful by then, so I brought Fortinbras back to the stable and barred the door. And then, in the morning . . ." He closed his eyes.

"You didn't think to tell anyone?" Inspector Rutledge asked.

"I didn't know he'd died," his voice wavered. "Not until this lady here," Rudy gestured to Mira, "came into the stable saying they found a man and needed to fetch the doctor back from the hunt. And then everyone said it was an accident."

"And what of the necklace? Hm?" Inspector Rutledge asked. "Did you and Miss Risewell plan to steal it together?"

Rudy frowned. "Necklace?"

"Jade and amethyst. Did you sell it for money to elope?" Rutledge asked.

He shook his head. "I don't know about any necklace. I'd given up hope long ago of ever eloping with Miss Theresia. It wouldn't be right."

"I suppose it will all come out in the trial," Rutledge said. "Rudolph Foster, you are under arrest for the death of Silas Treadway and perverting the course of justice."

Constable Welter produced a set of handcuffs and Rudy stood, offering his wrists.

Rutledge moved over to Byron and Mira. "I'm surprised he's cooperating so easily," he whispered.

"He said it himself: he wants to be rid of the guilt," Byron said, glancing at Mira and echoing her words. "He's a good man, but even good men will act wrongfully out of fear. If he is telling the truth, which I believe he is, his only crime was hiding the death."

Rudy paused at the door as the constables were leading him out. "Mr. Constantine? Will you let Mr. Sharpe know what's happened? I haven't finished filling the feeding troughs, and I don't want the horses to starve on account of what I've done."

"I'll take care of it," Byron said. "Don't you worry."

Rudy nodded.

The door of the stable opened and Theresia Risewell entered holding Verona's reins.

"What is going on here?" she asked.

"Mr. Foster has been arrested for the death of Silas Treadway," Rutledge said.

"What? But the inquest . . ."

"New evidence has come to light," Byron said.

"I'm sorry," Rudy said. "I should have told you."

"You mean . . . you killed him?"

"It was an accident, I swear it was. I thought . . . I thought he was being unfaithful."

"Speaking of which," Byron said. "I understand that you have recently sold a necklace, Miss Risewell."

Theresia paled. "I—"

"All I want to know," Byron continued, "is whether Mr. Foster was aware of what you were doing."

She hesitated before shaking her head. "I wanted it to be a surprise," she said, voice hollow.

Byron nodded. "There you are, Inspector. Rudy had nothing to do with it."

Rutledge's mustache twisted. "Assuming she's telling the truth."

"Even if she isn't," Byron said, "the necklace is easily taken care of. Walker?"

Walker pulled a small box from his pocket and handed it to Byron. He opened it, revealing the jade and amethyst necklace.

Walker said, "After telling the jeweler what the situation was, he sold it to me for the same amount he gave Miss Risewell."

Rutledge drew in a nasally breath, turning to Miss Risewell. "I won't charge you, though you lied to a policeman. Just ensure the money gets paid back to these men here. And tell your parents the truth before they decide to collect the insurance on it. Good day, Miss."

Rutledge and the constables left the stable, Mr. Foster in tow.

Theresia moved past the remaining party, leading Verona into her stall. After a moment she stepped out.

"I-I'm not sure how to take off her saddle."

Walker moved into the stall to help with the horse. Theresia stood at the center of the stable, looking aimless. Byron stepped closer to her, offering the necklace.

"I believe this is yours."

She took it with shaking hands. "What will they do with him? He won't . . . he won't hang for this, will he?"

Byron shook his head. "The current evidence shows it was a clear case of self-defense. Unless some other proof emerges, it will likely be a fine, or a short few months of time, for not coming forward about the death."

"Oh. I see."

"I'm sorry," Mira said. "You were going to elope, weren't you?"

Theresia went still, her shoulders tightening. "It doesn't matter."

She hurried past them and left the stable.

Byron took off his jacket, rolling up his sleeves.

"What are you doing?" Mira asked.

"I promised Rudy the horses would be taken care of," he said, climbing the ladder into the loft. "We can tell Mr. Sharpe about the situation after they've been fed."

They spent the better part of a half hour making sure the horses were settled. Mira brushed them down and fed them carrots and apples she found in a barrel, while the men handled the more strenuous activities.

In the end, they all smelled of horses and hay as they emerged into the chilled outside air.

Walker wiped the sweat from his brow. "Well, that's that

then. Mystery solved. Investigation closed. Now we can simply enjoy our time in Bath."

"Not quite," Byron said, linking his arm with Mira's and heading up the hill.

Walker caught up to them. "No, Constantine. We came here to solve a burglary. The burglar was found dead. The accidental killer has been arrested. What else is there to sort?"

"The woman at the gate," Byron said. "There's more than one thief."

February 13, 1889: Morning

DESPITE HAVING BEEN IN BATH FOR NEARLY a week, Mira hadn't seen much of the city. She walked a distance behind Walker and Liza as they made the rounds of Royal Victoria Park. Based on a brass plaque near the entrance, it had been Her Royal Majesty's first act to open the park when she was only a princess of eleven years old. The air was crisp and fine, but the temperature was the unfortunate sort that required a coat but caused you to sweat when you wore one.

Walker and Liza were the epitome of propriety and grace, standing a foot apart, perfectly content just to be together. In the past few months, Mira had ample opportunity to be chaperoned herself, but not much experience in being the chaperone. She had determined one thing from the hour and a half she'd spent in this new occupation.

It was dull as anything.

At least her chaperones had the intrigue of being witness to police investigations.

Perhaps she was being unfair. They had spent much of the morning exploring the city center, at least what they could see with the construction around the Roman ruins. After that, they had spent a good deal of time in the botanical gardens. A few flowers were beginning to bud and there was an abundance of friendly squirrels. But despite the beautiful landscape and architecture, she wished she were viewing it with Byron.

They had decided to let the case rest for a day or two, if only to appease their families. It was also quite possible that Silas Treadway's mysterious partner had already fled from Bath, and with no leads as to her retreat, it might be a fool's errand altogether.

It was nearing noon when they reached the obelisk commemorating Queen Victoria's eighteenth birthday. Walker and Liza stopped beneath it and called her over.

"Would you like to stop in on the Sherards before we go back to Davenguard for lunch?" Walker asked.

Mira frowned. "Isn't that a bit out of our way?"

"Not at all," Liza said. "The Royal Crescent overlooks the smaller portion of the park."

"I had no idea we were so close. I'd love to."

They followed the road past a copse of trees, and sure enough The Royal Crescent stood looking down on them from the top of the hill. It took only a few minutes to come to the door of number eighteen and knock. Greerson opened the door with a bow of his head.

"May I help you?"

"Yes, we are here to call on Mr. Sherard," Walker said.

"Mr. Sherard is still in London, sir."

"Oh, I mean the younger Sherard," Walker said.

Greerson nodded. "He, Mrs. Sherard, and Miss Sherard are out, I'm afraid."

"Out?" Mira said.

"Miss Sherard received a telegram half an hour ago from the police station. They left soon after."

Mira looked at her brother and he sighed.

"I suppose we'll be going to the police station, then."

WHEN THEY ENTERED THE POLICE STATION, CONSTABLE McGuire was manning the front desk yet again.

"I'd wondered when you'd show up, Miss," he said. "We've got a right old mess here. They're in as much of a fight as I've ever seen high-bred folks get into."

"What's happened?" Mira asked.

"Mr. Treadway's family has come to collect him. Except, they say that the corpse isn't him! Can you imagine that?"

Liza's mouth fell open.

Walker asked the obvious question. "How is that possible?"

"That's what they are figuring out now. The elder Mr. Treadway, Wilburn's his name, why, he thought Miss Sherard was playing a practical joke. Apparently they knew each other back in the day."

"Oh no." Mira's stomach twisted itself in knots. "Where are they?"

"They're in the inspector's office. You know the way."

"Thank you."

She, Walker, and Liza moved down the hall to the office. Walker did the honors of knocking. A man with a thin mustache answered the door. Rutledge sat behind his desk, Mrs. Sherard sat in one armchair, an unknown woman sat in the other, and Mary stood by a bookcase with Byron. He stepped forward upon her entrance.

"Miss Blayse, I didn't realize you were coming," Byron said.

He glanced back at Rutledge who gave a small shrug. "I didn't inform her."

"Greerson did, at the Royal Crescent," Mira said.

"Are we inviting everyone into our private affairs, now?" the unknown woman said.

"I'm Detective Constantine's secretary," she said, turning to Walker and Liza. "Would you be so kind as to wait in the lobby with Constable McGuire?"

Walker nodded and the two of them left. Mira stepped fully into the room and the unknown man, presumably Mr. Treadway, closed the door behind her.

Mira moved to Byron's side and he handed his journal and pen off to her, corroborating her secretarial half-truth. She skimmed over the last few notes he had made:

Man (Thomas Perch) from army contacted family six months ago. Silas dead.

No papers/letters from government indicating death. (Stolen papers?)

Corpse identity unknown.

Inspector Rutledge cleared his throat. "As I was saying, I understand that this has been a harrowing experience for you—"

"Harrowing?" Mr. Treadway said. "My wife and I were prepared to retrieve my son's body—a son, mind you, that we have thought dead for months—only to find the body of an entirely unknown man. And a thief, no less."

Mrs. Treadway dabbed at her eyes with a handkerchief. "I was not prepared to be pulled into such a scandal. To be attached to some unknown vagabond. When my dear boy is—"

she devolved into earnest sobs. "Dead in some foreign climate, who knows where."

Mr. Treadway moved to his wife, placing a hand on her back. Mary looked away.

"What we want to know," Mr. Treadway said, "is how this imposter was able to get hold of my son's papers."

"I'm afraid I don't know," Rutledge said.

"This man may have been a fellow soldier who took his papers when your son died," Byron said. "But it's impossible to prove it one way or the other."

"We will make an announcement that the man found dead at Wynmar had been masquerading as your son, so as to make it clear that you had no relation to him," Rutledge said. "Your family will no longer be connected with the thefts."

"I should think not!" Mrs. Treadway said. "Do people think we are connected?"

"Erm . . ." Rutledge squirmed like a tortoise who wanted to retreat into its shell.

"There are so many Treadways in England," Mira said, in an attempt to diffuse the tension. "The only people who know about the possible connection to you specifically are in this room. Save Castel, but he isn't one to gossip."

"Castel?" Mrs. Treadway said. "Who is that?"

"Castel Sherard. The next Baron Sherard," Mr. Treadway said, glancing at Mary. "And if memory serves, we can trust he will be reticent."

Mary blushed and cleared her throat. "I'm sorry that you came all this way for nothing."

Mrs. Treadway shifted in her chair, folding up her handkerchief. "I suppose it is better to know about this little incident now, rather than in a few months when rumors may have spread."

Mr. Treadway nodded. "It would have been much worse had we not known." He stepped over to Rutledge's desk and offered a hand. "We'll be staying in town for a few days, if something comes to light about our actual son or who this imposter is."

Rutledge shook his hand. "Thank you for being so understanding."

The Treadways left the room and the air was a little more breathable.

"Well. This is quite the strange situation," Inspector Rutledge said. "I have no idea where to even start."

Byron took the journal back from Mira. "I believe we ought to—"

"Ambrose," Mary said, voice terse. "Haven't you done enough?"

Byron's entire form wound tight like a spring as he turned towards his sister. "If you did not want me meddling with police affairs, you should not have invited me to Bath to investigate your burglary. Now, the burglar has been found dead, but his identity is unknown. We know he was working with a partner but have no leads on how to find her, and the jewels you asked me to retrieve are still missing. So no, Mary, I don't think I've even begun to 'do enough.' If you wish to return home, by all means leave us. But if you stay, please allow me to do my job."

Mary shut her mouth with a snap.

Mrs. Sherard stood. "Thank you for your patience in this matter, Inspector. If you need us, you'll know where to find us. Come along, Mary."

Once the office door had shut behind them, Byron took a deep breath and turned back to the inspector. "If we are to find out who our John Doe is, we can only work with what he left us. We need to return to his room at Wynmar Park."

For the fourth time in almost as many days, Mira and

Byron took the journey out to Wynmar, this time accompanied by Walker and Liza as well as the police.

In relation to the chaperone issue, Liza had said, "We shall chaperone you and you shall chaperone us. And besides, we shan't have time to be improper."

This time, the Risewells were much more surprised to see them, but readily agreed to their searching of Mr. Treadway's room. Inspector Rutledge stayed on the lower floor to ask them if they knew anything about Mr. Treadway's life before coming to Wynmar, while the younger investigators stormed the battlements, so to speak.

"This is so exciting," Liza said. "I've never been part of an investigation before. Not really."

Mira pulled all the clothes out of the wardrobe and set them on the bed to go through them more thoroughly. Byron and Walker were on the other side of the room on their hands and knees, checking for loose floorboards.

Liza picked up a jacket and turned it about.

"What are we looking for?"

"Any distinguishing marks. A tailor might have stitched in his initials or something. Or there might be something in the pockets that I missed."

Liza nodded and searched over all the stitching. "Did Byron teach you how to do this?"

Mira tugged on a loose thread in a coat. "No. I suppose this just seems to be one of the more logical places to start."

Liza shook her head. "I wouldn't have any idea of what to look for if you hadn't told me."

"It takes some practice," Byron said, knocking on the wood.

They spent the afternoon occupied with searching every square inch of the room for anything to identify their John Doe and came up with nothing. Until Mira shook out a coat and a button came loose, falling between the slats of a floorboard.

"I'll get it," Liza said, crouching. "Is there a pen or something thin on the desk? It's stuck."

Mira pulled a pin from her updo, a few strands of hair falling over her shoulders as she handed it over. Liza used it to fish the button out.

"Hold on, there's something else here . . ." Liza sat back on her heels, turning the item over in her hand. "It's a pretty little thing. A cufflink, I think." She handed it over to Mira, smiling.

Mira froze in place, her breath catching between her ribs. She looked up at Byron, who moved over to her side. "What is it?"

She placed it in his hand. "This isn't what I think it is, is it?"

It was a little gold pin with an encircled triangle at the center. Three little circles were at each point of the triangle.

"The symbol of Circe? I'm afraid so." Byron ran his thumb over its face. "Now just what was our John Doe tied up in?"

"Circe?" Liza said, standing. "What's that?"

Mira had quite forgotten that Liza wouldn't know. She furrowed her brow, trying to think of the best way to describe it.

Byron turned the pin over in his hand again. "Circe is a criminal organization that it seems we can never fully escape."

Mira's frown deepened. "If he was a member of Circe, surely there must be something more to the thefts. If Selene was right about what she wrote in her letter, they rarely steal just for money's sake."

Byron tucked the pin into his vest pocket. "Agreed. And it makes it all the more probable that our John Doe had more than one accomplice."

"You don't think that Monty fellow is in on it, do you?" Walker asked.

"No . . ." Byron trailed off, tipping his head to the side.

Mira jumped up. "But he might know someone who is! He may have left that life behind, but he may still have some connections."

Byron nodded. "He's our best lead at the moment." He turned to Walker. "Do you think you and Liza can keep the police and the Risewells busy long enough for us to speak with him?"

Walker smiled. "We'll do our best."

MIRA PACED IN THE BLUE ROOM. As no one was staying there, and it was unlikely that any of the other servants would disturb them, they determined it would be the safest place in the house to speak in. Byron had gone down to the servant's quarters to find Monty, but the longer he was gone, the more she wondered if the ex-thief had quit his position and fled.

She crossed to the window and pushed the curtain away, looking across the grounds to the stable. Was Theresia out there with Verona? Or was she too upset to ride? Her chest tightened. She hoped Rudy would be all right, for his and Theresia's sakes.

A soft knock came at the door and Byron stepped in with Charles Montague at his heels.

"I can't speak for long," Monty said once the door was safely closed. "Mr. Patterson will be expecting me back soon enough."

"We won't keep you," Byron said. "We only have a few questions."

"I thought the whole matter had been closed? First with the inquest, then with the arrest yesterday. Boh," Monty said. "I never thought Mr. Foster was that sort. He was always so nice and good at his job."

"It was an accident," Mira said. "But we're more interested in finding out more about the man who died."

"We found this in his room." Byron produced the pin from his pocket and held it out to Monty, whose eyes widened.

"He's part of . . . why I never." Monty licked his lip. "Goes to show what you know about people." He grinned, showing his gold tooth.

"You knew, didn't you?" Byron asked.

Monty's fake smile faded. "Not for certain. Never knew the chap but he had that sort of air about him. You can usually tell. And he looked kind of familiar, so we might have crossed paths before."

Byron nodded, tucking the Circe pin back in his pocket. "I know that you've left that life behind, but you wouldn't happen to know anyone still involved, would you?"

Monty sucked on his teeth. "I mean, there's Dennis, though I don't know where he went off to, and I'd rather not go looking for him. The farther he is from Bath, the better, as far as I'm concerned."

Mira stepped closer to him. "Is there really no one else? A thieves' gang, perhaps?"

He raised an eyebrow. "What'll you do with the information, eh? I may be a changed man, but loyalty is loyalty, even if it's to thieves I ain't associating with no more."

"We want to find out who the dead man really was," Byron said. "And we need to find out why Circe wanted him to steal from families here in Bath."

"Right." Monty sniffed. "You won't, eh, be arresting them?"

Byron shook his head. "Even if I wanted to, I don't have the jurisdiction."

Monty sighed. "I can get you in to talk with 'em, but not as you are. You'd need to be thieves bringing in things to sell. Or customers wanting to buy the stuff."

Byron nodded and adjusted his sleeves. "We'll need some way of bringing up Mr. Treadway in conversation. Otherwise we won't get the information we're looking for."

"Couldn't we show them the pin?" Mira asked.

"Ah, you mean pretend to be part of Circe?" Byron looked at Monty.

Monty twitched. "Circe would already know the meeting spot. They wouldn't need me to lead them there."

Byron hummed. "Do you think it would be reasonable to say that you recognized Mr. Treadway as someone from this local gang?"

"I suppose we could say that. Why?"

"Would it make sense for you to suggest someone to take his place?"

Monty begrudgingly nodded. "I'll see if I can get the night off. Mr. Patterson's got us footmen filling in for Mr. Foster, but I'll try. I'll meet you at the north side of the abbey if I can, tonight at ten. Don't be late."

February 13, 1889: Evening

"I don't know why I'm so tired." Mira gave an exaggerated yawn.

"You did walk with us through half of Bath today," Liza said.

Mira yawned again for emphasis.

"Goodness, child, why don't you just go to bed?" Aunt Eleanor said.

"I think I will," Mira said, standing. "Goodnight, everyone." She left the room, heading up the stairs. She'd already set out the clothes she would need for the evening's activities: a dark blouse and coat, split skirt, and riding boots. She changed quickly and moved to the window.

They'd discussed her plan for escape before returning to Davenguard. Walker and Liza were already enacting phase one of the plan: distraction. But the family had decided to adjourn to the sitting room near the front door, which left Mira with two options—sneaking through the house to the conservatory door or climbing down the ivy. If she climbed down the ivy, there was a guaranteed entrance back into the house and there was less of a chance of getting caught.

She opened the window and looked down. Dizziness came over her. It was rather far up. She pulled her head back in. If she left the window open, she could climb up the trellis on her return. That would be a much easier prospect than climbing down. Unless the trellis broke. However, if she went down now it still had a chance of breaking. Conservatory it was.

She slipped down the far stairs, wishing she knew which ones creaked. Most of the staff would be in the servants' quarters, so hopefully she wouldn't meet anyone on her way out. Halfway down the hall she heard footsteps approaching and ducked into the library. Her heart pounded in her chest. If she was caught leaving the house, it would be assumed she was going to meet Byron for some romantic interlude. It was only half true, but that sort of assumption could reflect poorly on Walker. Here she was, about to infiltrate a thieves' gang with ties to Circe, and she felt more anxiety about being discovered by a member of Walker's soon-to-be family.

She forced herself to breathe deeper and cast her eyes about the darkened room. The moon was full and shedding thin light through the windows. And a door. She smiled and, finding the key in the lock, she turned it, pocketed the key, and left Davenguard. Byron planned to meet her with a carriage at the end of the drive by nine, and by the watch on her chatelaine she had a little over fifteen minutes. The gravel crunched beneath her feet as she hurried to their meeting point.

What little breath she had clouded the air in front of her as she came to a stop beneath one of the giant stone lions at the front gate. Two pinpricks of light appeared down the road.

She rubbed her arms and hands to keep them warm as the light turned into the lanterns on a carriage. The horses came to a stop in front of her, nostrils steaming. The door opened and Byron stepped out.

"You look perfect for the part." He offered a hand to help her into the carriage.

"As do you."

He'd neglected to shave and had opted for a nice, but ill-fitting, wrinkled suit. They settled inside the carriage.

"That suit isn't yours, is it?" she asked as the carriage turned back towards Bath.

"Heavens no. I'd find a new tailor if it was. No, it's one of Castel's. Perish the thought if he ever finds out about it. I crumpled it up in all sorts of disarray to get it just right. Do remind me to have it pressed again before he gets back from London. I'm afraid I'll forget."

"I'll try. Has he written you at all to explain why he's gone?"

Byron shook his head. "It strikes me as the usual sort of bureaucratic nonsense."

They fell silent until the road changed beneath them to cobblestone as they crossed the bridge.

"You know," Mira said, "I am rather surprised that you didn't object to my coming with you. It wasn't even a question."

Byron took her hand and gave it a squeeze. "By now I have learned that there isn't much use in trying to stop you. Besides," he pulled his hand away, leaving a pearl necklace in her palm. "I think it will work in our favor to have both of us."

"Is this your mother's?"

"I thought it would add to our story."

"What story?"

"Well—"

They stood in the shadow of Bath Abbey as the tower bell struck ten. The gothic architecture loomed above them.

"Do you think he'll come?" Mira whispered, pulling the collar of her coat tighter around her neck.

"Hard to say," Byron said. "There aren't many people out, so it should be easy to spot him." He checked his watch. "If he isn't here in twenty minutes, we'll head back."

"Why do you think he chose here as the rendezvous?" she asked. "Do you think that the thieves meet somewhere around here?"

"I doubt they would meet this close to an Abbey. Too much guilt every time you walk by. Monty was smart in choosing it for us, though. Plenty of shadows to hide in, and since we look nothing like young hooligans ready to throw rocks at the stained glass, no one will think we're doing anything nefarious."

"We are lurking, rather."

"Well, that's only because of the shadows."

A dark carriage stood across the way. She wouldn't have paid it any notice, except every so often a person would attempt to hire it and the driver would wave them off. It struck her as odd, as they stood there in the cold waiting for Monty. Fifteen minutes passed, Mira's toes were quite frozen, and the carriage driver had waved off four potential fares. She was about to mention how odd it was to Byron when a man with Monty's build approached and the thought flew out of her head. The man's voice confirmed his identity.

"Sorry 'bout the delay. Had to borrow a prancer and couldn't find a place to hold it."

"You stole a horse?" Mira asked.

"Borrowed." Monty emphasized the word. "If I prigged it I would have said so. It hurts you don't trust me. I'm not in the horse stealing game, never was, never will be. Now do you want me to take you there or not?"

"By all means, lead the way," Byron said, gesturing out.

Monty nodded, walking past the carriage towards one of the northern roads. "What were the names you decided on?"

"Ernest and Rita Norman," Mira said.

"Ernest?" Monty raised an eyebrow, looking back at the two of them. "You're using a false name, and you chose Ernest?"

"Seems fitting," Byron said.

"I suppose." Monty shrugged and kept moving.

"Where are we going?" Mira asked.

"To one of the tunnels."

Mira swallowed. "Erm. Tunnels? You mean . . ."

"Under the city. Bath's been built over multiple times. There are tunnels all over. Connecting businesses. Hidden vaults built for structure back twenty or thirty years ago. You saw the construction over near the pump house? They're unearthing things from Roman times. Building it out so people can come and see it."

"Yes, I believe I heard about that," Byron said. "Didn't Liza mention it?"

Mira nodded. "They're building a museum, aren't they?"

"That's what they say. But the workers are only in there during the day, see? At night, it's a free meeting spot. The gang stay out of the areas that are being actively worked on. Don't want to accidentally leave a mark somewhere where one of them archaeologists will see."

He moved out of the moonlight, into an alleyway. A man dressed in workman's clothes and a thick coat stood before a set of descending stairs.

"What's your business here?" he said. "This is an archaeological site."

Mira's chest tightened.

"Here to see Sibyl," Monty said.

The man looked him up and down, then stepped aside so they could move past him.

"That's Adams. The gang pays 'im to look the other way," Monty whispered once they were down the stairs. They kept moving until they came to an archway that stretched into a tunnel.

Mira's breath stuttered. Byron took her hand.

"It'll be all right," he said. "I'll be with you this time."

She nodded. Monty looked back.

"Do you not like cramped spaces, Miss?"

"It's a little more than that."

"Don't worry, it opens up soon enough. There's even a space where you can see the sky."

She nodded and Monty stepped into the darkness.

"It'll be dark as pitch for a minute, shut your peepers if it bothers you, but just keep moving forward."

They followed him in, a metallic smell to the warm, humid air. Mira held tight to Byron as they kept moving, trying not to think of bones beneath her feet.

"Almost there, love," Byron whispered to her.

Monty wasn't lying, and before she knew it, there was light up ahead. Moonlight.

"Bit of a tight squeeze here," Monty said, getting onto his hands and knees and wriggling through the small opening.

"You go first," Byron said.

The stone was damp as Mira crawled through the narrow passageway and out into the night air. There was an overhang above where they stood, held up by doric columns. This new space was open to the sky with a large, rectangular pool that glowed green in the moonlight. Stars reflected on its surface. A colonnade stood above the overhang on the far side, braced with scaffolding.

"They're still working on this area," Monty said. "Apparently those Roman coves used to bathe together here."

Byron brushed himself off. "Fascinating."

Monty led the way around the pool and up a couple of stairs. "The gang'll be meeting back here."

This tunnel was much shorter and led to a room with wooden planks built up as walkways. An orange-tinged waterfall rushed out of the wall at the far side and disappeared beneath the ancient brick floor.

"Is that where the famous Bath waters come from?" Mira asked, raising her voice to be heard over the rushing water.

Monty nodded. "All those gentry morts and rum cullys in the Grand Pump Room drinking water from ancient times. Strange to think."

An archway led out of the room into another small chamber. Two women stood behind cases that folded out into little tables displaying an array of glittering goods that were being inspected by a man in a long, black coat. An alcove stood at the back with a basket inside it, and another woman sat on a stack of thick brick slabs that had likely been recently unearthed. The woman had wild, curly, brown hair that she had attempted to stuff under a white cap and wore a dirty blue and red dress. When she saw them she stood, arms folded across her chest.

"What are you doing back here, Fitzwilliam? You didn't go and lose the job did you? You don't need more papers, do you?"

"No, not at all Miss Sibyl. No one questioned the papers."

"Course they didn't." She looked over Monty's shoulder. "And who'd you bring, eh?"

Monty's hand shook a little as he gestured to them, and Mira wondered how he'd ever made it as a thief.

"This is Ernest Norman and his wife Rita. They're interested in talking to you about the business."

Sibyl raised an eyebrow. "We don't need anyone else."

Byron stepped closer to her and she flinched back.

"Please, Miss," he spoke with a prominent lisp. "We've tried working on our own, but we don't have no one to sell to." He pulled out the pearl necklace and held it out. "Here's proof of what we can do."

Sibyl took it, running her hands over each pearl. "And?"

Byron took it back. "I'm a jeweler by trade. Least, I want to be. I ended my apprenticeship rather badly, so I'm hard up to get a supply of jewels to work with. I can steal or help take pieces apart and put them together again. Once we have enough money to buy a shop, then I can be your fence."

Sibyl looked him up and down, then over to Mira. "And what exactly do you do?"

A brief panic overtook her. They'd discussed the plan and she was prepared to have a false name, but she wasn't entirely prepared to improvise.

"I'm nimble and quiet, and handy with a lockpick," she said, not putting on too much of an accent for fear of losing it.

Sibyl moved over to her, her eyes narrowing. "You're educated. What're you doing with this sort of fellow?" She gestured to Byron.

She straightened her shoulders. Byron said that a good persona started from a place of truth. He didn't say whose truth it needed to be. "My parents didn't approve of him, but . . ." she looked over at him and let her real feelings show through. "We eloped. And I'll do what it takes to stay with him, even if it means stealing."

Sibyl's expression softened and she stepped away. "We have enough thieves. You'll do well to forget about this place and go find dealings elsewhere."

Byron clenched his fists. "That's a lie. Mr. Fitzwilliam here says that you just lost one of your thieves. Mr. Treadway. We can help you."

Sibyl turned to Monty. "How do you know about that?"

Monty fidgeted with his sleeves. "When I was cleaning out his room I found his pin."

Byron pulled it out, handing it to her. "This one. He says it's a symbol of your group."

Sibyl scowled. "Not our group, no. One we're obliged to work with." She gritted her teeth and threw the pin on the ground. "And that man weren't one of ours. Not anymore."

"But he was, once?" Mira asked.

"Before he joined up with Circe," Sibyl said. "And brought the rest of us under their eye. We'd heard of them, stayed out of their way, and he goes and brings them to our doorstep." She turned away from them, wincing. "If you're smart, you'll stay away from them. Otherwise, you'll always be at their beck and call."

Byron's gaze flicked to Mira. "You don't want to work under them?"

Selene's letter came to Mira's mind. Most gangs had no desire to work with the Crescent, but were forced to for one reason or another.

Sibyl whirled towards them, gaze narrowing further. "You're asking an awful lot of questions." Her hand rested on the knife at her belt. "I'd suggest you leave before I'm tempted to ask some of my own."

Byron stepped in front of Mira. "Just one more. If you could be free of Circe, would you?"

Sibyl froze for a moment before moving over to the other two women. She pushed in front of the man examining the wares and closed up the stands. "Shop's closed. Get out."

The man protested as she escorted him to the archway before turning towards them again.

"You're from the Crescent, aren't you?" She sent a glare Monty's way, tightening her hold on her knife. "Well, what do you want from us? You already got one of us killed for those documents. You going to kill us too?"

Mira's heart raced. There was a crazed look in Sibyl's eyes.

"I think you've misunderstood," Byron said, stepping

between her and Mira with hands out in front of him in a placating gesture.

Sibyl pulled the knife, brandishing it in front of her. "Not another step. Not until you tell me who you really are and why you are here."

One of the other women pulled out a gun. "Sibyl, you need to sit down," she said, inching towards the archway. The second woman pulled out a knife and nodded in agreement.

"I'm fine," Sibyl all but growled. "Now tell us."

They were pinned in on two sides with no possible exit.

A tense few seconds passed. Mira didn't know what to do. Her eye caught some of the dirt on the hem of Sibyl's skirt. Except it wasn't dirt. It was blood. Mira swallowed, finding it difficult to breathe.

Monty broke first. "I'll tell you! I'll tell you. Just put the weapons away."

Sibyl shook her head. "Tell us first."

"I'm sorry, really I am," he said, and Mira wasn't certain who he meant to apologize to. "This is Byron Constantine. That detective. He's promised not to arrest anyone, he just needs to know about Mr. Treadway."

Sibyl faltered, lowering the knife by a fraction as her brow furrowed in confusion. "You mean, the gent who got you arrested for stealing paintings?"

"The very one," Byron said, standing a bit straighter and speaking in his normal, albeit tired, voice.

Sibyl raised the knife again. "You aren't from Circe?"

"Not at all. In fact, I do believe we share the same sentiment about them."

Sibyl gestured to Mira. "And who's she meant to be?"

"I'm his secretary," Mira said, stepping to Byron's side. "We really are only here to find out why Circe ordered all those burglaries and who Mr. Treadway was."

The knife made a sharp "schink" as Sibyl sheathed it on her

belt. "I don't need to answer nothing." She moved past them, back over to the vendors who also put their weapons away and began packing up.

"Take it out to the carriage," Sibyl told the other women. "We're done for the night."

"But won't he—"

"I don't care. We're done."

"We're working to stop Circe," Mira said. "You could help us."

Sibyl scoffed, crouching to latch one of the cases. "And I could kill the three of you and be done with all the questions."

Monty shook his head. "It's not worth it, Mr. Constantine. Let's leave."

Byron looked between him and Sibyl. "Perhaps we should go," he told Mira, taking her arm and leading her away. As they reached the archway, a cry sounded from the basket in the alcove and Sibyl rushed towards it. Mira turned, letting go of Byron's arm.

"A baby," Mira whispered. Sibyl held a bundle in her arms, gently bouncing it and shushing.

"Get them out of here," she said. "I don't care how."

The other two women stepped towards them, weapons once again at the ready.

"You can kill us," Mira said, "But murder is messy. Someone will come looking for us, and they'll find you."

"We'll be gone by then," the woman with the knife said.

"Maybe. But is this really the life you want?" She called out to Sibyl. "Is it the life you want for your child? To always be on the run? To always live in fear?" Mira stepped forward. "We can't promise you anything, but if you help us, at least you'll be fighting back. You would have a chance at freedom."

"You don't know what you're talking about," the woman with the gun said. "Now leave!"

Byron gently pulled Mira through the archway. There was no sign of Monty.

"Wait!" Sibyl called from behind them. She stepped up to the archway, still bouncing her baby. "I'll tell you what I know."

February 14, 1889: Early Morning

The two other women, who they learned were named Lucille and Elvina, stood guard outside the archway. Mira, Byron, and Sibyl sat on stacked stones or on top of the closed folding cases. The baby had calmed, and Sibyl rocked him slowly.

"The man you know as Mr. Treadway was my husband," she said, voice cracking. "His name was Enoch Hand. When I first married him, I didn't know he was a thief. I found out when he was arrested for stealing at the market in London. While he was in prison, I needed a way to pay the bills." She swallowed. "No one would hire me. But I met someone who worked with a gang in the city."

"The Forty Elephants?" Byron asked.

Sibyl nodded, looking away. "I was only going to do it until

Enoch was released. But when he got out he just went back to stealing again. He's been in and out of prison for over five years. The last time he was arrested was in July. Before we even knew about this one." She shifted the baby in her arms.

"While he was in prison, he met some men who worked with Circe. Prison guards, if you can believe it. They offered him a lot of money and an early release if he would help them and he agreed. They released him in August, six months early. He began working for Circe in London, but after a few months they ordered us to move out here, to create our own gang of thieves, and steal from the wealthy socialites. We could sell anything we liked and keep the money, as long as we continued to steal. A man from the Crescent would come by every week, they said to help, but he was more like a watchdog, making sure we followed orders. It soon became clear that there was more to the plan than just simple burglary, but I didn't know the details at first."

Byron finished jotting down a note. "When did your husband take on the role of Silas Treadway?"

"A few months ago."

"Do you know why?" Mira asked.

Sibyl gave a short nod. "A-a man who Enoch used to know came to Bath. He had been a part of Circe for years. He recognized Enoch, found out he had started working for Circe and well . . . he decided he wanted a cut. He came to one of the meetings at our house and spoke with the man from the Crescent. Together, the three of them came up with a plan to send Enoch into the center of society here. De—the man Enoch used to work with, it was *his* idea to use false papers. Apparently Treadway had died in a war somewhere, and no one would know. Enoch became Silas and it gave him more freedom to move as he needed, to meet wealthy people, be in their homes. A month or so later, they decided he needed more help, so they brought on another man to act on the inside too."

"Do you have names for any of these men?"

Sibyl averted her eyes. "I don't know the name of the man from the Crescent. And I've never met the man they brought in to help Enoch. And the other, who Enoch knew before, was part of the first gang my husband was in. He—" She broke off. "I don't think I should tell you. He'll find out, one way or another. He'll tell the Crescent. And I-I just can't risk that." She pulled her baby closer to her.

"You don't have to tell us," Mira said, reaching out and putting a hand on Sibyl's arm. "You are brave to tell us anything."

Sibyl softened. "I've probably said too much already. But . . ." Her eyes darted to the door.

"Go on and tell them," Elvina said. "If they can help . . ."

Sibyl took a deep breath. "I'll tell you this: I know what they're after. It isn't about the jewels at all. They are looking for political documents."

"How do you know?" Mira asked, eyes wide.

"They hold meetings at my house. I'm sent upstairs so I don't overhear or see anything, but the fireplace goes through both floors. I can hear through the chimney."

"Do you know what sort of documents they are?" Byron asked.

Sibyl lowered her voice. "It has something to do with the Treaty of San Stefano. The one signed in 1878. I think it has something to do with the Ottoman Empire."

Byron nodded. "It marked the end of the Russo-Turkish War." He tapped his pen on his cheek. "Why would Circe be concerned with that, I wonder?"

"They mentioned something about a new war and how these documents could stop it," Sibyl said. "They've been searching for them for over ten years and are starting to get desperate."

Mira frowned. "How have they not found them yet?"

"They sent in a package to some woman here in Britain.

I don't remember the name, but apparently it was sent to the wrong address or something. I remember distinctly that—"

The baby started fussing and Sibyl broke off mid-sentence to calm him. After a bit of shushing and some more rocking, she said, "Where was I?"

"The package was sent to the wrong address," Mira said.

"Oh yes. In one of the recent meetings, my husband asked if they hadn't got the wrong person again, but the man from the Crescent assured him that they had it right this time. It's taken them all this time to track the package to that woman and then to learn where it was sent after that. They still haven't found where the documents are hidden."

"And they are using the burglaries to cover up their attempts at searching," Byron said, starting a new page in his journal.

"So who has the documents now?" Mira asked.

"I don't know," Sibyl said. "I wish I could tell you more, but Enoch kept most of it a secret from me. And I can't risk *him* finding out that I told you anything."

"You've told us more than we could have hoped," Byron said.

Mira nodded. "I am so sorry for your loss. It must be terrible, especially now that you are looking after the baby all alone."

Sibyl gave a halfhearted laugh. "It feels as though Enoch was never around from the start. First with being in prison all those months and then out playing suitor to other women. I gave birth two weeks ago, and he never came back to see the baby. I know that Elvina told him about it when she went up to the manor to take jewels from him last week." She sniffed, looking down at her little one. "His son. And now he's dead and I've had to rush back into all this." She gestured vaguely to the chamber and shook her head. "I don't need anything else from that man. He's already put us in enough trouble."

Mira's mouth fell open. "You only gave birth two weeks ago?"

"Two weeks tomorrow," Sibyl said, standing straighter. "But don't you worry about us. We're used to taking care of ourselves."

"You don't have to." Byron tore a small piece of paper from his journal and wrote something on it. "I'll ask you again, do you want to leave Circe?"

She swallowed, looking up at the two women. "It isn't safe to. He—they'll find us, bring us back."

Byron passed the slip over to her. "Just the same, if you want help, don't hesitate to visit this address. You can have a new life."

Sibyl took the slip and tucked it into her pocket. "I'll think about it. But I don't need charity."

Byron nodded and stood, helping Mira up as well. "Thank you again for your help."

They went to leave, but Byron stopped once more on the threshold of the room. "I forgot to ask. Might I take a look at your wares? I'm quite prepared to pay for a few of them."

Sibyl smiled. "Certainly."

It was well after one in the morning by the time they caught a carriage back to Davenguard. The Sherard family jewels were tucked safely in Byron's jacket pocket.

"I knew that the thefts had to be more than just burglary if Circe was involved," Mira said, yawning. "These documents must be quite extraordinary if they are still looking for them after almost eleven years."

"It will be interesting to see what they contain," Byron said. "But first we'll need to find them."

"Right." She sat up straighter. "I've been thinking about

that. What if Enoch wasn't courting Theresia at random? Her father works with Sir William Arthur White, the ambassador to the Ottoman Empire. If someone were sending documents about that treaty to anyone, wouldn't they send them to him?"

Byron hummed. "I didn't realize the connection."

"Theresia mentioned it in the stable. Her family was meant to attend Sutherland's party back in October but had a previous engagement."

"I see." Byron drummed his fingers on his leg. "We'll need to find an excuse to visit Wynmar again."

Mira laughed a little. "You've forgotten. They are having a party on Valentine's Day. Perhaps I can arrange with Theresia for us to come visit again at a better time to talk with Mr. Risewell. So, we only need to wait a few days."

"Valentine's Day is today, love."

Mira blinked. "Is it really?"

He laughed and reached into his pocket. "If it wasn't, I wouldn't have brought this with me, presuming we might be out all night." He pulled out an envelope and handed it to her.

Mira opened it and pulled out a little heart-shaped card with a rose printed on it. She smiled as she read Byron's swirling hand:

A rose for my Rose

Her heart warmed. "I'm surprised you didn't forget," she said. "I certainly did."

His eyes twinkled. "I try not to forget important things."

"I'll have to make it up to you," she said as the carriage slowed to a stop.

"You'll be all right getting in?" he asked.

"I have a key to the library door," she said. "You don't think you'll have any trouble with your family?"

Byron shook his head. "My mother sleeps soundly and

Mary's room is at the front of the house. I'll slip in through the garden."

She leaned over and gave him a kiss on the cheek. "Goodnight, my dear Mr. Constantine."

"Goodnight, my Mira."

She slipped out of the carriage and dashed across the lawn, wanting to get in bed as soon as possible, cheeks warm despite the chill of the night.

February 14, 1889: Morning

No one was the wiser to their little escapade, but Mira was absolutely exhausted the next morning at breakfast. Walker and Liza managed to carry the conversation, though they kept sending curious glances her way. She was certain she would be interrogated the moment it was appropriate.

"Now, we do have the Valentine's party this evening at the Risewell's," Mrs. Renaldi said. "Did you bring one of your pink or red dresses, Liza dear?"

"I thought the red one would be nice," Liza said. "Especially if you wear your pink one, Mira."

"I'm glad I brought it," Mira said. "I completely forgot about Valentine's Day."

"How could you forget when you finally have a Valentine?" Walker said.

"I suppose I was a bit more concerned with—" she stopped herself before she said "the burglaries," and feigned a little cough. "With everything else. Bath has been such a change, hasn't it?"

"I won't be going to the party," Aunt Eleanor said. "Not to that house of death."

"Eleanor," Mrs. Renaldi said, "The Risewells can't be blamed for such an unfortunate accident."

"No. But they can be blamed for not looking into that man's background before allowing him to be in such close company with their daughter. We don't even know what his name was!"

"What?" Mrs. Renaldi said, laughing a little. "Wasn't his name Treadway?"

Eleanor picked up the morning paper from where it lay on the table and handed it to her sister-in-law. "They made an announcement this morning. No one knows who he is."

Mira set her napkin on the table, finding she no longer had an appetite.

"Mira, are you all right?" Walker asked.

She forced a smile. "Yes, I suppose I just wasn't as hungry as I thought I was." She stood. "I think I'll go make sure my dress is ready for tonight."

She left the dining room and headed up the stairs, feeling sick all over. The general public would never know the name Enoch Hand. And they would never know about his wife and child, either.

Somehow, that made her feel guilty about it all. Even if Sibyl hated him, it must have been terrible to learn that her husband had died, leaving her alone to raise their son. It was courageous to share her story at all, especially since her husband's accomplices were still at large. But because of her candor, Mira and

Byron now had something substantial to go off of to stop this newly revealed Circe plot.

She stopped halfway up the stairs, changing course for the library. She didn't know anything about the Treaty of San Stefano. If they were looking for documents related to it, it would be good to know more about the situation.

A little light was coming through the windows, but not enough for reading small print. She lit the gas lamps and went in search of the encyclopedias. With any luck, there would be an edition printed after 1878. That couldn't be too much to ask, could it?

She found a row of encyclopedias and pulled out the one labeled "ROT-SIA." She opened the front cover and smiled, seeing it had been printed in 1882. After checking for "San Stefano" and only finding information on the city, she took volume "T-UPS" from the shelf. There, she found the Treaty of San Stefano.

> *"The Treaty of San Stefano was signed on 3 March, 1878 at the conclusion of the Russo-Turkish War. It was an agreement between the Russian and Ottoman Empires and provided for the establishment of an autonomous Principality of Bulgaria. It also granted the independence of Serbia, Montenegro, Romania, and the Vilayet of Bosnia. The provisions of the treaty were later changed in July of 1878 after other European powers determined the treaty to be damaging to their holdings. (See Treaty of Berlin)."*

Mira frowned. If the treaty had been changed, what business did Circe have with the documents related to it? She flipped to an earlier listing and found the Treaty of Berlin. Skimming it, she learned the changes were mostly related to the amount of land granted to each of the new independent nations, but the new treaty revoked the Vilayet of Bosnia's independence.

The new wording kept Bosnia under Ottoman rule, but was placed under Austrian-Hungarian occupation. Her brow furrowed. That didn't make sense, but then again, she didn't have much experience when it came to international relations. She certainly couldn't discern why it would be important to Circe. She closed the encyclopedia, replacing it on the shelf with a sigh. She came looking for answers and only found more questions.

THE RISEWELLS KNEW HOW TO THROW A fine party. It was all swishing bustles, laughter, and flowers. The amount of red roses in the vases scattered around had likely depleted every greenhouse for miles. Mira walked along the outer wall with Liza and Walker, keeping a lookout for either Byron or Theresia among the waltzing partners. The Sherards had yet to make their appearance and it seemed Miss Risewell had not come down yet.

"You are such a worrier," Walker said. "We have all night to find her and I'm certain she'll agree to let you visit tomorrow."

"I'm not so certain," Mira said, smoothing down the lace on the front of her rose-colored evening dress. "Remember, I'm part of the reason why Mr. Foster was arrested. I'm sure she hates me for it."

"Once you explain this whole thing with" —Liza lowered her voice and hid her face with her fan— "Circe, why, I'm sure she'll understand."

Their little group stopped near the fireplace. Mira caught sight of Maureen and Bertie dancing near the center of the room. Bertie's demeanor was rather personable, and Maureen was in much better spirits than the last time she saw her.

The Risewells were by the stairs, but their daughter was not with them. Mira itched to sneak off to try and find the documents herself. But not only would that be bad manners, it would be foolish to expect to find them immediately when Circe had been searching for them for over ten years. She burned with curiosity. What could possibly be so important?

The song ended and Liza beckoned Maureen and Bertie over. Maureen looked an absolute vision in dark crimson silk.

"I much prefer a ball to a soiree," Maureen said, fanning herself. "Though one does get rather out of breath."

"I'll fetch some refreshments," Bertie said.

Walker nodded. "Good idea."

The men left their company and Mira tilted her head to the side. "Mr. Corbet is being rather attentive to you."

Maureen broke into a grin. "He's been just wonderful. I think he's finally decided that Theresia will never be interested."

"Does Admiral Hoddle approve?" Liza asked.

"I don't really know," Maureen said, adjusting a silk rose on her hip. "I'm not sure he realizes. He's been so preoccupied recently. He's become obsessed about taking a trip to Wells, which is strange because I really thought he was attached to the house and there isn't anything nearly as interesting to do in Wells."

Mira's heart sunk. If she remembered, Wells was where the asylum was located. Surely the doctor wouldn't admit her there when she was doing so much better, would he?

"Does he really care so much about the house here?" Liza asked, completely oblivious. "I find that so odd."

Maureen nodded. "It's the strangest thing. Though perhaps he's a little over-vigilant."

"Here we are," Walker said as he and Bertie returned with the drinks.

"Goodness, Walker, you'll give us all a fright!" Liza said, taking a drink from him.

"Sorry." He winked at Liza while turning to Mira. "By the way, I just saw the Sherards come in."

Mira nodded, trying to figure out a way of broaching the asylum question. Maureen took a goblet from Bertie and took a sip.

"Oh, this is much better than the last two I had," she said.

"Who's over-vigilant?" Bertie asked.

"Admiral Hoddle," Maureen said. "He's mentioned so many times that he's grateful no one has tried to burglarize the house here, especially with all the other thefts happening in Bath. And of course, we had so many break-ins at the house in London, so I think it makes him nervous."

Even with Maureen's improved mood and disposition, Mira was surprised to hear her speak so candidly about the break-ins. Perhaps it wasn't so difficult to speak about the burglary in terms unrelated to her father's death. Or perhaps she was a little affected by whatever was in the punch. It smelled of brandy.

"Wait," Walker said, "break-ins, plural?"

Maureen nodded. "There were two before . . ." She trailed off, her smile slipping. She cleared her throat and continued. "Two before the one where father was killed. And two after we moved. Though the police think the last two were just some nosy children who thought the home was abandoned."

"Was anything stolen?" Liza asked.

"I don't think so."

A strange theory began to form. Mira set her drink on a nearby table, trying to keep her excitement in check. "Maureen, what was it that your father did for work, again?"

"He was a journalist." Maureen took another sip. "He'd travel all over to write stories, mostly political ones. He often worked with the Foreign Office."

Mira swallowed, her mind whirling. "Did he receive many foreign letters or packages?"

"What a strange question." Maureen frowned. "I suppose he did."

"Excuse me." Mira stepped away from the group. It wasn't Mr. Risewell who had the documents, but Mr. Harris! Circe must have been trying to steal them back. That was why there had been so many break-ins and why Mr. Harris had been shot.

She had to find Byron. She moved to the stairs and climbed a few to get a better look around the ballroom. Her cursory glance availed nothing, so she returned to the floor and resumed her path along the wall. She doubted that he would be dancing, so she would either find him on the outskirts or have to search other rooms. She knew there were some men playing billiards and there were certain to be women in the drawing room. Perhaps he had found Mr. Risewell and was questioning him about any packages he'd received.

She ran into Admiral Hoddle at the edge of the ballroom before she found any of the Sherards. Her stomach dropped. She hadn't even thought about the implications of her realization. Was Hoddle involved in the whole conspiracy? It would explain why he was trying to get Maureen committed. But they didn't have any proof.

"You seem to be in quite the hurry, Miss Blayse," he said. "You'll trip over your hem if you aren't careful."

Mira laughed a little, trying to skirt around him. "I've done it before, I assure you."

"Why aren't you dancing? A fine young lady such as yourself should be wearing out her dance shoes."

"I haven't found my partner yet."

"Oh, yes, the young Mr. Sherard? I spoke to him a little earlier. I think he was with Mr. Risewell."

"Thank you very much, sir." She was about to pull away when a thought occurred to her.

"I hear that you might be taking a trip to Wells."

He narrowed his eyes a moment, then let out a good-natured laugh. "Why, news travels fast in this town. I thought it might be good to get Maureen out of Bath for a little while. I wouldn't want to go too far, as it seems she's formed an attachment." He gestured to where Maureen and Bertie were slipping away from the ballroom. "Looks like they are heading to the music room. 'If music be the food of love, play on,' and all that. I'd better go fulfill my duty as an upstanding guardian."

He wandered off, leaving Mira with more questions. She couldn't tell whether he was truly concerned for his ward or whether he was hiding a more nefarious motive. But she couldn't dwell on unknowns when she may have discovered who really had the documents. She stepped into the hallway, intent on searching all the adjacent rooms. He was not in the billiards room or the parlor or the library. She didn't expect him to be in the drawing room, but she decided to check it just the same.

As she approached the door, she found Mr. Wilburn Treadway exiting, which was rather curious. She was surprised that the Risewells had the forethought to invite him. She poked her head in, hoping that Byron would be there, and found Mary sitting on the sofa, hunched over. At the creak of the door, she looked up, eyes rimmed with red.

"What are you doing here?" Mary said, her voice thick but tinged with anger.

"I-I was looking for Byron."

Mary scoffed. "The two of you had plenty of time together last night."

Mira's cheeks burned. "I beg your pardon?"

"Don't play the fool. I waited up for Ambrose, and I know you were out past two in the morning. Don't you have any sense of decency at all? What if the servants saw you together? Or what if the carriage driver spreads gossip?"

Mira's jaw tightened. "You are assuming the very worst, not just about me, but about your brother. There was a very good reason why we were out last night. In fact, as you are wearing the necklace that was stolen, I assume you already know that we were investigating the very burglary you asked him to look into."

Mary stood, pacing away from Mira. "It doesn't matter what you were actually doing. Don't you see what it looks like? You could bring condemnation on the entire family should someone misunderstand your actions." She turned, shoulders straight, her mouth in a thin line. "Miss Blayse, I have not had much contact with my brother these past few years and even I am thoroughly aware of your impropriety. I know how often the two of you are alone together. How often you ride together in a closed carriage. If I am aware of it, I cannot begin to imagine the number of rumors spreading through society circles. Don't you care at all about his standing? About our family?"

"Of course I—"

"This sort of scandal is exactly the sort of thing that could affect Castel and the succession of the barony."

Mira clenched her fists. "Scandal? What scandal? If you have heard rumors about us, Miss Sherard, I have not encountered them. Is your family's image really so fragile?"

Mary approached her, nose wrinkled with derision and fury. Mira found it difficult to stand her ground.

"You have no sense of what our family's position is. No sense of the delicate balance that we have kept for generations. Your family is nothing. Has nothing." She leaned even closer. "It's a pity that Ambrose has regained his memories. If he hadn't, it would be all too simple to stop this madness. Simply separate you and let his memories of you slip away. Why, if I had known of your relationship to him sooner, I could have done something. He wouldn't even know you existed."

Mira's eyes burned, she couldn't breathe.

"How dare you," Byron said from the doorway.

They both turned towards him, watching as he stalked forward. He stepped between Mira and his sister.

"You have no right to speak to her that way." Byron's entire body was tense, his chest heaving.

"I have every right, as your sister, to ensure your future," Mary said, though her voice faltered.

Byron laughed, but there was an edge to it. "I am not aware of such a sisterly duty. But I do know that a sister is meant to be supportive, is meant to love her younger siblings instead of disparaging them. A good sister would not deride her brother's choice of wife or profession. And she certainly would not wish injury upon her brother or the woman he loves."

"I—"

Byron clenched his fists. "Would you really rather I went back to forgetting? Never knowing one day from the next? Not even remembering to write you or mother?" He gestured behind him to Mira. "I would not be here if it were not for Miss Samira Blayse. I would not have recovered my memories, save for her patience."

Mary shook her head. "I'm grateful that you've recovered. But can't you see that this woman is actively ruining your position in society? The way you run around together is disgraceful, disregarding all sense of propriety."

"As if you didn't act the same when you were courting," Byron said. "I may have been six at the time, but I had eyes."

"We were engaged," Mary said, voice tight. "It was an entirely different situation."

"For heavens sakes! Is that what this is about?" Byron said, turning to Mira. "Will you marry me?"

Mira blinked. He wasn't serious, was he?

Goodness, he was.

"Y-yes. Of course, I will." Her emotions were in all sorts of disarray. Shock, frustration, excitement, anger, and love all muddled together.

His shoulders relaxed by a fraction and he took her arm. He

turned them both towards his sister in a united front. "There. We're engaged."

"You can't—" Mary spluttered.

"We just did. I am sick and tired of playing society's games. Now will you leave us alone?"

Mary stood taller. "You are being ridiculous. Be honest with yourself, Ambrose. Do you love her or are you merely infatuated with the first woman you could remember after your accident?" Mary threw her hand out. "Have you considered her character at all? What sort of respectable woman lowers herself to take on a secretarial job and willingly chooses to engage in detective work? From my first impression of her I—"

"I know well enough what your impression of me is." Mira stepped forward, heat rising within her. "I have heard every insult, every snide comment of derision, and I have tried to keep the peace, because believe it or not, I love Byron and would never want him to lose his family in loving me." Tears sprung to her eyes. "I know what it is like not to have a family. I've longed to have a mother, to have a sister, and I thought we might have had that relationship, but clearly that was never meant to be." She wiped the hot tears from her face, shaking her head. "From the moment I met you, I found you to be judgmental, disagreeable, and myopic. You are so focused on how others perceive you, that I can't imagine you even know who you are."

"How dare—"

"How dare I stand up for myself? It is a wonder, isn't it?" Mira's heart raced. "I'll admit that we haven't taken the most pains to be proper and perhaps that is a failing. But I find your hypocrisy to be a worse one. I understand that you have had a terrible time at love, and I expect that you still feel the pain of losing it. So how can you possibly pass the same judgement that hurt you so terribly onto your brother?"

"Ambrose—"

"His name is Byron," Mira said. "It is his first name. The name given to him by his mother. It's the one he prefers to use, and you refuse to use it even in private. Do you know your brother at all? Or are you too busy judging him? Judging him because you are afraid and he is not."

"Of course, I know him!" Mary yelled, turning to face her brother again. "I can't allow you to give away your entire birthright based on what you think is love."

"Think?" Byron said. Mira had never heard him say something with such vitriol. "I don't think you know what love is, Mary. If you did, you wouldn't have let it walk out the door twenty years ago. You would have fought for it. Who cares if he didn't have a title? You could have convinced father."

"No." Mary took a few shuddering breaths, her eyes filling with tears, as she stepped away from them. "No, I couldn't." She ran past them, rushing headlong into Mrs. Sherard, who stood in the doorway. Mary pushed past her mother, escaping from the tension in the drawing room.

Mira suddenly felt quite dizzy. Byron stood beside her, shocked. Mrs. Sherard considered them a moment.

"That was unfair to your sister," she said after a short silence.

"Unfair to her?" Byron said, letting out a laugh. "She has been—"

"I know very well what she has been," Mrs. Sherard said. "But relationships go two ways," she paused, her gaze softening as she looked at him. "Byron."

Byron's mouth gaped. Mrs. Sherard cleared her throat. "I had better find Mary and take her home before she runs into the Treadways."

"They're here?" Byron frowned.

"Unfortunately." Mrs. Sherard sighed. "I ran into his wife in the hall."

Mira grimaced. “It’s too late, I’m afraid. Mr. Treadway was leaving just as I entered the drawing room.”

“Heaven help us.” Mrs. Sherard looked towards the ceiling. “I expect the two of you will be staying on to investigate whatever it is you’re getting into now?”

“Yes, Mamma.”

“Well. Carry on, I suppose.” Mrs. Sherard left the room.

Mira sagged into an armchair.

“Are you all right?” Byron said, moving over to her.

“I-I think so. Everything happened so fast . . .”

“I wish I had come sooner. How long had she been yelling at you before I came?”

“Not very long. How did you know to come?”

He gestured to the open transom window above the door. “I heard her as I came down the hall.”

“Oh no.” Mira felt sick all over. “And I said all those terrible things . . . Do you think anyone else heard?”

“I don’t think so. Most people are in the ballroom. And she deserved it after what she’s put you through.”

More tears surfaced. “I still shouldn’t have said anything. But I was so angry.”

He crouched in front of her, taking her hands in his. “I was just as bad, if not worse. I never should have brought up her relationship with Mr. Treadway.”

“You wouldn’t have needed to if I had kept my mouth shut.” Mira shook her head. “I so wanted your family to like me. And now I’ve ruined any chance.” She swallowed back a sob. “I don’t want you to have to choose between me and your family.”

He reached up, cupping her face with his hand. “I won’t have to. We’ll make it work.” He brushed a tear away with his thumb.

“How can you say that? Your sister, your mother—how can they respect me after that display?”

He looked towards where his mother had stood moments before. "Well . . . Castel came around."

Mira sniffed. "I suppose if he can, then anything is possible." She laughed a little through the tears.

"We ought to get back to the party before someone thinks the worst of us," Byron said in jest, smiling and offering her a hand up.

Mira stood, wiping her tears away. "You forget. We're engaged now. We can be alone in a room together as much as we like."

"Oh yes! And we no longer have need of a chaperone, do we?"

"Not in this setting. No, I believe we are quite free."

He took her hand and lifted it to his lips. She forgot her tears as warmth spread from her hand to her heart.

"You know," he said, "we ought to have gotten engaged a long time ago."

She ducked her head. "It wouldn't have been appropriate."

"And since when do we care about propriety?" He stepped back. "Do you know, this week has been one of the more insufferable experiences of my remembered life?"

"Has it been so bad?"

"I've felt as though I've been trying to do everything with both hands tied behind my back. We can't get nearly as much done when we're always under someone's eye, dragging our chaperones along to crime scenes. And I've had to keep up the ridiculous charade of living up to the Sherard name."

"I thought you said you didn't put on a persona with them."

"I don't. Or I don't mean to." He ran a hand through his hair, pacing as he continued. "It would have been so much easier if I had been Detective Constantine all this time. There would have been no need for elaborate lies about headaches when speaking with the doctor or trying to find a way to search the dead man's room without appearing unseemly. It's been unbearable."

"Yes, but if there is a member of Circe running in these circles, isn't it better that he doesn't know who you are?"

Byron sighed. "I suppose. So we'll keep up the act. But thank heavens we are at least free from half the shackles while we finish this investigation."

Mira gasped. "I forgot! I have news! About the documents, I mean. I was coming to look for you when I stumbled on Mary."

"What a coincidence. I was looking for you after talking with Mr. Risewell. He doesn't seem to know anything about the political documents. Either he's lying or he doesn't know he has them."

"I don't think the Risewells have the documents."

"Then who does?"

"Maureen. I was just in conversation with her, and she told us that her house in London was broken into five times in the past year."

Byron whistled. "Five times?"

"Yes. Two before her father died, the one where he was shot, and then two after she moved to Bath."

"Curious. Was anything taken?"

"Not that she knows of. But her father was a journalist who worked with the Foreign Office. Is it possible that the documents were meant to come to him with instructions of him passing them along?"

"And the other burglaries are covering for when they make the real theft," Byron said. "Do you think you can get an invitation to Henrietta Street?"

"I can certainly try."

He offered his arm, and they left the drawing room together. Halfway down the hall, the sounds of discordant piano music hit their ears. They followed the noise and found Maureen

Harris in the music room, at the piano, hammering out the racket. Mira recognized the pattern as the piece Maureen had tried to play for her and Liza that past Sunday. Bertie Corbet stood nearby, trying his best to not wince and failing. They were alone in the room, which was strange since Admiral Hoddle had mentioned chaperoning them.

Maureen stopped abruptly, her speech slightly slurred. "That's all I have memorized and it's simply dreadful. I don't think I'm playing it right."

Bertie shook his head. "No. You aren't. I don't know what it is meant to be, but surely it isn't meant to sound like that."

Maureen sniffed. "You're meant to lie and tell me how much you loved it."

"You want me to lie to you? That sets a bad precedent."

"Everyone else lies to me. Why not you?" Before Bertie could answer, Maureen looked past him, finally seeing Mira and Byron in the doorway. She greeted them louder than necessary, a strange expression on her face. "Mira! Mr. Sherard. We were just speaking of you."

"Were you?" Mira furrowed her brow.

"Well, we were. Before I tried playing my piece again. Did you like it? I think I've gotten better."

"Erm . . ." She looked at Byron and an idea sprang to her mind. She smoothed her discomfort into a smile. "I really know nothing about music, but did you know that Mr. Sherard plays the piano quite well?" She took his arm and pulled him closer to Maureen. "What if we came over tomorrow and you showed him the sheet music? Maybe he could help you figure out how to play it!"

"Oh, would you?" Maureen gushed. "That would be wonderful."

Byron smiled one of his knowing smiles. "I would be delighted."

February 15, 1889: Morning

THE NEXT MORNING, MIRA SAT IN FRONT of the vanity in her room at Davenguard, staring at herself in the mirror. It wasn't a practice in conceit, but rather a moment of reflection, of realization.

On a cognitive level, Mira knew she was engaged, but it had yet to sink in. She didn't feel any different. She'd always thought it would be a big romantic gesture, and she would be an entirely new person. But she felt exactly the same. Was it because she and Byron had been practically engaged for months? She'd known she would marry him at least since December. Maybe even before then.

She put her left hand out in front of her, flexing her fingers. He hadn't given her a ring. But was it the ring that made it an engagement or the answer to the question?

Had he asked Cyrus for permission first? Did he need to?

It all was rather anticlimactic, even though it had happened in the heat of an argument. They were courting and now they were engaged and that was that.

Somehow she was angry. This wonderful, beautiful thing had happened and she couldn't feel happy about it. Obviously, Byron had been planning to propose. They'd been tiptoeing around the question for weeks. And just because his sister was an incorrigible, overbearing shrew, he had to go and propose in a fit of pique.

Truth to tell, were Mira in the same position, she probably would have done the same. Anything to get his sister off their back. It was exhausting to be under someone's constant judgment and it had been a great relief to finally say what she really thought.

At the same time, she felt beastly about how their conversation had ended. There was no telling how Mary's *tête-à-tête* with Wilburn Treadway had gone, but the tears in her eyes when Mira came into the drawing room suggested it had been painful. And then to have that awful confrontation with Byron, to have everything brought up all over again, must have compounded her distress.

Her future sister-in-law had been in love, engaged, and then forbidden from marrying. Mira couldn't begin to imagine the pain Mary had felt.

The anger bled away and she came back to herself, staring at the mirror. Maybe it didn't matter how Byron had proposed. Though, it would have made her life easier had he given her a ring. She opened her jewelry box and sifted through it, hoping to find a ring that Walker wouldn't recognize. She didn't usually wear rings, so perhaps it was an easier prospect than she was making it out to be.

She chose a simple band with a ruby on it and slipped it onto her left ring finger. It felt strange, foreign even. But as far as anyone was concerned, she and Byron were engaged, so she needed to make a show of it.

A knock sounded at the door.

"Come in."

Liza poked her head in, her face reflected in the mirror. "Byron is downstairs. He mentioned that you were going to visit Maureen today?"

Mira tucked a loose strand of hair into her updo. "We're leaving after breakfast."

"Have you talked to Aunt Eleanor about it? I'm not sure Walker or I are allowed to chaperone you anymore after we returned from our walk on Wednesday without you."

Mira spun on the seat, facing her. "I don't think we'll need a chaperone." She lifted her hand.

Somehow, Liza's gasp made the engagement real.

BYRON AND WALKER WERE ALREADY IN THE dining room when they came down. Liza was a bouncing bundle of nerves since Mira had told her Walker didn't know yet.

The men stood as they entered. Byron took Mira's hand and moved to kiss the back of it, pausing when he noticed the ring. He raised an eyebrow and she just smiled.

"So what's the adventure of the day?" Walker asked. "Surely a visit to Henrietta Street with both of you is more than a social call."

Mira glanced over at Mrs. Renaldi and Aunt Eleanor. Her brother should know better than to hint at detective work in front of his future family. She didn't know how they would react to their daughter being even remotely involved with it. She kept her expression neutral and focused on the eggs in front of her.

"I thought Mr. Sherard might be able to decipher that bit

of sheet music Miss Harris demonstrated for Liza and me last Sunday."

"It sounded more like a jumble of notes than actual music," Liza said. "I doubt finding the right key will improve anything."

"There might be some underlying *secret* to the music," Mira said, hoping her brother would understand that they shouldn't speak so openly.

"Yes," Byron said. "And that reminds me of a different sort of secret."

"Oh?" Liza said, leaning forward, her eye on Mira's ring. Walker, as usual, was oblivious. It didn't particularly matter, though, as Davenguard's butler, Thorebourne, stepped in, interrupting the flow of conversation. "A gentleman at the door, madam. Another Mr. Sherard."

"Show him in, then," Mrs. Renaldi said.

Thorebourne bowed and left to do just that.

"Wasn't Castel in London?" Walker asked.

"That was my understanding." Byron dabbed his frowning mouth with his napkin.

Castel strode in and considered the group. His shoulders lowered by a fraction when he locked eyes with Byron. "I apologize for the intrusion, but I need to speak with my brother."

"Of course," Mrs. Renaldi said.

"In private?" Byron asked.

"As you like," Castel said. "Though it does relate to your occupation."

Mira's stomach twisted.

Byron nodded, standing. "Miss Blayse, if you'll come with us?"

"This is highly unusual," Aunt Eleanor said. "It is not appropriate for a young lady to be alone in the company of men."

Castel raised an eyebrow. "Have you not told them the news, sister?"

Walker choked on his breakfast. "S-sister?"

Mira averted her gaze. "I was going to tell them after breakfast."

Walker leapt to his feet, moving to her. "You're engaged?"

She nodded.

"How long?"

"Just last night," she rushed to say. "I wasn't keeping it a secret from you, I promise."

He pulled her into an embrace, with a laugh. Once within earshot, he whispered, "Byron's been planning it for ages. This means I need to move up my own plans."

She pulled back, grinning. "I'm so happy."

Castel cleared his throat. "Mira?"

"Sorry." She stepped away. "We can talk later," she said to Walker as she followed Castel and Byron from the room.

"Who told you?" Byron asked once they were safely in the sitting room.

"I stopped by the Royal Crescent hoping to catch you there. Mary was sulking and mother was quick to inform me of your upcoming nuptials. Congratulations, by the way."

Byron pursed his lips. "Thank you. Now, does your news have something to do with your abrupt departure on Monday?"

"Indeed it does. To get straight to the point, I left to consult the Admiralty. There is no such person as an 'Admiral Hoddle' in their records. I thought you might want to know."

His statement hung in the air for a few moments. Mira's heart raced. So Hoddle, whoever he really was, had been working with Silas, or more precisely, the thief, Enoch Hand. So many fake identities. Did everyone wear a mask?

She turned to Byron. "It's him, isn't it? He's the one working with Circe."

"It's a reasonable assumption." He drummed his fingers on the armrest. "What led you to investigate him, Castel?"

"The stories from his supposed time in the Navy. He said

he was captain of the *Serapis* for decades, yet I knew for a fact that Captain Arthur Dupuis ran the ship aground in 1884. Dupuis was suspended and then took command of the *Carysfort*, which happened to be my last assignment in the Navy."

"There's just one thing I don't understand," Mira said. "If there is no such person as Admiral Hoddle, how did he become Maureen's guardian? If Sibyl Hand is telling the truth, Circe hadn't tracked down the documents until last year, and that wouldn't be enough time for an imposter to become Mr. Harris' oldest and dearest friend."

"Has Maureen mentioned meeting Hoddle before her father died?"

Mira frowned. "Not that I remember."

Byron nodded. "We'll need to look into the solicitor then. It's possible that someone made a change to the will after her father died. Or after her aunt, Mrs. Callan, died, for that matter. I'll need to contact Chief Inspector Thatcher to look into it."

Mira's heart dropped. "Oh dear. You don't suppose they murdered her aunt too?"

"You mentioned yesterday that her house in London was broken into after Maureen had moved to Bath," Byron said. "Consider this scenario: For whatever reason, it took Circe over ten years to track down where the package with the documents was sent, and sometime last year they discovered they were in the custody of Mr. Harris."

"Excuse me," Castel said. "Which documents?"

"We aren't exactly certain," Byron said. "It's something to do with some treaty. Saint something or other."

"San Stefano," Mira said.

Castel frowned. "I suppose this has some connection to the burglaries?"

"It's the entire reason for them. To continue my theory, last summer, Circe began their search at the Harris house in London. They broke into the house in the middle of the night but found nothing. Each time they were a little more brazen. During the third burglary, Mr. Harris caught them, was shot, and died. Maureen Harris moved to Bath to live with her aunt, but the house and most of its contents remained."

"Hence the other two break-ins?" Mira said.

"Precisely. But no matter how many times they searched, they couldn't find the documents. The only explanation was that Maureen Harris took them. But it would have been incredibly suspicious if the burglaries had continued in Bath. Much better to have someone on the inside to search without too much question. They murdered Maureen's aunt and found some way of arranging for one of their own members to be assigned as guardian."

"Admiral Hoddle," Mira said, feeling queasy. "That must be why he is considering sending Maureen to the asylum in Wells. No one would question it and it would be even easier to search for the documents with her out of the house."

"And the other burglaries here in Bath?" Castel asked.

"A red herring, so that when he does find the documents, they can blame their disappearance on the thieves." Byron stood, pacing away. "I am glad you found us before we left for Henrietta Street, Castel. Otherwise we may have tipped Hoddle off without realizing."

"I would have come sooner, but I wanted to be thorough."

"And here I thought you disliked detective work," Mira teased. "When all the while you've had the makings of a rather fine sleuth yourself."

Castel rolled his eyes. "I shan't make a habit of it, I assure you."

Byron rubbed his hands absentmindedly. "Might I make use of this change in attitude before you revert to your proper self?"

"That all depends. What do you want me to do?"

"Can you keep Hoddle occupied while we make our search?

It should be enough if you can keep him in the sitting room. We don't want to make him suspicious."

"Certainly. Though, I hope it doesn't take you long. I'm not the best at making useless conversation."

"It's hard to say. Circe has been searching for a decade already. I'd imagine it will take us more than one afternoon."

"We have something they don't," Mira said.

"And what's that?" Byron asked.

"A good relationship with Maureen Harris. If anyone knows of a mysterious package that Mr. Harris received before his death, she would."

"We'll see what we can do with the time we have," Byron said, consulting his pocket watch. "We had best get over to Henrietta Street by noon."

"To think, if Hoddle had only boasted about something else, you never would have known," Mira said, following the men from the room.

Castel shook his head. "I would wager the barony that that man has never been on the sea for anything more than a pleasure cruise.

February 15, 1889: Midday

The ride to Henrietta Street was fraught with tension and nerves. There were too many possibilities in how the investigation could play out, too many uncertainties. The main factor was whether or not Castel could adequately distract Admiral Hoddle while they made their search. And then there was the matter of Maureen, about which Mira and Byron did not agree in the least.

"It would be much easier if we just told her the truth," Mira said. "We can't exactly ask her the right questions if we are still hiding your profession."

"It would be simpler, yes. But it would put her in danger. Think of what would happen if we told her and then didn't find the documents today. She would be left with the knowledge that her guardian is an imposter and have the burden of keeping it a secret."

"But if we tell her, won't we be more likely to find what we are looking for?"

Byron sighed. "I'm not prepared to take that chance. It is bad enough she is under his guardianship as it is, and we don't want to give him reason to harm her."

Castel folded his arms. "I still don't see why we don't turn the matter over to the police."

Byron's expression pinched. "If this is another slight towards my choice in—"

"Not at all. I am merely suggesting that if Hoddle were arrested for, say, impersonating an officer, then you would be able to search the house at your leisure."

The carriage fell silent. It was certainly something to consider. If Admiral Hoddle was arrested, they wouldn't have to worry about Maureen. And yet . . .

"Do we trust the police here in Bath?" Mira asked.

Byron sucked in a breath through his teeth. "I don't have enough experience with them to know. But I can't imagine it would be an immediate arrest. There would be a larger investigation into the man, and in that time, Circe could make other arrangements to secure the documents," he said. "I'd rather work with a known enemy than an unknown one. Besides, we don't want to risk the police finding the documents during the investigation. After all, Circe is awfully keen on procuring them. I'm sure they would find a way to convince the police to part with them."

"I'm interested to read them myself," Castel said. "It must be quite the secret."

"WHAT A PLEASANT SURPRISE!" ADMIRAL HODDLE SAID as

he let them into the house. "Did Maureen know you were coming?"

"She asked us to come round to listen to a piece she's been working on," Mira said.

"Oh, lovely! I do believe she's already in the music room. We can all go up together."

Castel opened his mouth as if to say something, but nothing came out. Byron took pity on him.

"My brother here isn't particularly fond of the piano, but my mother insisted on him coming to chaperone."

Mira tucked her hands behind her back and swapped her ruby ring to her right hand while Byron continued making excuses.

"Would you mind entertaining him while we talk with Maureen?"

"Why, I thought . . ." Hoddle let out a laugh, round and full. "Of course, I'd be happy to keep you company, Mr. Sherard. Do you play billiards?"

Castel visibly relaxed. "I certainly do. Lead the way, sir."

The two men walked down the hall and Mira let out a breath of relief.

"That's settled then. Now to find Maureen."

Byron nodded, gesturing for her to lead the way upstairs. "I'll need to fulfill my promise of looking at her music, so you'll be the one to guide the conversation. If you can find a way to divert the subject to her father, I think that will be our way in."

Mira nodded. "I'll do my best. Though I don't know how we'll convince her to let us look through his files."

"You are forgetting how clever we are when we work together." His eyes twinkled. "We'll find a way."

The door to the music room was slightly ajar, so Mira knocked on it, pushing it open.

"Miss Harris?"

Maureen turned from where she sat on the chaise lounge with a book.

"Why, Mira! And Mr. Sherard! I had forgotten you were coming." She closed the book and stood, coming over to greet them.

"I did promise to have a look at your sheet music," Byron said.

"So you did. Though I'm not sure you'll be able to make anything of it. Come in, please, and take a seat." Her dress glided over the floor as she moved to the credenza and retrieved her folder.

"I thought that perhaps I have been playing it in the wrong key, but I've tried just about every configuration, so maybe there's something else to it." She passed the folder over to Byron.

He opened it and scanned over the notes. He tapped his fingers on his leg, humming to himself.

"It is so good of you to come," Maureen said. "I hardly remembered that we'd made an appointment."

"Yes, you were rather preoccupied with Mr. Corbet last night," Mira said.

Maureen flushed. "I do hope I didn't make a fool of myself."

"He didn't seem to mind."

Byron stood, gesturing to the piano with the music in hand. "May I?"

"By all means," Maureen said.

He crossed the room, set the music on the stand, and stretched his fingers. Mira turned back to Maureen, mind spinning for a way to bring the conversation to her father and his correspondence. She winced as Byron began to play, the musicality sounding as poor as Maureen's attempts.

"Admiral Hoddle seems to be in good spirits," she said, unable to come up with anything at all to steer the conversation.

"Does he? I haven't seen him today."

"Do you not spend much time together?"

Maureen shook her head. "He's always in the study with his papers."

"I would have thought with him being your father's friend that the two of you would be more familial." Mira's stomach twisted. She'd found her segue, distasteful as it was to her. "My late godfather was my father's closest friend and he was practically a second father to me."

"Oh, I didn't even know who Admiral Hoddle was before my aunt died and he was appointed to be my guardian."

"I can't even imagine it. Did your father never speak of him?"

"Not that I remember. But he knew so many different people. It was hard to keep track of them all. I was surprised, though. My father had such a tight relationship with Mr. Corbet, Bertie's father, I expected to become his ward after my aunt died."

Byron stopped halfway through the piece and leaned forward, squinting at the notes.

"With all the people your father knew, I'm sure he received so many—" Mira started to say before Byron interrupted.

"Why, there's a musical cryptogram here."

"A what?" Maureen said.

"Musical cryptogram," Byron repeated. "It's a motif composers use in a piece to represent names. This is a very common one. B flat, A, C, B natural." He played the notes out. "It spells Bach, like the composer. I thought this was all nonsense until I came across it here in measure twenty-three. Makes me think maybe there is more to this."

"Like a secret message?" Maureen asked.

"Well, no. It's just the one motif here. A musical cipher would be . . ." he trailed off. "Well, depending on the way it was encoded, it could very well sound like this piece—all a jumble, with little rhyme or reason." He looked up at her. "Where did you say you found this?"

"My great-uncle sent it to us back in late July. Or, rather, it was finally delivered."

Mira blinked. "What do you mean by that? Had it been delayed?"

"From what I understand, it was sent to our old house in Hertfordshire just after we moved when I was nine. The new mistress of the house, Mrs. Meadle, meant to send it on to us, but kept forgetting. It wasn't until she was getting ready to move herself that she found the package and sent it on."

Mira's mouth went dry. Maureen would be turning twenty soon. "That would mean she'd had it for almost . . ." she tried to do the math in her head.

"Eleven years, yes."

Mira locked eyes with Byron. Slowly, he said, "It was in a package?"

"Yes. Wrapped in brown paper and string with a postmark from Austria-Hungary. Mrs. Meadle didn't even open it. The strangest thing about it was the package was addressed to my mother, Elizabeth Harris."

"That makes no sense," Mira said. "I thought your mother died."

"Yes. Giving birth to me."

"Perhaps the sender didn't know?" Mira offered.

Maureen shook her head. "It was from my great-uncle and surely father would have written to let him know. I didn't even know I had a great-uncle until we opened the package."

"What was in it?" Byron asked.

"There was the sheet music, a letter, and the musical box over there on the credenza. Father gave me the musical box, and then locked himself in the music room for hours working on the piece. Of course, he spent more time poring over it than playing. That was only a few weeks before he died." She swallowed. "So you see, that's why I've been trying so desperately to learn how to play it. It's the last connection I have to my father, really."

Byron's mouth twitched a little at the corner. "You wouldn't happen to still have the letter, would you? It might have some insight into how to play it."

Maureen's eyes brightened, and she jumped up. "I never thought of that! Yes, I have it in my room, if you'll wait here."

Once Maureen left the room Mira let out a laugh. "It's the music. The music is the document."

"It's quite extraordinary. But of course, whoever sent it had to do it covertly. And I'm certain there are so many women named Elizabeth Harris in England. That's why it's taken Circe all this time to find out who had it."

"Do you think Mr. Harris was decoding it?"

"I presume so." Byron began playing a little tune from memory. "And with his connection to the Foreign Office, he would be able to deliver the information directly. But he died before he could decipher it fully."

"What now?" Mira said.

He spun on the piano bench, facing her. "We need to convince Maureen to let us take it out of the house. It will take some work, but if we can decode it, we'll have the information we need to hand over to the Foreign Office. Then, and only then, can we work to remove Maureen from Hoddle's guardianship."

Mira nodded. "Do you think—"

Maureen's heels clicked down the hall and Mira fell silent.

"Here it is," Maureen said, handing over an old sheet of paper.

Byron skimmed it, sitting next to Mira so she could read it too.

My dear niece,

I know how much you enjoy Mendelssohn, so I knew you would enjoy this little musical box. It plays one of his songs without words, Book 1, Op. 19b No. 1 in E minor. I always find that his music contains more than any words can convey.

Did you know that Franz Joseph Haydn had a brother? I used his work and Bach as inspiration for my own song without words. I'm worried that all I've done is created words without a song. If you would kindly give me your opinion on it and write me back. Give my love to Sanford.

- H.M.

"What a strange little note," Mira said.

"I thought so too," Maureen said. "My mother didn't play the piano. Why would he send her sheet music?"

"Do you know a Sanford?" Byron asked.

"That's my father."

Byron hummed again. "I do believe you were right about there being a hidden message here, Miss Harris."

Maureen's eyes widened. "Really? It isn't just a jumble of notes?"

"Your great-uncle was quite obliging: 'words without a song,' suggests it isn't meant to be music at all. Do you have some fresh paper and a pencil I could use?"

Maureen nodded and moved to the credenza, bringing back the writing implements. Byron wrote the alphabet down the long side of a sheet of paper, A to Z.

"Usually with these sorts of musical ciphers, A is always A," Byron said.

"And B is B and so on?" Mira asked.

Byron paused, tapping the pencil to his cheek. "Possibly, but whoever wrote this used the BACH motif. In which case, B is B flat, C is C and B natural is H."

"I don't follow," Mira said.

"In some German compositions, the seventh diatonic scale note is denoted as H. So in C major: B flat, A, C, B natural spells BACH." Byron played the alternating notes on the piano. "But then, of course, we have the rest of the alphabet to account for."

Mira frowned at his explanation. It was rather technical, and she wasn't certain she understood it. But Byron fell silent and she didn't want to interrupt him as he consulted the score and wrote in possible notes next to each letter. Every so often he would move to the piano and play something out before coming back to the paper.

"This is exactly what my father did," Maureen said.

"That bodes well for us," Byron mumbled before returning to the piano again.

After a little while he had a complete cipher. He pulled out a fresh sheet of paper and flipped to the beginning of the score.

"Now to test it."

He wrote out each letter as it corresponded to the music notes in his neat, consistent hand. After a line or so he sat back, frowning.

"It's not making any words. Though . . ." he flipped forward a page in the score. "Perhaps the cipher doesn't start until after the BACH motif."

He went at it again, beginning after that point in the music, but a few letters in he stopped again. "No, that's not right either. I suppose it's possible that B natural isn't H after all."

"None of it makes sense to me," Mira said, leaning over. "Wouldn't it make more sense if the alphabet was in order instead of skipping around?"

"Well that would be an entirely different cipher." He ran a hand through his hair and let out a breath. "One I've never heard of. But there's no harm in trying it."

He continued in this manner for nearly an hour, with Mira or Maureen offering occasional suggestions, but every attempt yielded a stream of nonsensical letters. Nothing they tried worked.

"Maybe we were wrong about it being a cipher," Maureen said. "It could just be that my great-uncle is a terrible composer."

Byron shook his head. "There's more to this, I'm certain. Might I borrow it to work on at home?"

"As long as you promise to bring it back," Maureen said.

"You have my word." Byron tucked the score into the folder along with the letter. "Best go check on my brother and your guardian, eh?"

"Oh, I do hope they are getting on well," Mira said.

They descended the stairs with Maureen leading the way to the billiard room, but as they approached there wasn't a sound. No voices or laughter or billiards crashing into one another. A sense of dread settled over Mira as they turned the corner into the room.

At first, they noticed nothing amiss, aside from the unoccupied room. Byron moved before Mira had realized what was wrong.

"Castel!"

His brother was slumped in a high-backed leather armchair, a brandy glass on the floor beside him, a dark stain spreading out from it on the rug. Byron rushed to his side, holding his head up to check for a pulse. Mira stood frozen in the doorway, Maureen beside her.

"I-is he . . . ?" Mira stuttered.

"He's alive and breathing well." He picked up the glass and smelled it, making a face. "An Old fashioned, I think. Which means anything bitter would have been masked." He took his brother's hand and slapped the back of it, hard, a few times.

Castel groaned, shifting in his chair.

Mira slumped against the door. "Will he be all right?"

"I think so," Byron said. "Though we ought to get a doctor just to be safe."

"How did it happen?" Maureen said, voice shaky. "Where's Admiral Hoddle?"

Mira glanced at Byron, at a loss for words.

"We can explain everything, but can you send for a doctor first?" Byron said.

Maureen nodded, finally taking her eyes off of Castel as she rushed down the hall.

Mira rubbed at her arms, stepping into the room. "I never thought that he would be in any danger. I didn't realize—"

"Neither did I," Byron said. "And I should have known better."

Maureen's steps sounded down the hall, coming back.

"I don't understand," Mira said. "The only reason why Admiral Hoddle would do such a thing is if he knew who we were, but we've been so careful."

"H-he did know," Maureen said, stopping next to Mira, still bewildered. "Bertie Corbet told us last night."

"He . . . what?" Mira said.

"Bertie was boasting about how he helped the famous Byron Constantine search Silas Treadway's room and figured since the murder was solved that keeping it secret didn't matter anymore."

"Why didn't you say something before?" Byron asked.

"Since you hadn't told me yourself, I thought you'd rather I didn't mention it. But what does that have to do with Admiral Hoddle?"

"You may want to sit down," Mira said.

Maureen did as she was told, confusion and concern clouding her features.

"Your guardian is not who he said he was," Byron said. "This may sound ludicrous, but he's an operative working for a criminal organization intent on stealing political documents from your father's papers."

"Oh," Maureen said, quite still. "You mean . . . that's what everything has been about?"

Mira nodded. "That's why there were all those break-ins in London. And then your aunt. And now . . ."

"Yes. Yes. I see. This . . ." Maureen swallowed. "I'm sorry, that's just a lot to take in."

"I'm so sorry," Mira said.

Maureen shook her head. "I knew something was wrong. There was always something off about him but I didn't know what it was. Is . . . is this the reason my father was killed too?"

"I'm afraid so," Byron said.

The tension in Maureen's shoulders dropped and she let out a breath. "Well then."

"Are you certain you are all right?" Mira asked.

Maureen frowned. "Somehow I feel better knowing the truth, awful as it is. I never understood why I was placed under Hoddle's guardianship. Now I know." She looked up at them. "It's because of those documents you mentioned. You don't suppose he found them, do you?"

"I doubt it," Byron said. "If he had, I don't think he would have been here to greet us this morning. He would have brought them straight to Circe and never returned. And all this," he gestured to his brother, "would have been avoided."

Castel mumbled something in his sleep.

"The question now is what is Hoddle up to?" Byron said. "He knows who we are and took the effort of dosing Castel, but where did he go and why? Circe wouldn't give up on the documents so easily, not after searching for them for a decade. What's his play?"

February 15, 1889: Afternoon

By the time Doctor Turpin came, Castel was mostly roused. The doctor identified the symptoms as likely caused by a dose of morphia or laudanum and determined that there wasn't much to be done other than wait for the effects to dissipate. After sending Maureen in a carriage to stay with the Renaldis at Davenguard, Mira, Byron, and Castel left for the Royal Crescent.

Castel dozed for most of the trip, so they couldn't get much out of him as far as what led up to Hoddle administering the drink. Once they reached the house, it took both of their support to get him inside. They brought him into the sitting room where Mrs. Sherard was sewing. She looked up as they came in and immediately set her things aside, coming to meet them.

"What's happened?" She placed the back of her hand to Castel's forehead. "Is it a fever?"

"No, Mamma," Byron said as they deposited his brother into a chair. "He's all right, just had a bit of laudanum."

"A bit? He can't even support himself."

Byron huffed and explained the situation. Mrs. Sherard went back to her seat by the fire, wide-eyed.

"Forgive me, but I wouldn't think Hoddle capable of such a thing," she said. "He's always seemed so vapid."

"He's not an admiral," Castel said, his words slurring as he came to for a moment of lucidity. "I checked the admiralty."

"I suppose it all was an act," Mira said.

"And we have no idea where he's gone now, or why he thought it necessary to subdue Castel," Byron said.

The latter grumbled in his sleep, shifting in the chair.

Mrs. Sherard smiled fondly at him before frowning and looking up at the two of them. "Where's Mary?"

Byron blinked. "Mary?"

"Yes. A carriage came for her just over an hour ago. The driver said you sent him to fetch Mary for something."

Mira's stomach dropped. "We never sent a carriage."

Byron stood. "Do you remember what the driver looked like? Was there anyone in the carriage already?"

"I-I'm afraid I don't remember. I noticed he wore a muffler. There might have been someone in the carriage . . ."

Byron swore under his breath. "If it was Hoddle . . ."

"Why would he take her?" Mira said.

"I don't know." He paced away. "And that's more frightening than knowing. It's possible he received a message from Circe." He shook his head. "No. There wouldn't have been enough time between when he learned I was a detective and now for him to write his superiors and receive orders back."

A knock sounded at the door and Greerson came in with a letter on a tray. He brought it to Mrs. Sherard.

"This just came, Madame."

"Thank you. Would you fetch some tea for us and water for Castel?"

Greerson inclined his head and left the room. Mrs. Sherard slipped a letter opener through the top of the envelope and pulled out a card. After reading the first line, her hands began to shake.

"Byron," she held the card up and her son took it, reading it aloud.

Detective Constantine,

I have your sister, Mary.

If you cooperate, she will live.

I know you will find the documents that we have been searching for. You will drop them in PO Box 18 by sunset on February 17th or your sister will die. If you involve the police, she will die.

If you deliver the documents, your sister will be released within twenty-four hours.

"It's not signed," Byron said, throwing the note on the table.

"What documents is it referring to?" Mrs. Sherard asked.

"Political documents regarding a treaty." He rubbed his temples.

"Do you have them?"

"No, not exactly," Byron pulled the folder of sheet music

out of his bag and threw it on the table too. "It needs to be deciphered. But even once we have it, we can't just hand it over."

"We don't know what it says," Mira said. "Maybe once we decipher it, we'll see that the message isn't important after all."

"It has to be important, otherwise Circe wouldn't be after it." He mussed up his hair, looking over at Castel. "If it was Hoddle, he left from Henrietta Street and then came here. Where would he go afterwards? Where would he take her?" He stared blankly out the window.

There were several tense minutes where no one said anything at all. Mira's chest heaved. Castel teetered in his chair and Mrs. Sherard stared off into space. Byron had a hand over his eyes.

What was she meant to do? Everyone was reeling from the shock of it all. She moved over to Byron and set a hand on his arm.

"We'll find her."

"It's my fault that my family is in this mess," Byron whispered, his voice thick. "What if we can't find where he took her?"

"We'll take it one step at a time. But we need to start now."

He looked down at her. "Yes. Yes. Goodness, what am I doing? We only have two days." His voice cracked as he pulled away from her, beginning to pace again. "We'll need to talk to the postmaster and determine if anyone knows anything about Hoddle. He had to have arranged for the PO box. We can't be too obvious about our questions though." He whirled towards his brother.

"How are you feeling?"

Castel alternated shaking his head and nodding. "It's all a bit fuzzy."

"Let me know when you have your faculties back. I think I'll need you for the search."

"He needs to rest," Mira said. "And you should work on

decoding the documents, Byron. We'll need them to fall back on."

Byron grimaced. "I hate the idea of handing them over to Circe, regardless of what's in it. We should be out searching for Mary."

"We can't make a decision one way or the other if we don't know what the documents say. And Hoddle certainly won't accept the sheet music on its own."

"But we need to—"

"I can go to the post office," Mira said. "And check with carriage drivers and messengers."

"I can help too," Mrs. Sherard said.

"Mamma . . ."

"No, I shan't sit here waiting for all of you to do something. You may be the detective, she may be your sister, but she is my *daughter* and we are going to get her back." Mrs. Sherard stood, holding her cane in front of her. "Miss Blayse is right. We don't have much time. If we are to be successful, we need to divide and conquer. You are the only one here who can decode whatever it is they are looking for. The two of us can make inquiries ourselves. And Castel . . ." She looked over at her other son who had drifted out of consciousness again. "Well, we had better get him to bed."

AFTER TUCKING CASTEL IN AND ASSURING BYRON that they would be all right, Mrs. Sherard bundled herself and Mira up and led the charge out the door.

"The post office will be closing soon," she said to Mira as they climbed into a carriage. "If we're to discover anything, we need to do it now. I don't want to make an after-hours call to the postmaster's house. His wife prattles on and we'd never get away." Mrs. Sherard adjusted her gloves. "What do we know about Hoddle? Perhaps we can think of a lead as we drive."

"Well, we know he isn't actually a friend of Mr. Harris or the family. And he isn't an admiral."

"That is who he isn't. Which is useful in its own way. But who is he?"

"We don't know much. Only that he is working with Circe to find those documents."

Mrs. Sherard pursed her lips. "He strikes me as a rather desperate man. And desperate men don't think things through. Already, he's made a mistake in showing his hand. Why, I doubt that he realized you knew about his false identity, and yet he's taken such drastic actions. What might push him to go to these lengths?"

Next to her, Mira sat open-mouthed. In the span of the last hour, Mrs. Sherard had shown an entirely different side of herself. She really shouldn't have been surprised, having only known the woman for not quite two weeks, but it was baffling nonetheless. The stern, cold and calculating woman that Mira thought Mrs. Sherard to be was melting away. Or rather, she was seeing those attributes in a different light. She was stern because she was resolute and disciplined. Cold because she was pragmatic and could set her feelings aside to get things done. Calculating because she analyzed everything she came across.

She reminded Mira so much of Byron.

These thoughts rushed through her head in an instant and she pushed them to the side, focusing on the matter at hand.

"I imagine he was under quite a bit of stress," Mira said. "If Circe is intent on getting these documents and has been searching for so long, they are likely pressuring him to finish the job."

Mrs. Sherard tipped her head to the side in a familiar way. "You said that he recently discovered my son's occupation. That could explain the change in approach. Byron is a visible threat to his success, but also a possible chance for relief. If the renowned detective is on the case, surely he will find the documents and save Hoddle from the wrath of Circe. But only if he can find a way of convincing Byron to hand them over."

Mira frowned. She hadn't told Mrs. Sherard about Circe or its aims, and she didn't remember Byron mentioning it. And yet, his mother wasn't asking any questions about it.

"Did Byron tell you about Circe?"

Mrs. Sherard shook her head. "I was the one who told him."

Mira blinked, disoriented, as if the world had tilted on its side. "What . . . how?" Panic surfaced as the notion of the Sherards being part of Circe crossed through her mind.

Mrs. Sherard chuckled. "When I was a girl my father was a sea captain who traveled frequently to Jamaica. He'd tell me stories of pirates who sailed under the flag of Circe, the enchantress. Swashbuckling tales of adventure, of which he was always the hero."

She sighed. "My father died when I was still young and it was many years later that I went through his trunks and papers. In his old journals I found that he had documented little things in the mercantile industry that didn't make sense. Cargo disappearing. Ships that could enter port without documentation. Payments for goods that didn't exist. Each and every one of them led back to an organization called Circe. There was nothing I could do, so I tucked them away.

"When I had my own children, I told them the same stories of their grandfather and his daring exploits. And when Byron was older, he found my father's papers too. Shortly afterwards, he started working as a detective, using the information in the journals as a starting place. So you see, *I* was the one to tell *him*." She looked out the window, her shoulders sagging.

Mira sat back, the new information swirling in her mind. Was this why Mrs. Sherard disliked Byron's choice in occupation? Was it guilt?

"Did you—" She cleared her throat. "Do you ever regret not destroying your father's papers?"

"Never."

The carriage rumbled beneath them, rushing towards the common goal of this tenuous new alliance. Perhaps they were seeing each other clearly for the first time.

THEIR INVESTIGATION AT THE POST OFFICE YIELDED nothing. No man matching Hoddle's description had mailed anything that day. Mira wasn't particularly surprised. If she were wanting to send a ransom note, she would have hired a boy off the street. They asked every carriage driver they could find whether they had driven a man like Hoddle or a woman like Mary in the past day. None of them could tell them anything.

After two hours of investigation, they stepped into a tea house to warm up and regroup. Mira blew over the top of her cup, urging the tea to cool down so she could drink it faster.

"If this man really is part of Circe," Mrs. Sherard said, "he is not unconnected. They create a web of deceit, one strand leading to another. If we can only find one connection, we might be able to find him."

"Yes, but like a web, touching any part alerts the spider," Mira took a sip and winced as it scalded her tongue.

Mrs. Sherard hummed. "There must be someone we can talk to."

Mira gasped. "There is! Sibyl Hand."

"And who is that?" Mrs. Sherard frowned.

"The man who died was not Silas Treadway, but a thief named Enoch Hand. His wife, Sibyl, might know something. She's the one who told us about the documents in the first place."

"Will she warn the spider, do you think?"

Mira sat back, the warmth of the teacup radiating into her hands. "I don't think so."

"Well then," Mrs. Sherard set down her cup. "Where can we find her?"

THEY ATE A LIGHT SUPPER IN THE tea house while they waited for the cover of night. Mira led the way from the Abbey, through the streets, to the tunnel within the alleyway. The same man, Adams, stood guard.

"What is your business here?"

"We're here to see Sibyl," Mira said.

Adams puffed out his chest a little. "She's not here. Not yet. Do you know where the chamber is?"

Mira nodded.

"Wait there, then. If she ain't there by ten, she ain't coming tonight."

He stepped to the side, letting the women pass.

"It's a little cramped up ahead," Mira said, steadying her nerves. "And dark. But it does open up once we are through."

"A little darkness never hurt anyone."

"The footing is a little uneven too."

"I hope you aren't suggesting that I turn back."

"Not at all."

They moved in silence the rest of the way through the tunnel. Once Mira was in the open room with the blue-green pool, she reached down to help Mrs. Sherard through. Byron's mother took her hand, using her cane to help her up and out of the tunnel.

"Why, this is quite extraordinary," she said, looking about at the pool and colonnade. "Is this where the thieves meet?"

"It's a little further on."

"I suppose Mr. Davis, the architect, knows nothing of this skylarking?"

"I would assume not."

They ventured into the tunnels that led to the antechambers, but as the light dwindled, so did Mira's nerves. She took some deep breaths, feeling altogether unsettled as her mind reminded her of all the ways the Roman construction was like the Parisian catacombs. She jolted as Mrs. Sherard set a hand on her arm.

"Why don't we go back and wait in the room with the pools, hm? This Sibyl will need to come the same way we did."

"We don't know that," Mira said.

"If she didn't, then how would that man out there know whether she had come or not? Come along."

They retraced their steps, coming back into the open where the cold, moonlit sky stared down at them. Mrs. Sherard hoisted herself up onto one of the low walls, making a little seat. From the waist up she looked the picture of elegance, but her legs dangled in the air like a child's. In the moonlight, Mira could see Byron's profile in his mother's face.

"There. That's better. I can breathe a little easier in all this fresh air," Mrs. Sherard said. "I'm afraid I'm not used to these sorts of things."

Mira hesitantly hopped up onto the wall next to Byron's mother. "It isn't exactly a society party, is it?"

"I gather that you don't think much of society?"

Mira averted her gaze. "I never know how to behave, what I am meant to do."

The silence spread between them, thick and uncomfortable. After a moment, Mrs. Sherard said, "The great secret of society is that no one knows what they are meant to do. Things are always changing. Even the cutlery can't manage to stay consistent. You think you know what each fork and spoon is meant to do, and then you visit the duke's and he shows off his new set of tomato spoons. Yet another thing to remember, and all you want to do is ask why the dickens anyone would want a spoon used exclusively for one particular fruit."

Mira couldn't help but laugh. "Are you speaking from experience?"

"Very recent experience, I'm afraid. I bit my tongue to avoid saying anything rude. Mary ordered a set of tomato spoons the very next week. We have a reputation to uphold, after all."

Both of their laughter petered out at the mention of Mary.

"I do hope Sibyl knows something," Mira whispered.

"As do I."

It was nearing ten and Mira's extremities were tingling. Mrs. Sherard stood, pacing back and forth in front of the pool.

What if Sibyl didn't come? Would Adams know where she lived? Or worse, what if she had left town, never to return?

It was doubtful Monty would know where Admiral Hoddle would retreat to.

The skittering of rock against rock had them both turning towards the tunnel entrance. A woman Mira recognized scrambled through and froze upon seeing them. It wasn't Sibyl, but rather one of the other thieves, Elvina.

"Are you back to purchase more goods?" Elvina asked, setting her things down. She struck a match and lit the lantern she had brought.

"We're waiting for Sibyl," Mira said.

"You're out of luck." Elvina picked up the lantern in one hand and her case in the other. "She won't be coming for at a few days at least."

"Why?" Mrs. Sherard said, glancing at Mira.

"She didn't say. But when I stopped by earlier today, it seemed she had company."

Mira couldn't dare to hope. "Was he tall, with grey hair and mutton chops?"

She narrowed her eyes. ". . . yes?"

"It's Hoddle, it has to be." Mira stepped closer. "Please, can you tell us where Sibyl lives?"

"I'm not sure I—"

"It's my daughter," Mrs. Sherard said, coming to stand next to Mira. "That man has abducted my daughter. Her life is at stake. Please."

Elvina sighed. "She lives in a cottage near Old Bridge. I'll write the address down for you."

THE LIGHTS WERE STILL ON WHEN THEY returned to the Royal Crescent, address in hand. Once stripped of their winter clothes, Mrs. Sherard headed upstairs to check on Castel while Mira went to the sitting room, where she found Byron slumped over the low, Japanese-style table, fast asleep. Beneath him were pages of various ciphers, the sheet music, and scribbled notes. Mira picked up the one closest to her, but it was a mess of gibberish. She crouched beside him, placing a hand on his back and rubbing in slow circles.

"Byron?"

"Hm?"

"It's time for bed, love."

"Hrngh." He lifted his head, eyes bleary. "Mira?"

"Yes."

He let out a breath. "You're safe."

"Of course I am."

He sat up, considering the papers scattered around him. "What was I doing? I . . . I'm afraid I don't remember."

Mira's heart ached and she stood, reaching a hand down. "You were going to bed."

"Was I? No, I recall now, I was . . ." He rifled through the stack and picked up a packet of papers. "Right. Did you find—"

"Not exactly. We can talk about everything later."

He nodded and let her help him stand. He leaned over and kissed her on the cheek. "Goodnight."

"Goodnight. See you in the morning."

He took one last look around, tucked the packet of papers into his jacket pocket, and padded out of the room, still half asleep.

Mira slumped onto the sofa, rubbing her temples. Even though they knew where Hoddle was keeping Mary, there still was no guarantee of getting her back safely. She picked up the stack of the papers Byron hadn't taken with him. Dozens of attempts and none of them revealed anything. Maybe Maureen was right about it only being a poor composition.

They had two more days to figure something out. Two more days or Mary would die.

Footsteps shuffled down the hall and Mrs. Sherard came in, looking as exhausted as Mira felt. She sat beside her on the sofa.

"How is he?" Mira asked.

"Still sleeping, but he woke up when I came in. The glass of water I left on the nightstand was empty, so that's a good sign. Where's Byron?"

"I sent him up to bed. He was in that fuzzy state between wakefulness and sleep and his memory wasn't particularly clear."

Mrs. Sherard frowned. "I thought his memory had healed. Doesn't he remember things from day to day now?"

"He does. But that doesn't mean he remembers everything." She let out a wistful sigh. "I do believe he will always be my forgetful detective."

Mrs. Sherard smiled. "I'm so grateful that he has you."

Mira's breath caught in her chest. "You are?"

"From the moment I met you, I have seen how you've cared for him." Mrs. Sherard stood, moving to close the curtains. She paused at the window before turning back to Mira, straight-backed, hands folded in front of her. "Do you know why Mary dislikes you so?"

Mira swallowed. "I believe there's a list."

Mrs. Sherard shook her head. "It's the detective work. It always comes back to that. If you had been any other girl, she needn't have been so afraid. But you don't merely encourage his work, you engage with it. I'm not sure you are aware, but I have buried three grown daughters, an infant son, and a husband."

"Byron mentioned the loss the other day. He said that was why Mary was so protective of him."

"Detective work is dangerous. We've always known that. But when the accident happened . . . He didn't die, but we lost him just the same. Every time we would visit, he couldn't recall anything we had talked about the time previous. He may not remember it, Miss Blayse, but we visited him every week for a year. When his external injuries had healed, he got the notion that he could go on the case again. That was when we stopped coming, because Mary couldn't bear to see him destroy himself."

Mira swallowed. Everything that had happened in the past twenty-four hours only corroborated his family's fears. They may have asked Byron to come investigate the theft of their jewels, but Byron brought the danger of Circe to them. Now Castel had been drugged and Mary abducted.

"That's why you disapprove of the detective work?" Mira said. "It isn't because of what society will think, but because it is dangerous?"

Mrs. Sherard paused, moving over to a set of drawers built into the bookcase. She opened one of the drawers and returned with a rectangular book, sitting next to Mira and handing it to her.

Mira opened the cover and found a page pasted full of newspaper clippings.

Detective Constantine Solves Meerdown Murder.

Princeline Diamonds Stolen. Constantine on the Case.

Constantine Finds Duke of Shirland, Missing Three Weeks.

At the bottom of one of the later pages was the advertisement that had initially brought Mira to Byron.

The Central News September 17, 1888

Something troubling you? Are people following you in the street? Sounds that can't be explained? Mysterious letters in your postbox? Perhaps a loved one gone missing? Look no further. Come to 27 Palace Court, London. Can't miss it. Oh, and yes, I'm a private detective if you were wondering.

She ran a finger around its edge, smiling fondly. "You've saved all of his cases . . ."

"The ones the papers wrote about. I'm sure there are more. I don't disapprove of his detective work. He's brilliant. I couldn't be prouder of him. But it is one thing to lose a child to illness, quite another to violence." She turned to look at Mira, her scrutiny not as intimidating as before. "I'm grateful to you because you've brought back his memories. And now I know there is someone looking out for him, someone who is brave enough to stay by his side and intelligent enough to keep up with him."

Mira's heart glowed as she closed the book and handed it back. "You mean, you don't think it is improper for a woman to be a detective?"

"There is a superstition that it is bad luck to take a woman to sea." A wry smile came to Mrs. Sherard's lips. "But I have taken many voyages myself."

Mira laughed. "How terribly I've misjudged you."

"One's character tends to show itself over time." Mrs. Sherard's eyes twinkled for a moment. But her gaze grew distant and her smile faded. "We ought to get to bed. We won't do Mary any good if we aren't well rested."

"Oh," Mira stood, "I'll need to call a carriage."

"Nonsense. You can sleep in Mary's room. Come along."

Mrs. Sherard led the way up the stairs and helped her find some night clothes.

"Thank you, Mrs. Sherard," Mira said.

Mrs. Sherard paused in the doorway. "Considering the circumstances, you may call me Mamma, if you'd like. Sleep well, Mira."

February 16, 1889: Morning

It was a long and fitful night for Mira. She tossed and turned, her mind repeating conversations from the day previous. When she wasn't dwelling on her improved relationship with Mrs. Sherard—Mamma, she mentally corrected herself—she was fretting over Mary. One sunset left. Would Hoddle really kill her?

The familiar ache of loss settled in her chest. It didn't make sense. Her interactions with Mary Sherard were fraught with vitriol and tension. The row on Valentine's Day was evidence of that. And yet, she was grieving her all the same.

Was she feeling this way because it brought up the memory of when she learned about Emilie's death? Perhaps it was because she could already sense how the loss of Mary would affect Byron's family. Or was it because somehow, despite it all, she had some sort of attachment for her future sister-in-law, even if Mary would never return such familial affection?

It was still dark outside, but Mira couldn't stand to lie in bed and wait. Her anxiety urged her to move. She rose exhausted, limbs drooping as she dressed for the day in her rumpled clothes.

As she buttoned her boots, she noticed some papers strewn on the floor near the hearth. Strange, considering that everything else in Mary's room was in pristine order. She hadn't seen the mess the night before due to her own fatigue and the darkness of the room. She took a seat on the floor and examined the disarray. A stack of envelopes had toppled, splayed across the floor with a loose ribbon beneath them. A few of them were open and set to the side, the pages of each letter scattered.

Against her better judgement, she picked up one of the stray envelopes and read the sender's name: *Wilburn Treadway.*

The evidence around her formed a scene in her mind's eye, so distinct and clear, it was as if Mira was watching it in the waking world.

Mary had returned from the Risewell's Valentine's party, devastated from the conversation—whether with Wilburn or Mira and Byron, it was impossible to know. She came into her room, unable to hide her tears.

There were certainly tear stains on the letters.

Opening a drawer kept shut for twenty years, she retrieved Wilburn's love letters. She pulled on the ribbon that held them and read each line, knowing that her future with him had been lost.

One of the letters was singed near the top edge, as if Mary had intended to burn it before blowing out the flame. There were enough empty envelopes that she had likely succeeded in burning some of them before this one. Did it contain something that convinced her to save it?

If it was a love letter, it certainly didn't start like one.

My dear Miss Sherard,

Thank you for asking after my wife and her recovery following the birth of our son. She is doing well, and so is the baby. Our oldest, Silas, is already doting on him.

I am troubled to hear of the death of your sister and cannot imagine the devastation your family must feel. It is such a tragedy to have lost all your sisters, and Alice so soon after Edith. I remember you telling me how much you valued your relationship with them, how important their confidence was. I am so sorry for your loss.

Please give my love to your family. Even after all this time, I still care for all of them, though society does not allow us to be friends.

Sincerely,

—Wilburn Treadway

Mira swallowed, setting the letter down again. She never should have intruded on Mary's correspondence. But there was a glimpse, a glimmer of a past Mary as seen through Wilburn Treadway's eyes. Mary loved her sisters dearly—loved her family dearly—and to lose so many of them had left her in ruins. It didn't excuse her behavior, not for a moment, but Mira could understand it.

The light finally crept over the windowsill, reminding her

of the impending deadline. One more sunset. Two more days. Sister or not, Mira would do everything she could to save Mary.

She crept downstairs and into the sitting room, finding the papers arranged as they were the night before. She gathered the ones that had fallen to the floor and sorted them in her hands. Soon, she'd stacked the various ciphers and attempts in piles on the low table. The sheet music was in its own stack and the letter that accompanied the package sat alone.

She picked it up, scanning it again. It really was a strange letter. For instance, if it were sent by Maureen's great-uncle to her mother, why was it signed "H.M." instead of "Your loving uncle," or something to that effect?

And why go to the effort of sending the letter, and the musical box too, if the sheet music sufficed in relaying the desired message? Perhaps the letter was a screen or disguise, in case someone opened the package, making it appear a harmless gift.

The letter mentioned three separate composers: Mendelssohn—whose piece was the focus of the musical box—Bach, and Haydn's brother.

Why would someone writing a false letter mention all three? If Haydn's brother and Bach were the inspirations for the sheet music, could their names be a clue? Or even a code in and of itself?

She brought the letter with her and went searching for a library. She had no doubt the Sherards would have one. Only a week ago, she would have assumed if they had a library it would merely be an ornament for appearance, but she knew better now after her conversation with Mamma.

The thought of calling someone "Mamma" again warmed her from head to toe. It all seemed like a dream, so strange and new. But she wouldn't have woken up in Mary's room if it were only a fantasy.

She found the library without issue and went encyclopedia

hunting again. Would Haydn's brother have his own listing? She pulled the proper volume from the shelf and flipped through the pages. Yawning, she skimmed over Franz Joseph Haydn's section until she found his brother's name: Michael. She licked her finger, thumbing forward a page or so. There. Michael Haydn.

She scanned the entry: Younger brother of Franz Joseph Haydn. Born in Austria. Skilled composer of church music. Intimate friend of Mozart. She yawned again, her eyes drifting over a small diagram showing a few measures of music with notes from G to a high B with every conceivable note—flat and sharp—between them.

Beneath each note was a letter of the alphabet. The notation

included every letter and some symbols which were unfamiliar to her. Her exhaustion melted away as she dragged her finger down the page to find the relevant paragraph.

> *In 1808, Haydn developed a type of chromatic cipher with symbols for thirty-one letters of the German Alphabet. Each letter corresponded with a symbol in musical notation. Due to enharmonic pitches, the cipher can only be understood as visual steganography, not via musical sound, which presents as atonal and dissonant.*

Based on the diagram, the letter A would correspond with the note G, and the letter B with G sharp. Was this what H.M. intended? She packed up the encyclopedia and the letter and returned to the sitting room, intent on finally deciphering the sheet music.

She settled onto the floor, arranging her skirts around her and turned over a new sheet of paper. With careful lettering, she wrote out Haydn's cipher, skipping over the parts of the German alphabet she didn't recognize. She was writing out the W line when Byron came into the room, yawning.

"So it wasn't a dream. You did stay the night."

Mira nodded, finishing Y with a flourish. "Mamma insisted that I stay in Mary's room."

Byron's eyebrows practically flew into his hairline. "Mamma?"

She smiled up at him. "Your mother and I have found common ground."

"I . . . see." He rubbed the back of his neck and stepped farther into the room. "And how did the search go?"

She set the pencil down. "We talked with Elvina, one of the thieves we met in the ruins? Apparently, an older gentleman that matches Hoddle's description is staying with Sibyl." She pulled out the slip of paper with the address.

He read over it. "You're brilliant, you know that?"

"It was a joint effort." She smiled. "I now understand where you get your investigative instinct from."

Byron tucked the address into his pocket, hiding his own tired smile. "Well, regardless, we have a lead now, thank goodness. I'm getting absolutely nowhere with the sheet music. But now that we know where he's holding her, we just need a plan of attack."

Mira shook her head. "He's expecting us to deliver the documents to his post box. If we show up at Sibyl's house, won't it be dangerous for Mary?"

"What else can we do?" He threw an arm out in frustration. "I've tried just about every combination of musical ciphers that I know—Porta's, Bach's, Philip's, Amadi's—and I can't make any headway on it."

Mira lifted the encyclopedia and set it closer to him on the low table. "I looked up Haydn's brother and found this."

He sat beside her on the floor, pulling the book closer to him. "A chromatic cipher," Byron mumbled and ran a hand over his face. "I've never heard of such a thing. Musical ciphers are meant to be heard in the music, not merely seen."

"Shall we try it?"

He let out a long breath. "Let's start at the beginning."

They worked through the first few measures of the piece and when no words became clear, they moved on to the measures following the BACH motif. It still didn't work.

"I'm beginning to believe there are no secrets in this music and the documents must be somewhere else in that house," Mira said.

"No, there must be something we're missing," Byron said. "Why did you look up Haydn's brother?"

"It was in the letter." She pulled it out, handing it over. "I thought it strange that Maureen's great-uncle mentioned three composers."

Byron pored over it again. "'Did you know that Franz

Joseph Haydn had a brother? I used his work and Bach as inspiration . . . ' Obviously, Bach is a reference to the motif. I'm certain Haydn's brother is referring to the cipher you found in the encyclopedia. It was H.M.'s way of informing Mr. Harris the method of decoding the music, but he needed to be cryptic in case it fell into the wrong hands."

Mira took the letter back from him. "If Mr. Harris regularly corresponded with this Mr. H. M., wouldn't he already know the cipher?"

"Not necessarily. Not if H. M. determined that these papers were important enough to change the cipher. Evidently, Circe was aware of the situation, enough to know the package existed. H.M. may have added another layer of encryption so that, in the event that it was intercepted, the information would stay safe."

"He must have encrypted it too well, in that case. Mr. Harris worked on it for weeks and still didn't decode it before he was killed. We have just over a day."

"There must be something else." Byron picked up the letter, standing and beginning to pace. "'My dear niece, I know how much you enjoy Mendelssohn . . . ' That's another composer. Have we accounted for him?"

"One of his songs plays on the musical box that was sent with the sheet music."

Byron rubbed his chin. "Why did H.M. send the musical box? It would have been much more expensive."

"I wondered about that myself. Perhaps it was part of the cover? If someone opened the package looking for political documents, they would only find sheet music and a musical box."

He hummed. "'Book 1, Op 19b No. 1 in E minor—'" He stopped still. "E. You don't suppose that's the key, do you? Not musically, I mean. But that the cipher starts at E, not G?"

"Maybe?"

He rushed back to the low table, kneeling beside her. She

handed him the pencil and they reworked the cipher together, heads close.

Once the adjusted cipher was written out they started at the beginning again, testing a few measures before moving forward to the measure after the BACH motif. Mira stood, pacing back and forth with the sheet music and reading out the notes as Byron translated them.

"D, F sharp, F flat, D flat, F sharp, D sharp, F flat—"

"Secret," Byron whispered. "The first six letters spell secret." He looked up at her, breaking out into a wide grin. A sensation of breathlessness came over her. They'd done it. They'd broken the cipher.

"Keep going," he said, making a slash after the word.

"C flat, B, C, E, D flat, D sharp, B, F sharp—"

"Compartment. I would bet anything it will say compartment."

"Let me finish the word!" she laughed.

They continued back and forth, with Byron reading out the words as he discovered them and Mira reading out the notes. After a point, he set down the pencil.

"Wait. Wait just a moment."

"What is it?" she asked, turning towards him.

"It's the musical box. That's where the documents are!" He jumped to his feet, and before she knew it he had lifted her into the air, swinging her around. She dropped the sheet music in surprise, letting out an unladylike squeal.

He set her down, handing the now crumpled deciphered message to her.

Secret compartment, box, blue, horse, twist, use key.

He slipped an arm around her waist, pulling her close to him and kissing the top of her head. "We've done it. We've solved it!"

She laughed, looking up at him. "The musical box."

He nodded. "The musical box."

The two of them devolved into sleep-deprived giggles which were only interrupted by someone clearing his throat in the doorway.

"I'm sure this is all very exciting, but can you have some consideration for those of us who are convalescing?" Castel wandered in wearing a colorful dressing gown and a scowl. He held a hot water bottle to his head.

Byron bounded over to him. "We've figured out the cipher! Mary is safe. Regardless of what happens, she'll be safe."

"Well, that's a relief," Castel said, moving to sit in his preferred armchair. He picked up one of the papers that had been inadvertently scattered on the seat and scanned it as he sat down.

"And now that you're feeling better, you can tell us what happened with Hoddle," Byron said.

Castel's gaze flicked up to him. "He got the drop on me, that's all. I didn't realize he'd put anything in the drink."

"What were you talking about?" Mira asked, closing the encyclopedia in triumph.

"His time at sea. I was questioning him about it. Thought it might give us some insight into what he was up to."

Byron's expression blanked. "You knew that he was working with Circe, didn't you?"

"Yes."

"Then why on earth did you think that was a good idea? It's no wonder he poisoned you! Why, that might be why he went after Mary!"

Castel winced. "Please, lower your voice. My head is killing me."

"You should be relieved it's the only thing trying to kill you." Byron returned to picking up the strewn papers.

A moment passed before Castel said, "Whoever wrote this

is musically inept. Book 1 Op. 19b No. 1 is in E *Major* not E *minor*."

Byron moved over and snatched the letter out of Castel's hands, reading it over again. "I missed that. How did I miss that?"

Castel adjusted his hot water bottle. "Anyone familiar with Mendelssohn would know it."

"Mr. Harris loved Mendelssohn," Mira said. "He would have known immediately." She picked up the deciphered message. "It must have been written incorrectly on purpose, to draw his attention to the key. It was a clue to help him with the cipher."

"And we unwittingly stumbled upon it," Byron groaned. "I should have noticed it before. We would have had it decoded much sooner."

"You don't suppose Mr. Harris solved the cipher before he died, do you?" Mira asked.

"If he did, Circe certainly wouldn't still be looking," Byron said. "No, he must have gotten hung up on one of the other clues. My guess is Haydn. The package was postmarked in Austria, so we can assume that the man who sent it, H.M., was Austrian. He would have been more familiar with Michael Haydn and his cipher. But Harris was English. It might have escaped his notice."

"Poor man," Mira said. "Spending all that time trying to decode the message, and then killed for it without knowing why."

"I think it's about time someone found out what H.M. was so adamant on protecting," Byron said.

THEY REACHED HENRIETTA STREET AND BYRON PULLED out his lock picks, fully determined to break into the house to find the musical box. But before he could use them, he found that the door was already unlocked.

"Am I forgetting again? Because I distinctly remember Maureen locking it."

Mira's chest tightened. "So do I. You don't think Hoddle came back, do you?"

"I don't know. Stay behind me."

The door creaked as they opened it. Every noise they made seemed amplified in the house. It wasn't until they heard laughter coming from upstairs that either of them relaxed.

"That's Walker!" Mira said, following the sound. They found Walker, Liza, and Maureen in one of the bedrooms. A steamer trunk was open in the center of the floor and they sat with the contents spread about them.

Walker looked up as they came in and grinned. "We were just wondering how we were going to track you down. I figured when you didn't come home last night, Mouse, that you'd been out sleuthing."

"Mrs. Sherard invited me to stay the night at the Royal Crescent. What's all this?"

"I told them about Admiral Hoddle and the political documents," Maureen said. "This morning, we thought we'd better do some investigations of our own. He brought this trunk with him when he came to be my guardian, and I always wondered what was in it." She picked up a pamphlet and held it up.

Byron took it. "A playbill for *Pirates of Penzance*?"

"He's an actor!" Liza said. "I haven't seen any playbills for anything past 1885, so I think he was rather hard up. We think his name is Maurice Suchet, because that's the only name consistent on each list of players."

"But if he's an actor, why is he working with Circe?" Mira asked.

"Liza already answered that question," Byron said. "If he is a failed actor, the opportunity to be paid for impersonating a naval officer would have had some appeal. And if it is all an act, perhaps Mary is safer than we realized."

"Mary?" Liza asked.

"She's been abducted," Mira said. "We received a ransom note asking for the documents to be delivered in exchange for her release."

Liza's mouth fell open. "Abducted?"

"Is that why you're here?" Maureen asked. "Did you decipher the music?"

Byron lifted the folder. "If we're correct, the documents are in the musical box."

The group adjourned to the music room. The air was charged with excitement and anxiety as they huddled around the credenza. Byron gently took hold of the blue horse and twisted the head off.

Maureen gasped. "You've broken it!"

"It will reattach," Byron said. "And now we simply need a key."

Sure enough, there was a keyhole embedded in the neck of the horse.

"Oh, it's right here." Maureen opened the drawer of the credenza and pulled out the wind-up key. They all held their breath as it slotted perfectly into the lock.

Click.

A hidden compartment popped open from the base. Byron did the honors of swinging the door open, revealing a small stack of papers within. He gingerly removed the documents.

"Those have been hiding there all this time?" Maureen said.

Byron nodded. "And now it's time to find out what all the fuss is about."

They all took seats around the room as Byron skimmed over the documents. Mira tapped her foot, nervous energy flooding through her.

"It's not about the Treaty of San Stefano," he said after

several minutes of reading. "It's about the one that came after—the Treaty of Berlin. These documents list the changes made at the conference and describe how they would lead to widespread war in Europe."

Mira swallowed. "What sort of changes?"

"Placing Bosnia under Austria-Hungarian occupation, Russia regaining access to the Black Sea region, dividing Bulgaria into three parts, and placing Macedonia back under Ottoman rule. It details how these changes are likely to result in uprisings and strife and if any revolutionaries attack their occupiers it would certainly spark war. This last page has a list of alliances between countries and who would be most likely to be brought into a conflict. And most damaging of all, it lists Circe by name as the force behind these changes."

"No wonder they wanted the documents," Liza said.

"What would happen if the government is made aware of this?" Walker asked.

"I'm not certain, but it would be a blow to Circe and that's enough." He folded up the documents and tucked them into his coat, turning to Mira. "If Hoddle really is an actor, I think the best course of action is the direct one. We go to Sibyl's house and ask to speak with him."

"And what if he turns violent?" Mira asked.

"We'll just have to think one step ahead of him. Liza, Maureen, would you be so kind as to inform Inspector Rutledge of the situation? If you need to send a telegram in my name, so be it, but we'll want men watching the docks and the train station in case he escapes."

Maureen frowned. "Don't you want the police to come with you?"

"We'll be able to handle Hoddle well enough on our own, and I don't want to risk him doing something foolish, like harming Mary, if he gets wind of his impending arrest. Walker, are you up to coming with us?"

“I’d be more than happy to.”

Byron’s mouth ticked up at the side. “I think it’s time we allow Maurice Suchet one last performance as Admiral Hoddle.”

February 16, 1889: Afternoon

Sibyl's cottage was on the outskirts of Bath, down near the river Avon with an attached waterwheel that was in such disrepair it no longer turned. The old millhouse was small and covered with ivy, flanked by thorny rose bushes whose leaves hadn't returned yet, and surrounded by tall, yellowing grass. A black carriage was parked beside it. A dappled horse tied to a post was straining its neck to reach whatever it could graze on. The sky was dim with grey clouds and Mira couldn't help the sense of dread that came over her as they climbed out of their own carriage and started down the path. Walker split off a few yards from the house and made his way around the side.

Once he was out of sight, Byron rapped on the door. It

opened a crack, revealing Sibyl's face, which paled upon recognition.

"What are you doing here?" she hissed.

"We're here to see Hoddle. Or Suchet. Whichever name he's using now. May we come in?"

Byron didn't let her answer, pushing through the door and pulling Mira along with him.

Hoddle sat at the table, a spoonful of soup halfway to his mouth. His eyes bulged at their sudden appearance, his stricken gaze skittering towards the stairs.

"Where's my sister?" Byron said, tone calm.

"You need to go," Sibyl said. "He'll kill her. I know he will."

Mira frowned. The way Sibyl spoke held the same desperation as when she'd talked about Circe in the Roman Baths. It was then, and only then, that she remembered Sibyl had mentioned three men involved with the burglaries. Not two. She stepped back. "Who will kill her?"

Sibyl kept her voice pitched low. "If you know what's good for you—and your sister—you'll leave and send the documents like he asked."

There was a creak from the floor above. "Who's there, Sibyl?" A man's voice called down. It was deep, raspy, and vaguely familiar.

"Just the milkman delivering some milk," Sibyl called back. She lowered her voice again. "You really must go."

Byron's eyes flicked towards the stairs. "Is my sister up there?"

Sibyl nodded. "Please, go."

A thump sounded above them, followed by a heavy tread on the stairs. A man descended, holding Mary in front of him, arms bound, mouth gagged, and a knife to her throat. He was broad-shouldered and had a ragged scar that ran from the corner of his eyebrow to below his cheekbone. He towered above them on the stairs, a sly smile on his lips.

"I didn't know you delivered milk, Detective Constantine," said Aaron Dennis.

Mira's breath caught in her throat. Had Monty known that his former partner was working with Sibyl?

"And I didn't know you drove carriages." Byron's voice was steely and cold as he pushed Mira behind him.

"I've driven you more than once, I'll tell you. To think that I was able to pull one over on the 'Great Detective Constantine.'" His smile spread into a toothy sneer and a chill spread across Mira's back. She glanced over at the hooks on the wall and found a grey muffler. They'd been driven across Bath so many times. How often had Dennis been the driver?

"Now hand over the documents, else this will get unpleasant."

"You would add another murder to your list of crimes?" Byron said.

Dennis laughed. "This is a familiar scene, ain't it? You and me, a dagger between us. And you said nearly the same thing back then, don't you remember?"

Byron's jaw tightened.

Dennis scowled. "I suppose you wouldn't. It's another day for you. I'd wager you never thought of me again after arresting me." His eyes darkened. "But I dreamt of this moment every night in that prison in Reading. I didn't think it would happen. I thought you would be smart enough to follow the ransom instructions. But here we are. Just the same as before. Though this time I've got insurance." His hold on Mary tightened. "And I am fully prepared to kill her if it means you'll hand over the documents."

Byron stood tall. "You assume that we've found them. You only gave us three days to find something your people haven't been able to find after eleven years."

"Well then, you made a mistake in coming here. Your last day has been shortened to ten seconds. If you don't hand the documents over in that time . . ." He pressed the knife closer to Mary's neck and she let out a muffled cry.

"Ten."

Byron stilled. Mira didn't know what they could do. It was his sister or the documents. Documents that might prevent a war and millions of deaths.

"Nine."

But it was his sister standing in front of them, her red, greying hair falling out of its style, eyes wide and pleading.

"Eight."

The police were waiting at the stations and the docks, not outside the house.

"Seven."

Walker might be able to stall him but there was no guarantee he could retrieve the documents.

"Six."

There was no reprieve, no other option.

"Fi—"

Byron reached into his jacket and pulled the documents from his inside pocket.

"Give them to Suchet." Dennis jerked his head towards the actor.

With slow, deliberate movements, Byron did as he was told. Hoddle brought the documents over to Dennis and held them up for him to see.

"We've done it," Dennis breathed. "The Crescent searched for eleven years, and we're the ones who've finally done it. The Serpent will be pleased."

In one quick motion he snatched the papers from Hoddle and threw Mary away from him, retreating up the stairs. Hoddle ran after him. Byron was just quick enough to catch Mary before she hit the floor. Mira turned to Sibyl. "Is there another exit?"

She nodded. "There are stairs at the back of the mill."

The sound of voices and a scuffle sounded through the wall. Mira ran to the window and found Walker in a brawl with the two thieves. He threw a punch at Hoddle as Dennis came from the side. A glint of silver flashed in the light. She rushed outside, just in time to see her brother fall backwards into the tall grass.

"Walker!"

Dennis and Hoddle mounted the horse as she ran to her twin's side. They escaped in a clatter of hooves and dust. Walker sat up before she reached him.

"Are you all right?" She checked him over for any blood.

"Why wouldn't I be?" He rubbed his jaw where a bruise was already forming.

"I saw a knife."

"Oh, you mean this one?" He held his other hand up, revealing Dennis' blade. "I managed to disarm him, but he had a lucky left hook."

Mira let out a breath of relief, hugging him.

"Careful now, I'm a bit bruised."

She pulled back to look him over again. "I'm just glad you aren't dead."

"'Course not. But I thought there was only going to be one of them. Did something go wrong?"

Mira's eyes widened. "The documents! Come on!" She hauled him to his feet and they returned to the house.

Byron was still in the process of untying his sister. "I presume they got away?"

Walker winced. "I wasn't ready for them."

"No matter," Byron removed his sister's gag. "They're not important."

"No, but the documents are!" Mary said, voice increasing in pitch and volume with each word. "I've heard them talking about it. They are planning a war, Byron! Who cares about me?"

"I care about you!" Byron matched her intensity, then said softly. "You may not think that, but I do."

Mary shook her head. "Of all the times to have family loyalty." She rubbed at her wrists, hands shaking. "You have to get those papers back."

Byron looked heavenward, reached into his jacket with his other hand, and pulled another packet of papers from his pocket. "I never lost them."

Mira's mouth dropped open. "What?" She took the stack and scanned them. It was the documents. "What did you give Dennis?"

"Last night when I was working on the cipher, I decided we needed a backup plan. I didn't think Hoddle would know what was in the documents, so I made it all up. Three pages of political rigmarole."

"A bluff?" Walker said, looking over Mira's shoulder.

"I'm only grateful it worked. I thought it worth the risk when we believed we were only dealing with Hoddle. I didn't have a choice but to try it with Dennis." He pulled his sister into a hug. "Are you hurt anywhere?"

"I'm fine," Mary said, pulling away from him. "A little rattled, but I'm fine."

"You were abducted." He stood and offered her a hand, pulling her up.

"I came of my own free will, thinking you'd gotten yourself in another mess. It wasn't until we got here that I realized my mistake."

"I'm afraid that still counts as abduction," Byron said.

The baby started crying and Mira realized they had completely forgotten about Sibyl. The former thief moved to the back of the room and picked up her fussing child, shushing him softly.

"Is Dennis why you were so afraid to leave Circe?" Mira asked.

Sibyl froze in place before giving a hesitant nod.

"You know him well, then?" Byron asked.

"Well enough to want to stay clear of 'im. He's a harsh one, and I was grateful when he was conscripted into the army. But in December he came to Bath, as I told you. Enoch had a habit of boasting about his current job in the pub and one night Dennis was there. Dennis recognized him and knew enough from what he was saying to realize Enoch had taken up with Circe. He cornered him and forced him to tell him about the whole plot. Once he heard what we were to be paid, he insisted on being brought on. He transported the goods in that carriage of his. It was his idea to kill Mrs. Callan and bring Hoddle into it too."

"You mean, Hoddle isn't part of Circe?" Mira asked.

"He wasn't. Though after their conversation last night, he might just join."

"What happened?" Byron asked.

"Hoddle barged in yesterday afternoon in an awful state. Said he'd just killed a man. When Dennis got him to talk, he said some Sherard fellow was asking him questions about being an admiral and hinting that he knew his secret. So, he put laudanum in his drink."

Mary gasped, paling as she looked at Byron. "Castel?"

"Has a headache. Otherwise, fine." He waved her off and turned back to Sibyl. "What did Dennis say?"

"He told him that Circe would make it right as soon as they got the documents, and they made the plan to abduct Mary." The baby's cries died down and Sibyl looked down at him. "I hate to think what they'll do when they realize the documents are fake."

"I doubt that either of them will be back any time soon," Byron said.

"But they left by horse," Walker said. "The police are at the docks and train station."

Byron shook his head. "Be that as it may, they'll be bringing those documents to the Serpent. I think Circe will impose a far worse punishment for their failure than the law will for theft and impersonation."

The implication hung between them. Sibyl sat down. "I'm free of him, then. Dennis and Enoch. Free of them both."

"My offer still stands," Byron said. "You can have a new life."

Sibyl smiled. "I may just take it."

February 22, 1889

The delicate tones of the piano filled the sitting room of Swan Walk, London. Uncle Cyrus had purchased the instrument when Mira and Walker were still young, but it hadn't ever been played properly. A few stray notes here and there when they would play act being musicians, but neither of them had taken much interest in learning the instrument. It was mostly there for show. For propriety.

Byron played it now and for the first time in a long time he wasn't playing from memory. He'd taken the Austrian's cipher and used it as inspiration for something entirely new. It was beautiful and haunting, but full of so much hope as he played the final notes.

Warm applause sounded from the other occupants of the room: Uncle Cyrus and Loretta, their children on their laps and at their feet; Mamma and Mary straight-backed but smiling widely; Walker and Liza covertly holding hands; Mr. and Mrs. Renaldi, Aunt Eleanor having stayed behind at Davenguard; and Mira, sitting closest to the piano in a high-backed armchair.

"That was wonderful!" Mrs. Renaldi said. "Just wonderful."

Byron smiled, moving to stand next to Mira, taking her hand. "I did have some help in arranging it."

"You never let me listen to the completed piece," Mira teased. "It was lovely."

Landon, who had been listening from the doorway, stepped in. "Dinner is served, sir, whenever you are ready."

"Thank you, Landon," Cyrus said, standing. "Shall we all adjourn?"

The table had far more people sitting around it than at the beginning of the month, and yet it didn't feel crowded at all. There was safety and connection in being surrounded by loved ones, old and new. It was one of the best nights of Mira's life. The whole family celebrating two engagements together—Walker had proposed to Liza the night before they had left Bath.

Or, rather, almost the whole family was present.

Halfway through the first course Castel came in, offering his apologies. "I had a meeting with the Under-Secretary of the Minister of Foreign Affairs."

"Oh?" Byron raised an eyebrow.

"Yes, and I finally found the right person to hand the documents over to. A Mr. Jonathan Wallace."

Mira frowned. There was something familiar about that name. Byron's expression suggested he had a similar recollection.

"Wallace, you say?" Byron pulled out his journal.

"Oh, stop your detective work," Mary said in jest, for once, instead of her usual scorn. "We're at dinner."

Byron stilled.

"What's wrong?" Mira leaned closer to peer over his shoulder.

"You're sure it was Jonathan Wallace?" he said, voice shaky.

"I'm certain of it. Why?"

Mira read the line above Byron's finger and her blood froze. It was the list of names that Selene had sent them. Operatives of the Crescent.

Byron snapped the journal closed and forced a smile. "Oh, nothing. Might someone pass me the mashed potatoes?"

After dinner everyone settled into various occupations and conversations. Mira snuck away to the parlor, trying and failing to not feel nauseated from the revelation. It wasn't long before Byron found her there.

"And who are you hiding from?" he teased.

"Not who. What." She sighed. "I can't believe it. After everything we did . . ."

He held out a hand. "Why don't we go for a walk?"

They quietly took their coats from the hall and slipped out the door. The sun was starting to set, bathing everything in golden light.

"What are we going to do?" she asked after a few minutes.

"There's nothing we can do," he said. "And even if the documents had reached the right hands, what could the government do about it? The treaty has been signed for a decade. Circe's plan has already been put in motion."

"Then why did we go to all that effort if it didn't matter?"

"The truth always matters, Mira. The overall outcome, a perfect ending, is never my goal. And yes, this war Circe is planning will likely still happen. But if our efforts may delay it a bit longer, I think it is worth it."

Mira sighed. It all felt so futile. Every time they took a step towards stopping Circe once and for all, another plot would surface. It was like a hydra. With every head they cut away, more took its place.

"By the way," Byron said, "Sibyl Hand came to Bolton Street yesterday. Castel related their conversation to me after dinner."

"Is Bolton the address you gave her?"

Byron nodded. "We've arranged for her and her son, along with Elvina and Lucille, to go to America. According to Castel, she seemed in earnest about leaving the thieving lifestyle behind."

Mira looked up at him. "First Grace Trimbell, now Sibyl. How many ex-Circe members have you two helped to escape?"

His eyes twinkled. "A handful over the years. But don't you see? This case had so much more to it than Circe and the treaty? If we had left it alone, Sibyl Hand wouldn't have had the opportunity to escape the Crescent. Miss Harris would likely have been sent to an asylum. She never would have learned why her father was killed. The truth mattered a great deal for them." He took her hand in his. "My work as a detective may have started because I wanted to stop Circe, but I have continued to do it because of the people I am able to help. It's impossible to right every wrong, but I will always chase the truth."

"And fight for it?" Mira asked.

"Exactly."

They fell silent, walking down the streets of London hand in hand. It wasn't long before they came to Westminster Bridge where the sunset was in full force, colors rippling over the Thames. It made her want to paint again.

"You know," Byron said, leaning over the balustrade. "This was where I wanted to propose to you."

"Oh?"

"When we are apart and I think of you, I like to think of you here. Of us, here. When it's just the two of us and the light shines through your hair making a golden shining halo. It's my favorite memory." He reached out and tucked a strand of hair behind her face, his hand brushing her cheek.

Her face flushed, unexpected tears pricking at the corners of her eyes.

He pulled his hand away, the warmth lingering. “I’d been planning it for weeks and then lost the opportunity because of that silly spat with Mary.”

“It’s all right,” she said, placing her hand on top of his on the balustrade.

He shook his head. “No. It isn’t. But I suppose there’s nothing to be done. The important thing is, we’re going to be married.”

Mira looked out over the Thames. It was beautiful. The perfect place. She took his hand and turned it over, pulling the ruby ring from her finger and placing it into his palm.

His brow furrowed.

“Are we engaged?” she said, trying to hide her smile. “I don’t remember you ever proposing.”

He stared at her for a moment. His confusion soon turned to realization, and his smile soon devolved into a hearty laugh. For a moment she was scared he would drop the ring. But then he smiled at her and tucked it away.

“You are quite extraordinary, aren’t you? You anticipate my every move.”

He reached into his pocket and pulled out a box.

“Samira Blayse,” he said. “I may not remember every moment we’ve shared, but because of you I know that love does not persist in memory or even in the heart, but in the soul.”

He kneeled and opened the box, revealing an intricate ring with three hexagonal cut sapphires in a row, with dozens of diamonds following the edge of the band. The position of the stones formed a rhombus that curved along her finger as he slipped it into place.

“The very essence of my being longs for you and I cannot imagine living without you. Will you marry me?”

"You already know the answer."

"What if I've forgotten?"

She cupped his cheek with her hand, leaning down to kiss him on the forehead. "Of course I will."

He stood, pulling her closer. Mira admired her engagement ring.

"Where did you get this? It's beautiful," she said.

"It belonged to my mother's mother, Lady Catherine Clarke. And one of the stolen goods we happened to buy back from Sibyl."

Mira laughed. "A family ring." She held it out in front of her and it sparkled in the dwindling sunlight.

"I thought it was appropriate," his gaze softened, eyes trailing over her features, "as you are to become Mrs. Byron Sherard."

Her stomach fluttered, her pulse racing. "And here I thought we would be Mr. and Mrs. Byron Constantine."

He leaned closer, voice barely a whisper. "We can be anything you like. As long as we're together."

Her breath hitched as his lips found hers, fervent and tender. Her legs fell limp beneath her, dizziness coming over her, but he caught her and pulled her closer to him with a touch on the small of her back. She fell deeper into his embrace and the heat of a thousand sunsets was nothing compared to the warmth between them. It was not their first kiss, nor would it be their last, but the memory would always burn within her.

Author's Invitation

Welcome to the end of the book! Since you've made it this far, I have a favor to ask. Whether you enjoyed the book or not, please leave an honest review on Amazon or Goodreads. It only takes a few minutes and makes a significant difference for the future of this book. Reviews are essential for its success and longevity, and you'll be helping other readers decide if it's worth their time. If you loved the book, don't hesitate to recommend it to your friends!

To make it even easier, scan the QR code below to go directly this book's page on Goodreads:

AND IF YOU WANT TO KEEP UP with my news and inklings, you can join my newsletter by scanning the QR code below.

LOOKING BACK, THIS WAS ONE OF THE most complicated books I have written. There were so many moving pieces, clues, and characters to keep track of. I knew from the start that the main mystery would involve the musical cipher. The challenge was weaving in each of the separate mysteries, the history, and the character conflicts in a satisfying way. I hope I succeeded.

But my success means nothing without the people (and instruments) who helped me orchestrate it.

Dax, thank you for arranging the writing retreat back in July 2025. I will never forget the awe of seeing your dungeons and dragons speakeasy for the first time, nor the thrill of writing the first chapter of this book by hand. This book started in your basement with fancy drinks and delicious Chinese food. We really ought to do it again.

I would like to extend my sincere thanks to both of my lovely writing groups for your input throughout the first draft:

Hannah, Rachel, and Mary—we may have met because we all write science fiction, but you have helped enormously with this historical mystery. Our group is the reason why Mira is so introspective and why she found those letters in Mary Sherard's room.

Becca and Merlin—thank you for continuing our little group over the years. Without you, I may not have been brave enough to revisit that last confrontation with Aaron Dennis to give it more teeth. The book may have been left without a proper climax.

This may be a strange inclusion, but I must acknowledge the impact of index cards on my writing. In this case, they were imperative for keeping clues, locations, and characters organized. I practically played Clue with them (i.e. Mira, in the music room, with the carousel musical box).

I would like to express my deepest gratitude to my editor, Becky. You take my oblong, rocky prose and help me break it open to reveal the glittering interior of a geode. You go above and beyond in your edits. I can't thank you enough for the research you've done on thieves' cant and for your keen eye when it comes to echoing words.

Anything remotely related to music in this book is only possible because of Connor. We've been friends for over half our lives at this point (which I just realized as I am writing this. Crazy.) and have been through a lot of shenanigans at the Space Center and around the D&D table. What a treat to collaborate on something more musically inclined. Thanks especially for introducing me to the BACH motif. Those with a sharp eye might have noticed it on the cover.

As always, I must thank my mother last of all. You support me in everything I do and were with me as I tore my hair out trying to figure out the minute details of this mystery. You sat with me as I lay on the floor, surrounded by index cards, and going mad. But the book is finished, and I have retained my sanity because of you. I love you forever and there are not enough words to say it. If I were Mendelssohn, I would compose you a song that could say more than I could ever write:

A Song Without Words.

About the Author

NATALIE BRIANNE grew up steeped in British mystery—from Poirot to Lord Peter Wimsey, she learned early to love a good twist and a cleverly placed clue. Some of her fondest memories involve curling up with her family, trying to out-solve the detectives on screen. When a friend floated the idea of an amnesiac investigator, she couldn't resist—especially once Byron Constantine walked into her mind, top hat and all.

While writing the first book, Natalie lived in London—walking the same streets her characters do, even staying at 27 Palace Court, the detective's future home. Her time there brought a tactile authenticity to the fog, cobblestones, and candlelight of 1880s London.

When Natalie isn't writing, she's drawing, trying to keep her cat off her keyboard, and forgetting that she has vegetables in her fridge.

Looking For More?

CONSTANTINE CAPERS SERIES:

The Pennington Perplexity
Flashes of Memory
There Comes a Midnight Hour
The Veil of Death
A Song Without Words

SHORT STORIES AND NOVELLAS:

FROM CONSTANTINE'S CASEBOOK

Byron's Oblivion
The Great Sheep Panic
In the Silence of the Catacombs

FROM SAMIRA'S SKETCHBOOK

The Forgotten Letter

GENERAL FICTION

The Glade of Sionn O' Shea

www.ingramcontent.com/pod-product-compliance
Lightning Source LLC
LaVergne TN
LVHW091114080826
845145LV00008B/1911

* 9 7 8 1 9 6 5 4 7 7 9 8 4 *